deep water

The closer we get to the man, the stronger my feeling grows that something's wrong. He doesn't stop staring at us as we approach, his pale eyes unblinking. As the wind whips at his unbuttoned black coat, I'm surprised to see a large silver crucifix hanging down the front of his purple shirt.

He recognizes me. I see it in his face when he looks at me. Yet I've never seen this man before. He crosses himself quickly and glares. I feel my skin come up in goosebumps. That's the second time in twenty-four hours someone's reacted like that. What's wrong with this place?

deep water

Lu Hersey

USBORNE

"We must be willing to let go of the life we have planned, so as to accept the one that is waiting for us."

Joseph Campbell

For my family

First published in the UK in 2015 by Usborne Publishing Ltd., Usborne House, 83-85 Saffron Hill, London EC1N 8RT, England. www.usborne.com

Copyright © 2015 by Lu Hersey

The right of Lu Hersey to be identified as the author of this work has been asserted by her in accordance with the Copyright, Designs and Patents Act, 1988.

Cover photography: Landscape © Stelian Porojnicu / Alamy; lightning © Johan Swanepoel / Alamy; sea © Sergey Orlov/Shutterstock; girl © Dmitry Laudin/Shutterstock

The name Usborne and the devices ♀ 🎈 are Trade Marks of Usborne Publishing Ltd.

This is a work of fiction. The characters, incidents, and dialogues are products of the author's imagination and are not to be construed as real. Any resemblance to actual events or persons, living or dead, is entirely coincidental.

A CIP catalogue record for this book is available from the British Library.

ISBN 9781409586104 03521/1 JFMA JJASOND/15

Printed in the UK.

chapter 1

The rain drums on my head as I run. Freezing water drips off my hair and under my coat collar. As I reach my street, I see the house is still in darkness. All the other houses have lights on already.

My fingers don't work properly because they're too cold. I fumble for my keys while next door's cat winds himself round my legs.

I open the front door carefully, but he's too quick for me. He shoots down the hall and disappears into the dark of the kitchen at the back of the house. As I sling my rucksack down and flick the light on, I hear him hissing. He bolts back down the hall, hackles raised and tail fluffed up, and runs outside. Cats are weird. Usually it takes me ages to get him out.

I shut the front door quickly and shiver. It must be warmer out in the street than it is in here. Surely the heating should have come on by now? I head straight upstairs to the bathroom, turning the shower on full blast so it's nice and hot by the time I've got my clothes off. The showers at the swimming pool are too small and cramped and there's only ever a trickle of lukewarm water. I want to get rid of the smell of chlorine.

I'm glad Mum's not here. It gives me the opportunity to stay in for ages, basking in the heat. She hates me wasting hot water. Serves her right. I don't like training after school every day, but she insists I keep going. She says the school think I've got real potential and could make the national team one day. I reckon it's just because she thinks it keeps me out of trouble when she's at work.

The doorbell rings while I'm yanking my clothes back on. I run down to answer the door with a towel still wrapped round my head.

"Okay, Danni?" Levi pushes past me into the hall, breathing out a cloud of condensation. He folds his umbrella and sticks it behind the door.

"It's bloody freezing in here. Can't you turn the heating on?"

Levi has the patience of a two year old.

"I was just going to. Give us a chance!"

He grins at me and goes straight into the front room to switch on the TV. I've known Levi since primary school, so he tends to act like he lives here. He's come round to watch an episode of a stupid kids' soap with me. Today's episode was filmed at our school last week, and Levi's convinced we're going to be in the background shots somewhere. I think he secretly dreams of stardom.

"Want something to eat?" I don't bother to wait for a reply. Levi never says no to food.

I unwind the towel from my head and shake my hair out before reaching out to switch the kitchen light on. As the fluorescent light flickers into life, I shove the towel in the washing machine. The kitchen smells different. I can't place it. A musty, damp smell. Something's not right in here and I try to figure out what it is. Everything's tidy as usual. Then I notice a puddle of water gleaming on the work surface near the boiler. It's at least as big as a dinner plate. I feel the hairs on the back of my neck rising.

I look up at the ceiling but can't see where it's come from. Hope the boiler's not leaking. I don't want to deal with it and Mum's not back yet. I push the boiler switch to override and the heating blasts into life with a reassuring *whoomph*. Strange. The water must have come from somewhere. I stick my finger in it to make sure it's water.

Levi shouts through from the front room.

"Danni? It's about to start. Hurry up. I need food to survive these arctic conditions."

"The heating's on now," I shout back. "Shut up moaning a minute."

Without thinking I put the wet finger in my mouth. Bleugh, it's salty. I spit it out in the sink immediately. That was stupid, it could be anything. Hope I haven't poisoned myself. Does bleach taste salty? I pour myself a mug of water and swill my mouth out just in case. Then I find a packet of biscuits and head back to the front room.

"When's your mum back?" Levi is stretched out on the sofa resting his trainers up on the arm.

"Dunno. I thought she went in early today, but she must be on a late shift."

I plonk myself down in the armchair next to him.

The show starts. We catch glimpses of some kids in our year and at one point I see Levi going past the science lab window.

"It's not me, dumb-ass. It could be anyone."

"Anyone your height, with cornrows exactly like yours."

In the end I have to admit you can't really tell from the top of someone's head, but I still think it's him.

At six Levi has to go.

"Better run, Mum'll have my tea ready."

"Lucky you. Looks like I'm cooking mine again."

"I'll come back afterwards if you're still on your own. We can watch a film."

"Great."

Truth is, Levi isn't coming back just because he wants to see me. He's got a little brother and a baby sister and his terraced house is no bigger than mine. I think it's quiet as a morgue round here, but he seems to like it.

I notice it's still raining as he heads off into the dark.

I close the door and call the supermarket where Mum works. I want to find out what time she's back and if she's bringing any food. If not, I'll get a pizza out of the freezer.

"Betterbuys Superstore, Hayley speaking. How can I help?"

"Hi, could I speak to Mrs Lancaster, please?"

"Mrs Lancaster? Oh, you mean Erin. Is that Danielle?"

"Danni. Yes it is."

I try to remember which one Hayley is. They all look the same to me.

"It's her day off today, Danielle, remember?"

Obviously I don't remember. Would I be phoning if I did?

"Oh, right. Silly me. Thanks, Hayley. Bye!"

Mum didn't tell me it was her day off, I'm sure of it. I call her mobile and hear her ringtone faintly. It's coming from upstairs in her bedroom.

Just for a second I imagine she might be unconscious,

dead even, lying on the floor upstairs the whole time we were watching TV. It's stupid but as I go upstairs, my heart's beating really fast.

Of course she's not there. I spot her phone flashing on the wooden chair next to her bed. The chair seat's covered in globs of water, like someone's knocked a glass over or something. I'm amazed her phone's still working. I pick it up and stare at the screen. It's flashing the missed call from me. I wipe the phone on my jeans and put it back down on her bed.

It feels empty up here, like something's missing. Mum's shoes are lined up on her shoe rack as usual and the stuff on her chest of drawers is all neatly arranged. I pick up her perfume and spray it towards the dressing table mirror. It smells of Mum getting dressed up to go out. The scent hangs in the still air and forms a slight mist on the glass. Crap. Now I wish I hadn't sprayed it and try to rub it off with my sleeve.

I stare at my reflection. My dark brown eyes look massive in this light and you can hardly see the whites. My hair has gone all straggly and looks like straw. Probably should have blow-dried it after my shower. I pull it back into a ponytail to see if it looks any better, but then I can't find a hairband. I let it fall back down. I'm hungry. Time to cook my pizza instead.

* * *

Levi and I watch a horror movie about sharks. There's no plot, but some of the special effects are gruesome. All the main characters get eaten, one by one. I really shouldn't watch films like this. I spend too much time training in the sea in summer.

At the end, Levi checks his watch. "Gotta go. Mum'll be on my case." He grins. "I told her you were helping me with schoolwork."

"Levi, you're such a liar. What if she finds out?"

"She won't. I'll do it over half-term."

"Are you walking to school tomorrow?" I ask.

"Yeah – do you want to take Cheryl to nursery with me on the way?" Cheryl is Levi's baby sister. We often take her to nursery because his mum starts work really early.

"Maybe. Call me to check I'm awake."

When I've seen Levi out, I decide to clear up the mess I've made in the kitchen so Mum doesn't have a go at me later. She's been really snappy recently. I wish she'd taken her phone with her. As I shove my plate in the dishwasher, I glance at the water on the work surface under the boiler. At least the pool hasn't got bigger.

I try to remember if Mum said anything about going out tonight. I'm sure she didn't. It's not like her to stay out without letting me know. Usually when she's out she drives me crazy, phoning all the time to check I've eaten properly and haven't burned the house down.

When I've finished in the kitchen, I head upstairs to bed.

I read for a while, then glance at my alarm clock again. It's eleven. Mum's never stayed out this late without ringing me. I wonder if she's got a date or something else she didn't want to talk about. She might at least have found a way to call.

I lie back on my pillows and stare at the ceiling. It's turquoise. When we painted it, I wanted the whole room this colour because it made me think of the sea, and I'd read in a magazine that turquoise was relaxing. Levi says it's lurid. He doesn't think much of my whale posters either. He says sleeping in here would give him nightmares about drowning.

Maybe the posters are a bit childish. I stuck them up a few years ago now, so it's probably time for a change. Perhaps I'll ask Mum if I can redecorate over half-term. I reach out and switch my bedside light off. Mum makes such a fuss about me getting enough sleep, she'll just get annoyed if she thinks I've waited up for her.

Midnight. Still can't sleep. I wonder if I should phone someone? Trouble is, I don't know who to call. Mum doesn't have that many friends and anyway, it's late. I rack my brains trying to think of where she might have gone. I wish I'd paid more attention to her this morning, but it was so early. I'm sure she didn't say anything about going out.

I could call Dad, I suppose, but I can't face it right now. I haven't spoken to him for a while and he'll ask loads of questions. Just thinking about it makes me feel tired. Mum's bound to come back soon. I didn't hear her say it was her day off, so I guess she probably told me where she was going when I wasn't listening. I close my eyes and wait for sounds of her return in the darkness. At some point, I drift off.

Something is washed up by the waves, something big. It rolls over and over in the surf.

Looks like a body. It can't be…

Mum.

Bubbles pop around her half-open mouth. A tiny crab scuttles out.

I must have screamed myself awake. My throat feels completely dry. It's not even light yet. My heart's thumping and my T-shirt's damp with sweat. It's the most realistic nightmare I've had for years. As I gradually calm down, I feel the silence ringing in my ears. I'm still the only one in the house.

Something is wrong. Seriously wrong.

chapter 2

My alarm clock says 5 a.m. I stumble out of bed and head out onto the landing. Mum's door is still open. There's no one in her bed. Just a dent in the pillow where her head should be. Tears of shock sting my eyes. I know Mum. She'd have found a way to contact me if she was going to be out all night.

Her room smells stuffy. I forgot to turn the heating off last night. Despite the room temperature, I feel cold inside and sit down heavily on Mum's bed. Her phone's still where I chucked it yesterday. Should I call the police? It's too early to call Levi to see what he thinks.

Suddenly it occurs to me to find out whether Mum took

her car or not. If she didn't, she can't have gone far. I get up and walk over to her bedroom window, my heart beating faster in anticipation. I look out onto the street. It's raining. The cars all look strange colours under the street lights but I can't see ours anywhere. Wherever she is, she probably drove there.

I still can't decide about calling the police. But it's definitely time to call Dad.

His phone's switched off. I'll have to try his landline. I hurry downstairs to find the address book in the hall table drawer. I'm panicking so much, I start looking under D and can't find him. It's Mum's address book. His name's Nigel. How can I be so stupid? I hesitate briefly, then call the number. His phone rings for a while before he answers.

He grunts sleepily. "Hello?"

"Dad?"

"Danni? What's wrong? It's the middle of the night!"

"It's nearly morning. Mum hasn't come home."

I'm so worried, my breath catches in a sob.

Dad's calmer and much more practical than I expected him to be. Maybe because he's half asleep.

"Sweetheart, stop panicking a minute. Let's talk about this sensibly. Did she take the car?"

"Think so. I can't see it outside."

"Well that's good…"

"Is it? Why?"

"She probably had a drink with a friend and couldn't drive back."

"But, Dad, she'd have told me."

"Have you tried phoning her?"

"Of course I have! I'm not stupid. Anyway her phone's still here. She left it behind."

"So that'll be why she hasn't phoned."

"She'd have borrowed someone's phone to call me. I know she would."

"Maybe there was no signal or something. Is her bag there?"

"Not sure."

He tells me to go and have a look, so I do a quick search round the house. He's still on the line waiting.

"Can't see it anywhere." I feel like crying.

"Well that's good. Sounds like she's got the car and her bag, so she had plenty of options if she got stuck. She could have gone to a hotel if she needed to."

"Why would she go to a hotel, Dad? And why wouldn't she call?"

He hesitates. "Maybe she was out on a date? I don't know…"

I consider it for a moment. It had crossed my mind too.

"I think it's unlikely…" I feel uncomfortable discussing it with him.

"Look, love, I'm sure she's fine. Try not to panic. Go back to bed for a while."

"Why? That's stupid. I won't be able to sleep."

There's a moment's silence.

"Okay, tell you what. I'll get up and come over. Shouldn't take too long. Mum'll most likely be back by the time I get there, but it would be nice to see you. It's been too long."

I sigh with relief.

"Thanks, Dad."

We say goodbye and I put the phone down. I feel calmer knowing he's coming over, but it hasn't stopped me worrying about Mum.

Dad has to drive over from Cararth in Cornwall. It's in the middle of nowhere. That's where he lives now, in a flat above his new shop, Cararth Crystals. Mum hasn't let me visit him very often since he moved there, but it's always further than I think. It'll take him at least an hour to drive here to Graymouth.

The house feels airless. I go into the front room and switch on the TV. The programme choice is either news or cartoons. I watch the news, in case they say something about motorway pile-ups or mass shootings or something. They don't. I guess it's a good thing. I'm not happy though. Something's happened. I can feel it.

After a few minutes, I open the curtains and look out to

see if I can spot her car again. Parking is difficult in our road and sometimes Mum has to park in the next street. No one has a garage because all the houses in this part of Graymouth are terraces. I go upstairs and get dressed. I'll walk round the block just to check.

You don't meet many people out at this time in the morning. I only see one dog walker on my way. I widen the search beyond anywhere I've ever known her to park, until the drizzle penetrates my clothes and I start to feel cold. I walk slowly back home.

I'm glad I left the TV on. The place feels less empty.

Dad calls again.

"I'm on my way, love. Just checking she's not back yet."

"No, she's not."

"And she still hasn't called?"

"No."

He doesn't say anything for a minute. I wonder if he was hoping he wouldn't have to come.

"Okay, won't be long."

"Thanks for coming, Dad."

"Don't be daft. Like I said, it'll be great to see you!"

In different circumstances, I'd be looking forward to seeing him too.

* * *

The phone rings at seven, and this time I'm sure it's going to be Mum. It's not. It's Levi asking if I want to take Cheryl to nursery with him on our way to school. School? I hadn't even thought about it. I tell him about Mum.

Twenty minutes later Levi is at the door with Cheryl in her pushchair. He's looking worried.

"Danni? Have you called the police?"

I shake my head. Levi rarely takes things seriously. He's making me panic again.

"Have you called anyone? Her friends maybe?"

"Just Dad. He's on his way."

"Has he called the police?"

"Don't think so."

"Well my mum reckons you should call them. Just in case. Listen, I've got to take Cheryl to nursery now. Call me later. I want to know everything's okay."

"Thanks, Levi."

"I'll tell the school what's happened. But you'd better call them as well if you get a chance." He smiles. "Try not to worry, Danni. I know you will, but she's probably fine, okay?"

I attempt to smile back. He walks away and I watch him pushing Cheryl up the road until they turn the corner, wondering what number you call for the police if it isn't an emergency. Or maybe it *is* an emergency?

I close the front door.

The phone rings again and I answer immediately.

The woman sounds official.

"Is that Danielle Lancaster?" My heart starts racing.

"Yes, I'm Danni. Who's that?" My voice is shaking.

"Hello, Danni. This is PC Barnes calling from Graymouth Police Station." She sounds super friendly, so I'm convinced it must be bad news. I can hear the blood rushing round my eardrums.

"Is your father with you yet?"

"No, but he should be here soon." I feel like I can't breathe.

"Okay, Danni, now try not to worry. Your father has informed us that your mother may be missing. I'm calling to let you know that we haven't any information about her yet – but that's generally a good thing. If she'd been in any kind of accident, we'd be likely to know."

But what if someone's killed her? Would they tell me now, or wait until Dad's here? The policewoman's still talking.

"If she doesn't turn up in the next few hours, we'll send an officer round to talk to you and Mr Lancaster, okay, Danni? As you're under sixteen we need to make sure someone's responsible for your care."

"Thanks." It feels so weird that there's a policewoman talking to me. Somehow what she's saying doesn't seem real.

"Meanwhile, perhaps you could find us a recent picture of your mum to help with our investigation?"

"Okay." The hall seems to be getting darker. I think I'm going to faint.

"We'll come round at about midday if we haven't heard from you."

"I'll tell Dad." My voice comes out as a stupid squeak.

"Please let us know if she comes back in the meantime, won't you?"

"Yes of course." I just want her to get off the phone so I can try to breathe, but PC Barnes insists I write down her number in case I need to contact her.

At last she's satisfied that I know what to do and I can put the phone down. I sit on the chair in the hall, unable to move for several minutes. My mind's whirring.

So Dad called the police. He must have done it straight after he last called me. Which means that now he's worried too.

I pace up and down, trying to think. I can't help imagining all the worst case scenarios.

After a while I go to the kitchen and pour myself some cereal to pass the time. I don't know why. I don't feel like eating, and the crunching sounds too loud in my head when I try. I give up and empty the cereal into the bin. All the while I keep an eye on the time. Everything seems to have slowed down.

I wonder if I should phone the school, but decide to focus on finding a recent picture of Mum first. There are a couple of photo albums on the bookshelves in the alcove in the front room. The photos won't be recent because we don't get many printed these days, but it's all I can think of. I move my swimming trophies out of the way and pull the albums down.

In one of them there's a series of pictures of me on the beach with both Mum and Dad. I wonder who took them since we're all in them. Must have been one of Dad's relatives. Mum doesn't have family. I'm about five in the photos. Mum and Dad don't look very happy. Probably just before they split. The colours are a bit faded as the prints are so old.

Apart from that, it's nearly all pictures of me at various ages. Some at school, some with friends. Lots of me at swimming galas. There's one of Levi with an afro. I remember his mum moaning about it and making him have it cut. No recent pictures of Mum though. I take out one of the beach photos and look at it more closely. You can make out Mum's dark brown eyes and her wispy fair hair. I guess she still looks like that, just a bit older. I wish I'd taken more pictures of her.

If she comes back, I definitely will.

When she comes back. I must try to stay positive.

I stare out of the front room window, thinking of all the

detective programmes Mum likes watching. Maybe the police will want to know what dentist she goes to? They always check dental records against unidentified corpses. I shudder and turn away from the window. I can't think about things like that. She hasn't been gone that long. Like Dad said, she's probably fine.

Some chef on TV is talking about his new book on Italian cooking.

I think back over the last conversation I had with Mum. I'm almost positive she didn't say anything about it being her day off yesterday. I'm about to call her work again to double-check, but the doorbell rings just as I'm going to the phone. I run to open it.

chapter 3

"Dad!"

Dad looks really pleased to see me. I throw myself at him and we hug for a moment. A familiar smell of incense wafts from his clothing and fills my nostrils. Then I notice.

"Dad? What have you done to your hair?"

Last time I saw him, his hair was mousy brown. And not in dreads.

"Thought I'd dye it."

"Okay…but why orange?"

My attention is diverted by a flurry of excited barking coming from Dad's car.

"Better let Jackson out before he injures himself," I say.

Dad's Jack Russell is bouncing up and down trying to see out of the window, and barking like a maniac. The car is a decrepit-looking Ford estate, which some previous owner once hand painted a nasty, lurid pink. Dad bought it at an auction a couple of years ago, amazed that no one else even bid for it.

We let Jackson out and the little black and white dog jumps up at me excitedly. I'm really pleased he remembers me.

Dad puts on Jackson's lead. "Do you think Mum will mind me bringing him into the house?"

"She's not here, Dad, so she won't even know."

I can see he's worried. He looks up and down the street as if he's checking Mum's not about to come round the corner. I don't like to tell him she'd be far angrier about him being in the house than Jackson. I'm just glad he obviously thinks she's still alive.

Dad shifts uneasily in his chair as he looks round the room. He hasn't been here for a long time. I think back to our conversation on the phone. He seemed so calm about it all while we were talking, as if it wasn't unusual for Mum to vanish for no reason.

"Dad, did Mum ever do this before, when you were together?"

"Well, you know how it was, Danni. I probably annoyed her…"

It's true. He did.

"But yes, she went a couple of times without saying anything. Came back the next day…"

I think about it for a minute. From what I remember, Mum and Dad used to row all the time. She probably just wanted to get away from him for a bit. But Mum and I rarely fall out. We've been arguing more since I told her I wanted to stop competitive swimming, but that's only because she always thinks she knows what's best for me. It's not the same as her and Dad.

"I think something really bad has happened this time, Dad." It's almost a relief to voice my fear out loud.

"Give her a chance, Danni. No news is good news."

But if he really believed that, he wouldn't have called the police.

There's nothing to do but wait. I can't stand the tension of being in the house any longer.

"Dad, the police aren't coming until midday. Let's take Jackson out for a walk or something. I'm going mad sitting here."

Jackson hears the word "walk" and races to the front door. Dad picks up his lead. Looks like Dad can't wait to get out either.

* * *

We walk round to the park and throw sticks for Jackson for a while. It's getting on for eleven when I think about Mum's work again. I suggest we call in before we go back, and Dad thinks it's a good idea.

It's only when we get to the supermarket, I realize I was half hoping Mum would be here, working as usual, and she'd make some feeble excuse for not contacting me. Of course she's not. As Dad and I stand in the store talking to her colleague, Hayley, I begin to think coming here was probably a mistake.

For a start, Hayley isn't concentrating on what I'm saying. She's too busy staring at Dad, transfixed by his ripped vintage Sex Pistols T-shirt and the orange dreads. Admittedly anyone who knows Mum is going to be surprised meeting Dad. They could be from two different planets.

When Hayley realizes I'm asking about Mum, she's suddenly all concerned. Mum hasn't called the store either and they were expecting her here for the 10–4 shift today.

"It's not like her not to call, is it? I hope she's all right," says Hayley.

I don't want to stay here a minute longer.

"Anyway, we've got to go now, Hayley," I say. "The police are coming round."

Her eyes widen with interest. I bet she can't wait to tell everyone the gossip. I've no idea why Mum likes her job here so much. She's even taking the Betterbuys Superstore management course.

At least, she was.

On the way out of the store I spot some framed photos under a banner that reads, *Our friendly staff – helping you at Betterbuys!* There's a picture of Mum in her supermarket overall, smiling. My heart clenches. It's a recent picture. I turn back to ask Hayley for a copy to give to the police, but she's disappeared already. Dad has lost no time getting outside, and I can see him through the plate glass busy untying Jackson's lead from a railing. Jackson's jumping up and down, barking. I can't face hanging round to find someone else to ask about the photo, so I just lift the whole frame off the wall and tuck it under my arm.

The police come round exactly on time. It's a policeman and a policewoman and they ask a lot of questions.

"Are you sure she didn't say anything about where she was going yesterday, Danni?"

"I don't think so. Maybe she told me when I wasn't listening. She looked as if she was going to work like normal when I left for school. But then I found out later it was her day off."

The policewoman smiles at me. "And you didn't have a row?"

"No. Definitely not. She made me a packed lunch to save me rushing, and I went off to school as usual." I think about the packed lunch. Mum always makes me healthy sandwiches with loads of salad in, even though I moan about it. Yesterday she put an orange in my bag too. I don't like oranges that much, but she said I needed the vitamin C. I get a lump in my throat and my eyes start welling up. "Do you think...maybe something awful has happened to her?"

"I doubt it," says the policeman. He smiles at me kindly. "Maybe she just needed a break."

He's wrong. I know it. The tears fall down my face and I reach for a tissue in my pocket. I tell him she's not the type to just disappear. He can ask any of her friends at work and they'll say the same.

The policeman wants to talk to Dad alone, so the policewoman offers to come to the kitchen and make a cup of tea with me.

She sounds all friendly but I can see she's looking round the room carefully.

"Are you sure she didn't leave a note, Danni?"

"I'm sure. That's where we always leave notes for each other – see?"

I point at a red London bus magnet stuck on the fridge. Mum bought it when she took me there on a day trip once. There's no note.

I realize the policewoman is talking to me. "And you say she left her phone here – she hasn't got another phone, like say, one for work?"

"I don't think so. She works in a supermarket."

The policewoman writes it down in her notebook and asks for the name of the store.

"Maybe you could fetch her phone for me, Danni? We may need to check it back at the police station."

I run up to Mum's room and grab the phone off her bed. I hesitate a moment, remembering the way Mum talks into the phone a bit too loudly, as if the person she's talking to is deaf or something. I often tease her about it. I feel like crying again. I hurry back down and hand it to the policewoman. She takes the phone and looks at me sympathetically.

"We may as well go back to the front room and join your dad," she says, putting the phone into a bag.

Back in the front room, Dad glances up and smiles, but he looks worried. I wonder what the policeman has said to him.

"Your father is going to take you to stay at his place for now," says the policeman. "We think this would be for the best, as you're still a minor."

"What do you mean?" I'm starting to panic. Surely I don't have to go?

"We can't allow you to be left on your own. How old are you? Fourteen?"

"Fifteen."

He checks his notes. "Oh yes. Well that's still too young."

"But that's stupid! I can look after myself. What if Mum comes back?"

Dad interrupts. "Mum will understand. She wouldn't expect you to stay here on your own. Anyway, it's not that far!"

He's lying. It's miles.

I'm so upset that I can't speak for a few minutes. I feel like I'm abandoning Mum. Like I'm already accepting that she's not coming back, even though it hasn't yet been twenty-four hours since I came home from school to find she wasn't here.

Dad gives the police his number at the shop and they say they'll let us know as soon as they hear anything. At the last minute I remember the photos from the album and hand them to the policewoman.

"They're a bit old, aren't they?" says Dad.

"I brought a more recent one back from the supermarket," I mumble. I bring out the frame from where I shoved it beside the sofa. I probably shouldn't have taken it from the supermarket without asking but I don't care. I just want them to find Mum.

* * *

"You'd better pack what you need for a few days, Danni, just in case." The police have gone and Dad wants to get back to Cararth soon. Even Jackson seems restless again.

"What about school?" Even as I'm saying it, I remember today's the last day of school before half-term. Suddenly I feel a glimmer of hope.

"Dad, can we take Levi?"

"If he's allowed, yes of course." He looks at his watch. "Will he be back from school yet?"

"Not yet, but I need to get some stuff together anyway."

"Okay. As soon as he's back, we'll go round and ask."

I look at Dad with his rainbow titanium nose ring and his glowing dreads. I almost have second thoughts.

If Levi's mum is surprised at Dad's appearance, she hides it well.

"It's nice of you to ask, Nigel. I know he'd love to come but I need him here when I'm working. He looks after the other two for me during the half-term holiday."

Behind her, Syrus and Cheryl are having a pillow fight with the cushions on the sofa. Levi picks them both up and pretends he's going to throw them out the window. They squeal with delight.

"Perhaps he could just come for the weekend then?" says Dad.

Her face brightens. "Are you sure? It seems like a lot of trouble…"

"It'll be a pleasure. Danni might want to come back to fetch a few more things anyway. In fact her mum will probably be back by then."

He adds the last bit as an afterthought.

He doesn't believe it either.

chapter 4

I wake up and stare at the ceiling. It's pink, and there are fairy stickers all over it. For a second I can't work out where I am. Then I remember. I'm in Michelle's room. She's my half-sister. I haven't seen her for ages. Dad's not with her mum any more either, but she gets to stay with him more than I do. I guess that's why the spare room here is mostly hers.

Dad's house is on Cararth High Street. The shop takes up the ground floor and his flat's upstairs above the shop. I get up, pull some clothes on, and go to the kitchen. I can't go in the front room yet as Levi's still sleeping. Yesterday I didn't eat that much because I was too upset, so now I'm starving.

I say hello to Dad as I walk past his room. He's working at his desk and looks up and smiles.

"Make us a cup of tea, could you, Danni?"

"Okay, Dad. One sugar?"

"Thanks."

Something smells like bonfires.

"What's the smell, Dad?"

"Sage."

A cloud of smoke wafts out of his bedroom.

"You'll set the fire alarm off if you're not careful. Why are you burning that crap?"

"I'm clearing negative energies."

Negative energies? My heart sinks.

Dad must have clocked my expression. "Don't worry, nothing to do with Mum. Just bills. I've so many outstanding invoices this month." He sighs. "Bring the tea through, could you, love? I need to finish up before the shop opens."

While I'm making Dad's tea, the bell rings downstairs. I immediately wonder if it's the police with news about Mum.

"Can you get that, Danni?" Dad's muffled voice comes from his room. "Just let him in, he knows what to do. Tell him I'll be down in a minute."

I run down the stairs and open the door. It's a boy. He's about my age, maybe a year older. He's beautiful.

Dark floppy hair, falling in his eyes. For a moment I just stand there open-mouthed like a goldfish. Then I attempt to speak.

"Oh, hi. Um, Dad said…"

I can't remember a word he said.

The boy smiles.

"You must be Danni. Nigel talks about you all the time."

I smile back. I'm still rooted to the spot. He shifts a little.

"Er, can I come in?"

"Of course, sorry. Dad said you know what to do?"

"Yes, I think so." He grins and brushes past me and opens the door that goes into the shop area. I follow and watch as he pulls up the blinds and turns the sign on the shop door round to OPEN. The air is filled with a heady fusion of aromas from the display of incense by the counter.

"Is the cash in the till already?"

He's asking me. Of course I have absolutely no idea.

"I'll just go and get Dad." I smile again and back out of the room, nearly falling over the display of incense on the way. My heart is beating faster. Suddenly, I find my brain and put my head back round the door.

"Um, what's your name by the way? Sorry, I forgot to ask."

"Elliot."

He pushes his hair back off his forehead. His eyes are the bluest I've ever seen.

"I'll be right back, Elliot."

Dad's still in his room.

"Is the cash in the till, Dad? Elliot wants to know."

"Oh, sorry – no. Here it is."

Dad reaches under his desk and hands me a heavy bag full of change.

"Do you mind? I won't be long…"

"No, that's fine."

It's the first time I've felt like smiling in over twenty-four hours.

Elliot is arranging a display of quartz clusters in the window when I get back with the money. He's focused on the task, so I get a chance to look at him. I'm transfixed by the skilful way he moves things round without knocking anything over. His fingers are really long. Mum would say that means he's artistic. He turns to acknowledge me with a smile and I suddenly feel embarrassed about staring at him.

When he's finished, he switches on the halogen lighting and the crystals sparkle. I hand him the bag.

"Thanks." He smiles at me again, and starts emptying the bags of change into the till. The coins clatter into the metal tray and he has to raise his voice. "How long are you staying with your dad?"

I hesitate.

"I don't know really. It's complicated. My mother's disappeared somewhere."

His expression changes immediately and he stops what he's doing.

"Seriously?"

"Um, yes…at the moment we've got no idea where she is."

"That's awful."

Even though I'm really worried about Mum, I realize I'm enjoying the attention. I suddenly feel guilty.

"The police are looking for her. Maybe she'll show up today." I try to smile. "Hope so anyway."

He stares at me for a moment.

"Well if not, you're welcome to come out with me and my friends tonight. We're going to the Chill Out. Might help take your mind off it for a bit."

My heart beats faster. Is he serious? I open my mouth to say something, but then don't know what to say.

"Chill Out?" I manage to squeak. Does he mean a nightclub? I wonder how old he thinks I am.

"It's a bit lame. It's a sort of club for young people run by the church in the next village, to try to keep us out of trouble. But nothing else happens round here, believe me.

I just thought, if you're staying, you might like to meet some people."

"Yes – that would be…um, great. Maybe. I'd better ask Dad."

"My father could give you a lift if you like."

I'm about to mention Levi when Dad comes down and starts talking to Elliot about all the deliveries he's expecting. I'm not sure whether to hang round or not. I start to feel awkward and go back upstairs. I can take Levi down to meet him later.

I start worrying about the invite. It seems weird arranging to meet new people when I don't know what's happened to Mum. At the same time I'm getting butterflies thinking about going somewhere with Elliot, which is crazy. After all, it's not like it's a date or anything.

chapter 5

"Any chance of some toast, Danni?" Levi's finally awake. He yawns and puts his duvet over his head again before I can tell him to make it himself. He can be such a slob sometimes.

"So who were you chatting up downstairs?" His voice is muffled by the duvet.

"What do you mean?" I can feel myself blushing, which is very annoying.

"I heard you talking. What's he like?"

"Elliot? He works in the shop. He seems okay."

Levi uncovers his head and raises one eyebrow at me. "And?"

"And nothing."

I walk out to the kitchen to avoid any more questions. Making toast for Levi is easier than trying to explain why I feel like this about someone I've only just met.

Dad buys unsliced wholemeal bread, so I search out a bread knife and start cutting the loaf to make toast. As I slice, the knife handle seems to be sliding from my grip. I look down, and stupidly nick my finger with the blade at the same time. I put my finger straight in my mouth, to ease the pain. I feel a trickle running down my arm. Surely it's not bleeding that much?

I take my finger out of my mouth to look at it. It's not blood. It's water. The cut is tiny and has stopped bleeding, but my hand is covered in water. I look at the knife handle. It's all wet too, like it's been in the sink. I feel uneasy. How come I didn't notice it was that wet? I dry my hand and the knife on a tea towel and start again.

Before I've finished cutting the next slice, drops of water start falling onto the loaf. I check my hands and stare at them in dismay. Water is welling up out of the lines in my palms. I can see it happening. I must be hallucinating. I blink hard and look again, then run into the front room in total panic.

Levi looks up at me from the sofa bed.

"Danni? What's up? Is it your mum?"

I feel like crying.

"There's something seriously wrong with me. My hands are leaking water everywhere."

Levi starts to laugh.

"Hey, it's okay, dumb-ass – stuff happens when you meet boys."

"What do you mean? I know loads of boys. This has never happened before!" I hold my hands out towards him. Levi glances at them. He doesn't seem that impressed.

"Danni, when you really fancy someone, you can sweat like a pig. Trust me. It happens to me all the time."

"Great. They must find that so attractive."

He grins. "So you do fancy him. Knew it!"

I wipe my hands on my jeans and look at them again. Nothing. The water's stopped. I start breathing again and glare at Levi.

"So what happened to breakfast?" he yawns.

I try to convince myself I was imagining things, but I know I wasn't. I don't believe that much sweating is normal, whatever Levi says. But I think it has more to do with worrying about Mum than meeting Elliot. At the back of my mind, I can't help wondering if I'll ever see her again.

When he's eaten the toast, Levi and I go downstairs to the shop to see if we can help out. I'm slightly worried about what Elliot and Levi will think of each other, but they seem to get on fine. Levi starts cracking jokes about crystal balls, and soon has everyone laughing, even Dad.

I'm relieved when Elliot invites Levi along to the Chill Out later too. I was feeling a bit awkward about it. A small part of me almost wishes Levi wasn't here so I could have Elliot all to myself, but that's stupid. Every so often I catch Elliot looking at me like he's checking me out, though it might just be that he feels sorry for me because of Mum.

In the afternoon, Levi and I take Jackson down to the freezing cold beach for a walk.

"Bet you're looking forward to tonight."

"What makes you say that?"

"Going on a date. That's exciting."

"Don't be daft. Why would I want to take you out on a date?"

"You don't but you're stuck with me."

There's a tiny bit of truth in what he's saying but I don't tell him that.

"It's not a date. Elliot wants us both to come along."

"But he likes you."

"Do you really think so?" I'm trying not to sound pleased but he picks up on it immediately. He imitates me, putting on a stupid simpering voice.

"Do you really think so?"

I push him into a gorse bush. We both start laughing and Jackson barks at us excitedly.

"I feel bad about Mum though."

Levi's serious for a change. "It's not your fault she's gone AWOL."

"But I can't really enjoy myself until I know what's happened to her."

He grins. "Maybe Elliot should take me to this club without you then?"

I give him another shove.

We hear nothing from the police all day. Dad calls them to check there's no news. Levi and I sit and listen to see if we can pick up anything from Dad's side of the conversation, but it's mostly just "aha" and "I see" and "thank you".

"What did they say?" I ask as soon as he puts the phone down.

"Not much. They're following up a few leads apparently. I'm not sure if that means anything. And they still haven't found her car."

"Do you think I should stay here instead of going out tonight, just in case?" For a moment I'm torn. Obviously I want to see if the police find out anything about Mum. At the same time I want to see Elliot and meet his friends.

"No, you go and have fun. They probably say stuff like that to look like they're doing something. It'll be good for you to get out and make friends your own age round here. Then maybe Mum would agree to bring you over more."

Somehow I doubt it. Mum's been refusing to drive me here since Dad bought the shop last autumn, and she's really stubborn. But at least Dad's talking like he expects her to show up again.

chapter 6

Levi and I stand outside Elliot's house.

"You look nervous."

"Hey, thanks, Levi. You really know how to make me feel better."

I sneak a look at my hands. Levi catches me doing it and grins. I ring the doorbell.

The door opens and a middle-aged woman answers. She's got a black coat on and she's clutching a handbag like she's just about to go out. She stares at us in horror, then crosses herself quickly.

"What are you doing here? We don't mix with you people."

I'm shocked that she reacts like that to Levi. I wonder if he's ever come up against such open racism before.

"We've come to see Elliot. Is this the right house?" I ask.

"He won't want to see you. Go away."

Now I'm totally confused. It's not Levi she's staring at. It's me. I'm sure I've never seen this woman before in my life. How come she thinks she knows me?

Elliot suddenly appears behind her in the narrow doorway.

"Aunty Bea? Can you let my friends in for a minute until Dad's ready to give us a lift?"

"You don't want that sort in your house," says the woman.

I catch Elliot's horrified expression.

"I thought you were just leaving, Aunty Bea. Can you please move out of their way?" Elliot spits the words out angrily. He sounds furious.

The woman pushes past us into the street, glaring directly at me as she passes. She brushes so close, I step back in alarm.

As she walks off towards the car park, I hear her hissing something under her breath.

Elliot looks at Levi. "I'm so, so sorry."

Levi grins. "Why apologize to me? It's Danni she didn't seem to like. Perhaps we should leave her out here?"

Elliot laughs and looks relieved. I guess he thinks Levi's joking.

"I can't believe she was that rude to you. Since we lost

Mum, she behaves like she owns the place and we can't get rid of her. Come inside."

I stare at him.

"You lost your mum?"

"She died. A while ago now." He smiles sadly.

"Oh no! I'm really sorry." I can't think what else to say. Poor Elliot. I get a dull ache in my heart suddenly, wondering how I'd feel if Mum was dead.

At that moment a man comes out of the kitchen, putting his coat on with one hand and jangling car keys in the other. He doesn't look much like Elliot, but he's obviously his dad. He grins at us all and tells us to follow him out to the car. No staring, no giving me the evil eye. At least he doesn't think he knows me too.

The Chill Out is in an old chapel building in Ancrows, a village a couple of miles away. By the time we get there, I'm feeling glad Levi is with us. It's difficult going into a new place with someone you've only met that day. I find it hard to talk to people I don't know.

When we get inside, it's obvious the place is still used as a church. The rows of pews have been pushed to one side, and we're greeted by a friendly woman with very flushed cheeks. She's wearing a baggy jacket over her clothes and there's a crucifix pinned on the lapel. Elliot introduces her as Mrs Goodwin.

"Welcome!" she says, smiling broadly. "I'm the minister here at Ancrows Chapel."

I wonder what kind of evening we've let ourselves in for. I hope it's not a Bible class or something.

It turns out Mrs Goodwin's really nice. She stays behind the scenes all evening, only coming out to bring snacks and drinks or help set up the pool tables.

Levi spends his entire time chatting to a friend of Elliot's. She's tall and slim and looks like a model. I overhear her talking about her school and get the impression she's the same age as me and Levi. I also find out that Elliot's already in sixth form, so I was right. He must be at least a year older.

The girl's called Sarah and she hangs on Levi's every word. I can't help smiling as he starts telling her exaggerated stories about life in Graymouth.

"Must be really boring for you here," she says. "I mean you can't even get alcohol – everyone recognizes you in the shop, so there's no way."

"I've got fake ID, but it can still be a problem," says Levi.

"Fake ID? Wow." Sarah looks impressed.

"Yeah my cousin told me how to get a fake driving licence. I got into real trouble though, so I stopped using it."

"No, really, with the police and everything?" Even Elliot is drawn into Levi's story.

"Nah, my aunty. Much more scary. She caught me in

the supermarket down the road trying to buy some cans for a party. I was grounded for weeks."

Everyone laughs, including me. I remember it well. His mum was furious with him.

"Glad I'm not the only one with awful relatives," says Elliot in my ear.

On balance, I'd rather deal with Levi's aunt than his any day. But I don't tell Elliot that. I just smile.

Elliot challenges me to a game of and I readily agree. It saves me having to think of things to talk about. I feel reasonably confident I won't make a total fool of myself because Sophie, a friend of mine at school, has a table tennis table in her basement. I've spent hours on wet Saturdays playing endless tournaments with her. On the other hand, playing with Elliot makes me feel shy.

At first, Elliot makes the game easy, but he soon realizes I can play. Once we start in earnest, my competitive streak takes over. I want to win. Then suddenly our hands touch as we move round the table. The contact throws me so much I lose the next couple of games. I can't stop blushing, especially when I catch Levi laughing at me.

"Let's stop and get a drink," says Elliot. He puts his bat down.

"Okay." I put mine down too. Elliot takes my arm and guides me towards the drinks table.

"Coke?"

"Thanks." My arm's still tingling where he touched me. I find I'm blushing again. I don't even like Coke, but I accept the cup he hands me gratefully and take a big swig.

I look hesitantly over towards Levi in case he's still laughing at me. Fortunately he hasn't noticed anything and he's got his arm casually draped around Sarah's shoulder. The way she's looking into his eyes, it's plain she really likes him. I'm pleased because it makes it obvious that Levi and I are just friends. The downside is I feel even more awkward with Elliot. I start asking stupid questions to cover my nervousness.

"What's that about?" I point at some words in a foreign language that have been carefully painted onto the wall in gold lettering. *In Nomine Meo Daemonia Eicient.*

Elliot opens his mouth to answer, but Mrs Goodwin chips in. I hadn't noticed she was standing so close.

"We've only recently opened the chapel again. We'll get someone to paint over it."

I've no idea why she wants to paint over it, but I nod anyway.

"What does it say?" I ask politely.

"It's Latin. It says, *They will cast out demons in my name.* My predecessor's handiwork of course. It's taken over twenty years for this place to open again."

"How come?" I've no idea what she's talking about.

"Surely you must know?" Mrs Goodwin stares at me.

"You've heard what happened with the Chosen?"

I shake my head. "Chosen what?"

She looks genuinely surprised. "Usually it's the only thing people know about Ancrows. It was a cult. Extremists of course. They're always bad news. Get Elliot to tell you about it on the way home if you're interested."

I realize Mrs Goodwin is encouraging everyone to leave. I glance at my phone and see it's ten o'clock already. Elliot and I go to find our coats, and gradually everyone starts moving towards the door. I can't believe the evening has gone by so quickly and I feel almost guilty that I've hardly thought about Mum until now. I guess there still isn't any news about her or Dad would have called me.

When we get outside, Elliot suddenly puts his arm round me. I catch the faint scent of something like pine resin. Maybe cedar.

"Are you okay, Danni? You seem a bit quiet. Are you worried about your mum?"

Feeling him so close, I'm no longer able to think about anything except him. My heart's beating so fast, I don't know what to do. I rest my head awkwardly on his shoulder. The smell of cedar gets stronger.

I realize someone's calling me.

"Danni?" Dad beckons to us from the car.

Great timing, Dad.

I feel awkward, but try to look casual as I move away from Elliot.

"Just going to fetch Levi," I call over to Dad.

Then I run back inside the chapel to find him, still tingling with excitement that Elliot put his arm round me.

It's annoying not getting a chance to talk to Elliot, but Dad insists I sit in the front seat next to him. As we set off back to Cararth, he keeps glancing at me like he wants to say something.

Suddenly I feel a wave of anxiety. "What's up, Dad?"

He coughs nervously. "Listen, love, I don't want you to worry, but the police called earlier."

I feel like someone's tipped a bucket of cold water over me.

"Have they found Mum?"

There's a short silence.

"Possibly…" He's staring ahead through the windscreen. He's avoiding looking at me.

"Possibly? Is she…?" I can't bring myself to say "alive".

"If it's her, yes, she's alive. But I don't want to raise your hopes…"

"If it's her? Dad, what do you mean *if*?"

"A woman matching Mum's description was found near here two days ago. But she had no ID on her, so the local police force have been working through national missing person reports and they only just made the connection."

For a moment I don't say anything. I don't get it. What does he mean, *found*? My mind's whirring. If it is Mum, why wasn't her bag with her? She takes it everywhere. Had she been attacked? And why was she here and not in Graymouth?

I want to ask a million questions but I feel so churned up I can hardly talk.

"Please can you stop the car? I feel sick."

chapter 7

I sit on the verge in the darkness. The cold air is making me feel slightly better, but I still feel ill.

"Of course it might not be her." Dad is trying to play it down. Maybe he's worried I'll be even more upset if the woman the police have found turns out not to be Mum.

"The police wouldn't have contacted you if they weren't pretty sure," I say.

"Hopefully you're right, Danni – Graymouth police won't tell us anything more until they confirm details with the local force over here. They just said the woman that's been found has some kind of amnesia. But she hasn't any obvious injuries."

I shiver.

"Why can't we go to see her right away? I don't understand!"

"Love, I told you. They won't even let us know where this woman is until they've checked out every possibility. They have to be thorough. I'm guessing they have a lot of safety measures in place to protect everyone involved. They've promised to call first thing tomorrow."

I start crying again in sheer frustration. "But if it's Mum, she'll want to see me now! What was she doing round here?"

"Danni, I haven't got any answers, I'm really sorry. There's nothing we can do until the police call in the morning."

I glance up at Dad's car, parked up by the side of the road. Elliot's staring anxiously in our direction from the back window.

I take a deep breath and stand up shakily. I can't stay out here all night arguing with Dad about it. We might as well get back in the car. I walk over and open the passenger door.

"You okay, Danni? Do you still feel sick?" Elliot sounds really concerned.

"I'm fine. Sorry to hold you up."

"It's no problem, really. If there's anything I can do…"

"Don't think so. But thanks." I slide onto the front seat and put my seatbelt back on.

Levi doesn't say anything, which shows he's worried. We stay silent for the rest of the journey.

When we drop Elliot off, Dad gives him a shop key so he can come and open up in the morning. We'll be setting off to see Mum – because it *has* to be her – as soon as the police tell us where she is.

I try to smile at Elliot.

"Thanks for taking us to the club this evening. See you tomorrow maybe."

"Hope so – see how you get on." He looks at Dad. "Don't worry about getting back in time for the shop, Nigel. I can lock up."

"Thanks," says Dad.

I wind up the car window.

Hope so. That's what he said. It's the only good thing I can hang on to right now.

Elliot raises an arm to wave as we drive off. The way he's standing, he looks so sad. I wonder when his mother died.

Then I stop thinking about Elliot and my mind floods with worry about Mum.

Dad wants us all to go to bed when we get inside.

"We're not going to do any good sitting here talking all night. We should get some rest. Tomorrow could be a long day." He wanders off to his room, yawning.

I still feel wide awake. I chat quietly with Levi for a while, but I can tell he's really tired too. He does his best to reassure me about Mum, and I realize it's pointless me speculating any more. I can't do anything until the morning. Eventually I decide I should leave Levi in peace and go to bed.

I climb under the duvet and lie back on the pillows. I'll never be able to sleep. I keep going over and over the few details we've been given. Maybe it's not Mum after all. I certainly can't think of any reason why she would have come here to Cornwall when she always avoids the place. Yet the police obviously think it could be her…

I close my eyes, just for a moment.

Under the waves, the rocks are mottled white like corpse flesh. A gold chain spirals in the dark green light. The current pulls me. I can't get away. I can't breathe. As I hit the rocks, I'm sure I'm about to die.

I wake up with a start. It's daylight, but only just. The image of the rocks is still seared on my mind. I even feel my head tentatively to check for bruises, then feel stupid. Of course there aren't any.

A few minutes later, Dad hands me a cup of tea. He's still in his pyjamas.

"Drink this, love. And don't rush. I don't want you burning

your throat. The police haven't called yet so you've plenty of time." He smiles encouragingly, but he looks worried. "Are you okay? I heard you shouting in your sleep…"

I nod. "I'm fine, thanks. Just a nightmare."

I hear Dad's phone ring a few minutes later while I'm in the shower. I grab my towel immediately and run out of the bathroom, dripping water everywhere.

Dad's standing in the kitchen still holding his phone.

"Good news, Danni! The police say the woman they've found is definitely Mum. They managed to confirm it using her medical records. She's in Bodmin hospital, which isn't that far from here. We can leave as soon as we're all dressed."

I should be overjoyed, but there's something about the way he said it.

"So what's wrong with her?"

He hesitates. "Apparently she's still got this amnesia thing. They said to warn you she's not making much sense yet."

"Perhaps she'll be okay when she sees me?"

"Hope so!" he says. His voice sounds a bit too bright and breezy, and somehow it doesn't ring true.

"Did they say anything else?"

"No, not really. That's all. Let's just get ready and we can go."

* * *

We pull up in the hospital car park. There's a moment of silence when Dad turns off the engine. I look up at the ugly concrete building in front of us.

I open the car door and get out. Levi climbs out of the back.

"You don't have to come in, Levi."

"Nah, it's okay. You need someone sensible with you."

I glance at Dad. His dreads glow even brighter in the early morning light. He's chosen to wear a diamanté nose ring today, to match his sequinned Blondie T-shirt. Worst of all, his jeans are way too short and he's wearing pink loafers. I wonder how he could possibly think that outfit was a good idea.

Levi is right. I do need someone sensible with me.

The foyer is dismal, though they've tried to cheer the place up by painting it buttercup yellow. A small notice says the framed pictures on the walls are all done by former patients.

"Pity they obviously needed therapy," observes Levi.

We troop up to the reception desk. Two middle-aged women behind the desk are discussing someone's wedding arrangements and it's a while before they notice us. One of them finally looks up.

"We've come to see Erin Lancaster," Dad says as he catches her eye. "The police said you'd be expecting us."

"The police? Oh! Is that the poor woman they found on the beach?"

Now we've definitely got their attention. They look at each other furtively and then one of them points us towards the lift.

"Go up to the third floor – the psychiatric unit. We'll let Dr Murphy know you're coming."

The psychiatric unit? They told Dad she had amnesia. I think of a horror film Levi and I watched recently, about a psychiatrist experimenting with people's brains. Levi and I laughed so much at the time. Suddenly it doesn't seem so funny.

As we walk into the lift, I see the receptionists whispering to each other. I think I hear the word *naked*. I'm beginning to feel like I can't breathe. One of them picks up the phone.

A woman in a white hospital coat is waiting for us when we reach the third floor. She looks too young to be a doctor. Her dark hair is scrunched back into a ponytail.

"Mr Lancaster?" Her accent sounds familiar but I can't place it. I'm not great with accents.

"Call me Nigel," says Dad, shaking her hand.

"I'm Dr Murphy." She turns to me. "You must be Danni. The police told us about you." Her eyes are different colours, one blue and one green. I nod and try not to stare.

"Is it okay if my friend Levi comes in too?"

She smiles at Levi before she answers.

"Yes of course. These things are much harder on your own – I'm glad you've brought a friend with you. I'll take you to your mum's room. We've put her in by herself at the moment, until she…well, just for now. I warn you, Danni, she's not really responding yet. We're hoping she'll improve soon – and maybe your visit will help."

We follow her down a long corridor which has lots of closed doors on both sides. Horrible wailing sounds come from behind one of the doors. The place smells of disinfectant. My legs start to feel like they belong to someone else. I want to run away but they keep propelling me forwards.

"You've got eyes exactly like your mum's," Dr Murphy says to me. "Same lovely velvet brown."

"Thanks." I smile nervously. "People often say I look like her."

"She's got my ears though," says Dad, trailing behind us along the corridor.

Dr Murphy glances back at Dad and doesn't say anything. You can't see Dad's ears anyway as they're hidden under the orange dreads.

"Where are you from?" I still can't place Dr Murphy's accent.

"Ireland – west coast. Have you ever been?"

I shake my head. "Sorry."

"It's beautiful. You should go sometime."

She stops by one of the doors. "This is her room. Now before we go in, keep in mind that she's not well, Danni. That's why she's here. She may not even recognize you, but try not to get too upset – it's still very early days."

My heartbeat sounds so loud in my ears, it's practically deafening me. Dr Murphy opens the door and we follow her into a small, stuffy room painted sickly green. It smells a bit like feet. A tiny window lets in some daylight but it's too high up to see out of.

Mum sits motionless on the metal-framed hospital bed, propped up against stark white pillows. I hardly recognize her because of the total lack of expression. But it's definitely her.

My heart plummets. It's a real shock to see her like this, even though I've been warned.

"Mum? Mum!" I go over to the bed and gently shake the sleeve of her hospital gown. She looks blankly at a point somewhere above my head. Then she just turns and stares up at the window.

"Mum?" I stroke her hair. She doesn't even blink.

This can't be happening. What's wrong with her?

"Just keep talking to her, Danni," Dr Murphy says quietly. "Don't give up. We're not sure if she can understand or not, but we think she can hear okay. Talking to her could be really helpful."

I feel uncomfortable and try to think of what to say. I glance at Dad but he just looks like a rabbit trapped in the headlights.

"I'm going to try and catch the consultant a moment so he can have a word with you," says Dr Murphy. "He's not in for long today, what with it being a Sunday – but you may be lucky."

She heads towards the door, taking her clipboard. She smiles at me on her way out.

"Don't worry, I won't be long. Ring this bell if you've any problems."

The door swishes closed behind her.

Dad seizes the opportunity. "Maybe I should go and grab a coffee before she comes back," he says. "Give you some time alone with Mum."

He leaves the room so fast I don't have time to argue, but I feel really angry with him. How can he just leave me here? I know it must be a shock for him to see Mum like this, but what about me?

Levi touches my arm gently. "Do you actually want some time alone with her, Danni?"

I calm down and think about it for a minute. At least Levi isn't running away.

"Yeah, maybe it's not such a bad idea. I'll probably feel

less stupid talking to her on my own. Looks like she's not too big on answers right now."

He nods. "I'll be right outside the door, okay?"

If only Dad could have said that.

I sit on Mum's bed and stroke her face softly. She's just staring at the wall. I find her hand and try to hold it. The hand is cold, even though the room is like an oven. It feels like there's no air in here.

Suddenly, she jerks her hand away, and I jump. She starts tugging frantically at her sheets, eyes flicking round the room like she's looking for someone. She doesn't seem to see me at all.

"What do you want, Mum?"

She's scaring me.

"Shall I ring the bell or something?"

She doesn't answer. I don't think she's even heard me. She's getting more and more agitated. I've no idea what to do. I keep wondering if I should press the bell.

"Where's it gone? Who's taken it?"

The sudden sound of her voice shocks me.

"Help me, you've got to help me...Mam?" She's getting louder.

Then she looks directly at me for the first time. "Find Mam for me?"

I've no idea what to do. This woman in front of me is

nothing like my mum. Yet it is Mum, of course it is. Levi pops his head round the door. He must have heard her shouting.

"You all right in there?"

I nod and try to smile. But I don't feel okay at all.

"The doctor's coming back."

I know he's trying to reassure me.

"Thanks."

He hesitates a moment, then disappears back into the corridor.

As soon as I'm alone with Mum again, she starts whimpering. I can't do anything to stop her.

I've never felt so powerless or sad in my entire life.

Through the window I hear the sound of a road drill somewhere in the hospital grounds. It seems strange that other people are out doing normal everyday things.

I try to get Mum's attention again. "What's happened to you, Mum? Are you still in there somewhere? Please don't do this. Please?"

I might as well be talking to a zombie. She doesn't look at me. I hear voices out in the corridor and bite my finger hard to try and stop the tears coming.

The door opens and Levi comes back in with Dr Murphy and an older man with thinning grey hair. The man stares at me through steel-rimmed glasses.

"Danni? I'm Mr Albright, your mother's consultant."

I nod and we shake hands.

"I understand you're the next of kin?"

I've never thought of myself like that, but say yes anyway.

"Do you have an adult here with you today?"

"My father. He's just gone to get coffee."

"You may want him here with you."

Mr Albright sounds impatient, a bit like my headmaster at school.

"Can I run and find him?" I feel nervous.

He looks at his watch, shakes his head. "No matter, you can tell him later."

Dr Murphy shifts uncomfortably and for a second I think she wants to get Dad for me.

"I'll go and find him," says Levi. He looks at me and mouths "Won't be long" as he leaves the room.

But Mr Albright doesn't wait. He starts talking the moment Levi's gone.

"As you can see, Danni, your mother is almost completely non-responsive to verbal communication. The good news is the brain scan we conducted when she was brought in didn't highlight any serious head injuries, just some localized bruising around the temple region, which may have led to a slight concussion. So it's a bit of a mystery. Perhaps you can tell us about her state of mind the last time you saw her? Did she appear very depressed, or upset in any way?"

I've been through this with the police already.

"She was no different from usual that morning. She was just fussing about me getting ready for school. Same as always…"

My voice trails off. Tears well up in my eyes and spill down my cheeks. I wish Dad would come back. He's so useless sometimes. I wipe the tears away quickly with my sleeve.

"We're only asking as her case is somewhat unusual," Mr Albright continues, stroking his chin. "Does she have a history of psychiatric problems?"

I shake my head. "I don't think so…"

He stares at me for a few seconds. "Hmm. Well I think the way she was found, and the lack of serious external injury, suggests that she's suffering from some form of acute stress disorder which has led to the dissociative stupor she's in now."

Dr Murphy chips in. "He means we think she's possibly had some kind of shock, Danni, and this may be her way of dealing with it. But you have no idea what that shock or upset might be?"

I shake my head again. I feel numb. Mr Albright moves towards the door.

"Then we'll wait a while longer to see if she improves,"

he says. "But we may need to discuss a more radical treatment for her on your next visit."

Something about what he just said makes me shudder. He mutters a few words to Dr Murphy and leaves the room.

"Has anyone told you where your mother was found?" asks Dr Murphy when he's gone.

"I don't think so. The police talked to Dad. I think they just told him that she was in here, suffering from amnesia."

"She was on the beach at a place called Porthenys. Did she ever mention this place? Does it mean anything to you?"

"Porthenys? No, I don't think so. I've no idea why she would go there. I just thought she'd gone to work…"

"The ambulance crew said they thought she'd been in the sea. She was starting to show signs of hypothermia. Her hair was still wet when they brought her in. Perhaps you can think of somewhere round here she might have left her things? She had nothing with her on the beach."

I shake my head. "No idea, sorry."

Mum starts calling out again.

"Mam? Please help me, Mam." Her voice cuts my heart like a knife and I start to cry again. Dr Murphy hands me a tissue and smiles sympathetically.

"Is it possible for you to bring your grandmother in with you next time? She asks for her a lot."

"But I haven't got one – not on Mum's side anyway."

"Oh? I'm sorry. I thought the way she kept asking… Never mind, it's great that you're here. That should help her a good deal."

Her words start me thinking. It feels like there's a lot I don't know about Mum right now. Like what she was doing around here, and what happened to her. And I realize that she never talked about her family or her past. But I'd know if my grandmother was alive.

Of course I would.

chapter 8

As we leave the hospital, I'm still angry with Dad. I can hardly bring myself to look at him. Why did he have to get a cup of coffee at the critical moment? If only he'd been there when Mr Albright was talking. Even Levi wasn't with me, because he was chasing after Dad instead. Already I can't remember half of what the consultant said.

"I've said I'm sorry, Danni. There'll be other chances to meet Mr...you know, the consultant. I just didn't expect him to come and go so quickly."

I don't bother to answer.

"Anyway, love, where do you want to go? No point in rushing back for the shop. Elliot's there until it closes.

We've got time to take Jackson for a walk before we drive Levi back to Graymouth."

It feels like it's been one of the longest days of my life and it's still only lunchtime. All I want to do is find out why Mum was in this area in the first place. She usually avoids coming anywhere near Dad's place if she can, and we never visited Cornwall when I was younger. I try to tone down my anger.

"Could we go to Porthenys – where they found Mum – or is it miles?"

"Porthenys? No, it's not far. We can drive there if you want."

I look at Levi. He shrugs and nods.

"Okay, Dad, I guess we may as well take a look."

I want to see if I can discover anything that might explain what happened to Mum. After talking to Dr Murphy, I wonder if perhaps her car's still there, or her bag, or something that might give me a clue what she was doing. I keep going over it in my mind. Whatever possessed her to go in the sea on a freezing cold day? I'm sure she must have left her things somewhere nearby.

The three of us huddle together against the cold wind in Porthenys car park. Dad's is the only car here. It looks almost luminous against the muted colours of the few houses down by the beach, but for once the bright pink is comforting. There's something dark about this place. Even Jackson is subdued.

There's a tourist information board next to a sort of thatched shed with a picnic table and benches inside. We read the board in silence.

The picturesque hamlet of Porthenys, with its excellent bathing beach, is also sometimes known as "the village that died". One tragic night back in February 1898, a terrible storm wiped out the entire fishing fleet of Porthenys and the male half of the village population with it. The village never recovered, and in time was abandoned completely.

Fortunately, times have changed. In recent years Porthenys has become a thriving holiday destination, and apart from a few remaining ruins by the side of the lane, most of the formerly derelict houses have now been fully restored.

Under the notice, someone has stuck an advert for Charming Traditional Cornish Cottages, listing a phone number to contact for holiday lets available in Porthenys.

"Wonder how many people died in that storm?" Levi is looking down towards the beach.

In the dull light, shutters closed fast against the biting wind, the cottages don't look very charming to me.

Dad shivers. "Think I'll stay here and check the car over if you don't mind. Need to find out what that ticking noise in the engine is all about."

I'm sure there's nothing wrong with the car apart from the colour. I reckon he's just ducking out again. He probably only agreed to come here because he felt bad about disappearing in the hospital.

"Take Jackson down to the beach with you." Dad raises the bonnet of the car with a clunk. "He needs a good run."

Jackson and I are nearly at the cottages by the beach when I realize Levi is lagging behind. I turn back to see him crouching next to a gap in the hedge.

"Danni? Come and take a look at this."

I walk back, dragging a reluctant Jackson, and crouch next to him. We peer through the gap. A couple of ruined cottages have been completely hidden by the high hedgerow and we're staring into what would once have been the front door of someone's home.

Ducking under the overhanging branches, we step inside. The cottage roof is long gone, but you can still see where the fireplace was. Dark stains in the brickwork show where a staircase led to an upper floor. The air is still because we're out of the wind, but it's icy cold in here. A pigeon suddenly flaps off from the thick ivy covering the back wall and I nearly jump out of my skin.

"Shall we go on down to the beach and take a look round?"

Levi nods.

I feel unnerved. I can't imagine why Mum would want to come to this place.

As we wander down to the beach, I start wondering who found her and called the ambulance. I wish I'd asked Dr Murphy if she knew. I might get Dad to ask the police later. Maybe they live in this village? I can see a few houses higher up on the cliff that don't look like holiday lets. Perhaps Mum was able to say something to whoever found her before she went to hospital. I'd love to find out.

The beach is narrow and rocky, enclosed on both sides by dark slate cliffs. The whole place smells dank and looks deserted. I can see from the line of seaweed that the tide comes right up to the slipway by the houses. It will have swept the beach several times over since Mum was found, and I'm disappointed. I doubt we'll find any trace of her here.

Jackson is determined to help us and keeps bringing me stalks of rotting seaweed and pieces of driftwood to throw. His barking echoes sharply off the rocks. The only other sounds are the gulls and the crashing waves.

I get an uncomfortable feeling that we're being watched. I turn back towards the village and notice the dark outline of a man silhouetted against the holiday cottages. I'm sure he was staring at us, but now he's looking towards the car park.

A large Rottweiler appears beside him and Jackson loses all interest in trying to get me to throw things for him. Before I can stop him, he races off towards the other dog. I feel uneasy.

"Jackson, come back!"

Jackson chooses not to hear me.

"Shall we go and fetch him?" Levi doesn't wait for a reply and starts running back up the beach. I run after him.

The closer we get to the man, the stronger my feeling grows that something's wrong. He doesn't stop staring at us as we approach, his pale eyes unblinking. He isn't smiling. It's possible he's annoyed at having to deal with Jackson, but I think it's something about us. As the wind whips at his unbuttoned black coat, I'm surprised to see a large silver crucifix hanging down the front of his purple shirt.

He recognizes me. I see it in his face when he looks at me. Yet I've never seen this man before. He crosses himself quickly and glares. I feel my skin come up in goosebumps. That's the second time in twenty-four hours someone's reacted like that. What's wrong with this place? I feel like there's something going on I'm expected to know about, but I've no idea what it is. It's starting to scare me.

"You need to control your dog." His voice is loud and authoritative, like someone used to giving orders and being obeyed. The Rottweiler growls at us. Levi steps back in alarm and I try to catch Jackson's attention so I can get him on his lead. Of course he ignores me completely, and keeps crouching and then leaping up and barking excitedly at the massive dog. The Rottweiler growls more loudly and bares its teeth. Jackson cringes and whines.

"What are you doing here?" The man sounds about as friendly as the Rottweiler. And what does he mean anyway? It's a public beach and anyone can go on it.

"Danni's mother was found here a couple of days ago." Levi is remarkably polite. "Did you hear about it? She's in hospital now. We've come to see if we can find any clue as to what happened to her."

I wish he hadn't said anything. I don't like the look of this man. I definitely don't want him knowing anything about me. He keeps staring at me. When he opens his mouth to speak, I can't help recoiling at the sight of his crooked teeth, stained dark with nicotine.

"You mean the poor lost soul on the beach? Gabriel found her. He's such an angel. I went straight back home to call an ambulance. Had to cover her with my coat first of course." He brushes his hand absently against his coat sleeve like he's wiping off some invisible dirt.

Gabriel has to be the dog, though he doesn't look like

any kind of angel to me. All the same, I'm glad he found her. She might have died of exposure if he hadn't.

"Thank you for helping her." I manage to force myself to smile at the man.

"Don't thank me. I was merely bringing a sheep back to the fold. It's my job. I'm a minister of God." He caresses the silver crucifix. I catch a whiff of his sour breath on the wind.

Jackson starts growling softly. A snarl from the Rottweiler silences him, but I know how Jackson feels. I don't like the man either.

"Well thanks anyway." I want to get away from him as soon as we can, but I still have to ask, "Did she say anything when you found her?"

"No."

Somehow I don't think he'd tell me if she had.

"Did she have anything with her? I wondered where she put…" My voice fades to silence under his cold stare. His eyes have virtually no colour. They're pale, washed out blue, like the circle round the yolk of a hard-boiled egg.

"Nothing."

"Not even her handbag?"

"Nothing. There's no point in you looking further."

His eyes keep flickering to the sea and back. He looks shifty suddenly, and I feel sure he's lying. The trouble is I've no idea why, or what about. I drop my gaze and bend down to grab Jackson. For once he keeps still. As soon as

I get the lead on, I turn to walk back to the car, a shudder rising up my spine. Levi loses no time in following me.

"What's wrong with everyone round here? Why do they look at you like that?" Levi is furious. "Some bloody minister he was. That guy was *naaasty*!"

The way he says it makes me smile despite everything. We walk back to the car park. Dad isn't even pretending to fix the engine any longer. He's sitting in the driver's seat reading a book on crystal healing. Levi thinks it's funny, but I don't.

Dad looks up as we approach the car.

"Find anything?" he asks.

I try to sound casual. "Just some psycho."

Dad picks up on my tone straight away. He stops reading. "Psycho? What sort of psycho?"

"One with a hellhound." Levi is right. That dog was vicious.

"You have to be careful of dangerous dogs. I hope you didn't get too close? Quick, get in the car out of the cold."

As we climb in, I see something out of the corner of my eye.

"Take a look, Dad. That's the man we were talking about walking up the road. He says he's a minister of God."

Dad looks to where I'm pointing. "A minister! That's okay then." He sounds relieved and leans forward to put his book in the glovebox.

"He told us he's the one who found Mum."

"Really?" Dad stares after him. "I should go and thank him."

Before I can stop him, Dad jumps out of the car and hurries over towards the lane. Levi and I watch him in silence. Dad looks up the lane for a minute, then turns and walks back to the car.

"He's disappeared. Couldn't see him anywhere."

I'm relieved. "He probably wouldn't have wanted to talk to you anyway."

"Don't be silly." Dad starts the engine. "Why ever not?"

I can't think of an answer, but I know I'm right.

Dad drives carefully out of the car park.

"Strange for a minister to have a Rottweiler," he says thoughtfully.

chapter 9

We drive home to Graymouth and take Levi back to his house. I wish he could stay at Dad's longer over half-term, but it's Sunday and he's looking after Cheryl and Syrus tomorrow while his mum's at work. After we've dropped him off, Dad drives to my house. I need to collect some clothes for Mum.

"I'll wait in the car, Danni. I don't know where she keeps anything anyway."

The rain lashing against the windows makes the place look really depressing. I'm not surprised Dad doesn't want to go in. Neither do I.

Dad reaches out to turn up the Ramones, then hesitates a moment.

"Is that okay with you?"

"I'll be fine."

It's stupid to be afraid of going back in by myself. I just wish we hadn't dropped Levi off before we came here. He'd definitely have come in with me.

The Ramones get louder as I shut the car door. Jackson must be deafened. I run to the house through the rain.

Inside it's freezing and the whole place smells musty. I stand in the hall a moment, wishing I didn't have to do this on my own. Then I pull myself together and head upstairs to Mum's room. It's already getting dark, so I switch the light on. Somehow the bulb isn't bright enough to disperse the gloom.

I try to collect her things together without getting too upset, but it's horrible having to go through all her clothes. It feels wrong. Finding T-shirts, jeans and jumpers is easy enough. I leave the underwear drawer until last. It's far too personal. Finally I have to brave it and I open it, trying to decide how much to take. I grab a big handful and dump it on the bed. A piece of paper flutters to the floor and I bend down to pick it up. It looks like a page from an old school notebook. I scan the page quickly. It's Mum's writing, but more childish.

Beryl says my sort end up in hell for definite. She's such a bitch. We haven't even done anything wrong. Not like her family.

Beryl says she's going to heaven because the new minister says so. He's a slimy toad. I told her I'd rather be in hell anyway if she's up there.

Beryl's a spiteful cow and I hate her. She knows people like me and Mam aren't allowed in the chapel now, even if we want to go. Which I don't anyway.

It's obviously from a diary Mum wrote when she was young. From the date I work out she would have been about twelve. I wonder who Beryl was. And why wasn't Mum allowed in the chapel? Anyway it's no use to her in the hospital, so I shove it back in the drawer.

Soon I've got everything I think she needs. I pull down a large weekend bag from the top of the wardrobe and cram in all the clothes I've piled up. I add a hairbrush, deodorant, and some face cleanser.

I can't find her make-up anywhere, so I guess it must still be in her handbag. I wonder if the police have found her car yet. Her handbag is probably still in the car, unless someone stole it from her on the beach. Either way it's not here, and I'm desperate to get out.

As I struggle to do up the zip, I look round to see if there's anything else she might want. No point in taking books or magazines. On impulse I snatch a framed school photo of me that she likes off her bedside table and stuff it in the side pocket. Stupid really, since she doesn't even recognize me right now.

I stagger downstairs with the bag and take a quick look in the front room. The box from the film Levi and I watched last week is still on the table. Suddenly I'm filled with a feeling of intense sadness. I leave as fast as I can, slamming the door behind me.

Dad opens his window to talk to me and turns down the Ramones.

"That was quick. Are you sure you've got everything?"

"Hopefully. Think I've got enough for now. Anyway, you weren't too keen to come in and help, were you?"

"That's not fair. I don't know—"

"Where she keeps anything. Yes, you said."

I go to the back of the car and open the boot so I can shove Mum's bag in. It's not worth picking a fight with him and I can't explain why I'm angry. I suppose it's not all his fault. I come back round and climb into the passenger seat.

"Dad?"

"Mmm?"

"You know when you left me with Mum at the hospital?"

"You're not going to have another go at me are you?"

"No, it's okay, honestly. I just want to ask you something."

"Go on then."

I hesitate, wondering how to put it. "Well, after you left the room, Mum started sort of making weird noises and shouting. The only thing I could really understand was that she was asking for her mother."

"Oh? You didn't tell me that."

If he'd stayed in there with me he'd know, but I manage to hold my tongue. This is more important.

"I keep thinking about it. She never mentions her mother normally. Never. What happened to her?"

"To be honest, Danni, I've no idea. I'm not even sure if she's alive or not."

My pulse starts to race. I turn to stare at him.

"Seriously? You mean I might have a grandmother that no one's bothered to mention before? That's just great."

"There's no need to be sarcastic. It's not my fault. When we got married, your mum said she didn't have family. I assumed she meant they were all dead, but maybe I was wrong. She refused to talk about them anyway."

"So where did she live when she was a child?" Already I'm starting to feel excited, even though I know it's ridiculous. Of course I don't have a grandmother.

"I'm not really sure. Cornwall somewhere, I guess."

"How can you *not* know, Dad? You married her. Didn't you talk to each other about *anything*?"

"Of course we did. But she didn't like talking about her past – it was a closed subject. She just got angry if I asked too many questions."

I know he's right. She did the same with me. But now I wish I'd asked her anyway, even if it did make her angry. Dad should have tried harder too.

Dad shifts in his seat and fumbles with the car keys. He glances at me quickly.

"Did you know her father drowned? I think that's the only thing your mum ever told me about her family. Often wondered if it was the reason she was so touchy about it."

"Yes, she told me that too."

Dad looks relieved and starts the car. I sink my head back against the headrest and try to remember the day she told me. I can't have been more than five or six. We were on a beach somewhere. She said my grandfather's fishing boat had gone down in a storm when she was a girl. I was upset because Mum was crying.

But there was something else. It was a long time ago and the memory keeps flitting away from me. I can't quite grasp it.

"I can probably find her father's memorial if you'd like to see it," says Dad, as we pull away from the house. "It's not that far from home. She showed me once just before we got married."

"Really?" For a minute I can't believe I heard him right.

"Are you telling me it's somewhere near your shop in Cararth?"

"Yes, I'm fairly sure it is. I didn't live there back then of course, but I think it's in the area."

My mind starts racing as the information sinks in. If the memorial to my grandfather is close to Cararth, surely Mum must have lived nearby. Could that be why Mum hates taking me to Dad's new shop so much? Maybe she thinks she'll see someone she knows, family even? I always thought her problem was with Dad not paying maintenance. That's what she told me. But perhaps things weren't that straightforward. After all, she never cared about that before he moved. Maybe there was another reason.

Dad turns to me, looking worried.

"I don't want you to get disappointed though, Danni love. I can help you find the memorial easily enough, but it doesn't mean you've got a grandmother, or that she lives round here. I've certainly never met her. And your mother's in a very confused state right now. Most likely she died years ago."

"I know, Dad. Thanks." I smile to reassure him.

But however rational Dad's being, the way Mum was calling for her mother in the hospital is haunting me.

I can't help thinking my grandmother might still be alive.

chapter 10

"She didn't save him!"

Mum sits next to me on the dark, wet sand, crying. The waves crash closer with the incoming tide.

"Why? Why didn't she?" Tears stream down her face. Water surges around our legs.

I'm scared. I stand up and struggle my way against the surf to the beach. Mum's not with me. I look round and see the waves close over her head.

I try to scream but I can't. I can only whisper.

"Danni? Danni, wake up!"

I open my eyes. Dad is leaning over me looking anxious.

"Are you okay, love?"

I blink up at him, and for a minute I'm not sure where I am.

"You were making such a strange noise. I thought you were choking or something."

"It was Mum, she was drowning."

"Well since you're awake, I'll make you a nice cup of tea." Dad pats my head gently as if I'm Jackson, and leaves the room.

I lie back on the pillows, thinking about the dream. Now I remember what Mum said that day on the beach. I leap out of bed and run to the kitchen.

"Dad, that dream just jogged my memory. When Mum told me her father had drowned, she said something else. Something like '*She didn't save him*'. She said it more than once. It didn't make any sense. What was she talking about?"

"I've no idea. Maybe you heard her wrong?"

"No, I didn't. Even as a little girl I thought it was strange. But you know what? That dream has brought it back to me. I see it differently now I'm older. What if she was talking about her mother?"

I'm excited because I'm sure I'm right. As if I somehow *know* it's true. I can't explain the feeling.

Dad looks at me. "Children often blame their parents for things that aren't really their fault."

I realize he's talking about me and him, but I haven't got time to deal with that now.

"Yes but this is different. Her mother couldn't possibly have saved him. He was out at sea in a fishing boat. It's mad."

"Sometimes children don't see things logically, Danni. Maybe she thought her mother should have stopped him going out fishing that day or something?"

That hadn't occurred to me. For once Dad could be right.

"Anyway, my point is that somehow Mum ended up blaming her mother for his death. Do you reckon that's why she stopped seeing her?"

Dad looks worried. "You really do think her mother might still be alive, don't you? I hope you're not going to be upset if she's not."

"No of course not. Just curious really," I lie.

Later on, Dad drops me by the hospital.

"Are you positive you're okay going in on your own? We could all go tomorrow instead."

"It'll be fine, Dad. Mum just needs some clothes. I'll meet up with you and Michelle later."

I guess Dad is trying to be nice to me. I think my nightmares are beginning to disturb him. But he's off to pick up Michelle, and I can't imagine my little half-sister wanting to spend much time here. Nobody would if they didn't have to.

I lift Mum's bag out of the boot.

"Catch you later, Dad. Thanks for the lift."

I manage to keep a smile fixed on my face as he waves and drives off. But I'm dreading seeing Mum again, if I'm honest.

A male nurse shows me the way to Mum's room. Today the corridor stinks of boiled cabbage and toilets. He knocks and opens the door to her room, waving me inside. Mum looks over in my direction, but her eyes don't focus on me. It's as if she's waiting for someone else. I feel a sense of despair. Nothing has changed.

The nurse points to the tiny cupboard next to Mum's bed.

"You can put her things in there if you like. Sorry there isn't more storage space. I'll be on the reception desk if you need anything else."

He smiles and leaves me on my own in the room with Mum.

Mum sighs and makes whimpering noises. I feel hopeless again, but this time I manage to stop myself crying by talking to her. I tell her where I'm putting her things so she can find them later, though I don't think she even hears me. I place the photo of me on top of the cupboard so she can look at it if she wants to. She doesn't say anything. She probably has no idea I'm here. I tell her what I've been doing, just to fill the silence. It's like talking to myself. It's so depressing.

I'm about to give up when Dr Murphy walks in.

"Hi, Danni. I heard you were visiting. How are you?"

"Okay I guess."

She looks sympathetic. "It always hits the patient's family hardest. I expect you were hoping she might be a bit better today?"

I smile. "Stupid, huh?"

"No, it's perfectly normal. I hoped she'd be showing signs of improvement too. Has she been asking for her mother again?"

"No. Not while I've been here, anyway."

"You realize she only behaves like that because she's not well right now?"

I nod. "Though when I left yesterday I found out her mother might be alive after all. At least Dad doesn't know if she is or not." I stammer to a halt after I've blurted it out.

Dr Murphy stares at me intently.

"That's very interesting, Danni. If it's true, why do you think she didn't tell you before?"

"I've no idea." I hesitate a moment. "Maybe she isn't alive. Dad just said he didn't know for definite. I could just be clutching at straws, but he's agreed to help me try and find out."

"Well I hope you find her," says Dr Murphy. She smiles at me. "I've a hunch you might do – but don't tell Mr Albright I said that. He's not a man who is big on hunches."

For some reason, talking to Dr Murphy is easy. But hearing the consultant's name reminds me what I wanted to ask.

"What did Mr Albright mean yesterday, when he talked about more radical treatment for Mum?"

Dr Murphy looks serious again.

"He wants to try a treatment we sometimes use in cases of chronic depression, but we need a more accurate diagnosis first. Don't worry about it for now." She looks at her watch. "I'd better check my other patients. Call in my office on your way out, if you've time, Danni. Your mother had some jewellery with her when she came in, and it's probably best you take it home with you. It's not really secure in here."

I try talking to Mum again when Dr Murphy's gone, then give up and put the radio on instead. I don't think Mum notices the difference. Dad has this radio station on in the shop sometimes and I wonder if it's on now. Dad told me Elliot's helping in there again today. I haven't had a chance to talk to him since Saturday night.

A hospital assistant comes in and helps Mum out to the

bathroom so she can be washed and changed into her own clothes. I choose an outfit for her, and try to make it something she would choose for herself.

By the time I have to leave to catch the bus, the assistant has got Mum dressed and sitting in a chair. She looks almost normal in her own things, but this makes me feel worse. What if this is as good as it gets? What will I do if she stays like this for ever? I can't bear to think about it. I kiss her quickly on the cheek.

"Bye, Mum. Try to be better next time. I don't want you getting Mr Albright's radical treatment."

I don't expect any response, but suddenly she looks directly at me.

"Mam? Find Mam for me?" Her voice is like a child's. I feel tears welling up. I have to find out if I'm right about my grandmother, and soon.

"I'll try, Mum. If she's alive, I'll find her for you."

My voice cracks and the tears pour down my cheeks. I leave the room. Mum doesn't even notice.

I walk quickly down the horrible cabbagey corridor wiping the tears from my eyes. I'm about to escape in the lift when I remember Mum's jewellery.

I ask the nurse on the desk for directions to Dr Murphy's office and he sends me back down the corridor. When I think I've found the right door, I knock.

"Come in!" Dr Murphy's accent is unmistakeable. Relieved, I walk in.

"Oh great, Danni, you remembered. Just a minute." She rifles through all the drawers under her desk and eventually finds a brown envelope with Mum's name and patient number on it. She hands it to me and smiles.

"Knew it was here somewhere. Unusual necklace, I seem to recall."

Mum doesn't have an unusual necklace. She tends to wear simple chains and stud earrings and often doesn't bother to wear jewellery at all. She hates drawing attention to herself, even though I reckon she's attractive for her age. I open the envelope quickly and tip the contents out onto my hand. It's a thick gold chain with a gold crucifix on it. Quite large. Looks like it belongs to a man.

"There must be some mistake. This isn't Mum's. I've never seen it before."

Dr Murphy looks at me carefully. "But she was holding on to it so tight, it took us a while to prise her hand open."

I don't know why, but I start to panic and I feel like I can't breathe. Worse, my palms start tingling. I look at the chain again. There's a weird lump of rusty metal hanging on the chain next to the crucifix. It takes me a moment to realize what it is. It's a key.

Then I see the water seeping out of the lines in my

hands, just like it did before. I close my fist quickly so Dr Murphy doesn't notice.

"I've definitely never seen this before," I say, my mouth going dry with fear.

"Strange thing to have on a chain, isn't it? The key I mean. It's so rusty, it looks like it's been under water a long time. Anyway, you keep it for now, Danni. It came in with your mum, and maybe when she's a little better she can say whether it's hers or not. I don't like to keep gold in here in case it gets lost or stolen." She smiles.

"Okay." I try to smile back, but I can't stop thinking about my hands. I push the chain into my jacket pocket, wiping my palms on my jeans at the same time.

"Better go. Got to catch a bus in a few minutes."

I run out before she gets a chance to ask me anything else.

I look at my hands again as soon as I get out of the hospital, dreading what I'm going to see. I'm so scared, I'm shaking. But the sweating seems to have stopped. They look normal. Maybe I'm going mad? It can't have been as much water as I thought.

I feel my jeans where I wiped my hands. They're still really damp. My heart sinks.

On the bus, I try to calm down. I'm not going mad, I'm just worried about Mum. It's nothing.

After a while, I take the chain out of my pocket to look at it more closely. I've never known Mum wear a crucifix. I reckon this one's solid gold. I turn it over and notice there's an inscription on the back. I hold it up to the window to see it better.

In Nomine Meo Daemonia Eicient.

Strangely, the words look familiar. I think they're the same as those on the wall at the Chill Out, but I don't know Latin so I can't be sure. It can't be Mum's. I'd have seen it before. It's the kind of thing you'd really notice.

I shove the chain down to the bottom of my rucksack so I don't lose it, and stare out of the window. I hope she's well enough to explain everything to me herself soon.

chapter 11

JOSEPH PENGELLY, FISHERMAN
CAST UNTO THE LORD'S NET AND HAULED UP
TO HEAVEN.

Dad, Michelle and I stare silently at the dark granite slab set into the turf. Michelle arrived yesterday. It's Dad's turn to look after her for a few days.

We're standing in the graveyard of a small church just outside Ancrows, the village where Levi and I went with Elliot to the Chill Out club. Someone's put a bunch of flowers under the inscription. They've wilted a lot so it was probably a few days ago. Michelle leans down and flicks a slug off.

My heart clenches and the graveyard suddenly feels colder. Maybe Mum left them here before she went to that beach. The date engraved on the memorial is the same day she went missing. It's also the anniversary of her father's death, twenty-two years earlier. Are the dates connected? Is that why she came to Cornwall?

The smell of the decaying flowers hangs in the air. I guess this memorial meant a lot to her, yet she never once brought me here. I feel hurt. I know I asked her several times where her family came from, and she always evaded the question. She said it was a nowhere place she preferred to forget. Once she even told me it wasn't on the map, which I found really annoying. Everywhere is on a map.

I was hoping this memorial would say something about my grandfather's wife, or maybe where he came from, so I'm really disappointed. The inscription tells me nothing new, apart from when he died. If I could only find out my grandmother's first name, it might help me trace her.

"Do you two want to look inside the church while we're here?" Dad's breath comes out in a cloud of condensation.

"I'll stay out here and look after Jackson for you," I say quickly. I want to be left on my own out here for a minute, even though it's freezing cold.

Michelle yanks at Jackson's lead to stop him peeing on a gravestone and grins at me. She's got a lovely, cheeky little face and her green eyes are sparkling.

"Here you are, Danni." She hands me Jackson's lead and I make the effort to smile back at her. She and Dad trudge off along the paved path towards the church. They seem totally comfortable with each other and I feel a slight pang of envy.

I hear them chatting as they get to the big porch at the front of the church, then the clack of the latch on the church door as they go in. I look down at the engraving again. I wish it told me more. I crouch down and trace the inscription with my finger to see what it feels like. The granite is rough and icy cold. I poke the flowers. They're all floppy and the stems are going slimy. Being here makes me want to cry. But practically everything makes me want to cry at the moment, especially thinking about Mum.

Jackson keeps straining at his lead and whining excitedly.

"What's he to you then, girl?"

I jump in alarm and look round. I didn't hear anyone coming. Jackson is wagging his tail and trying to make friends with the man standing behind us. I pull Jackson back but he keeps straining to get closer. I glance up at the man and realize he's a tramp. The hair under his hat is long and tangled and his clothes are full of holes and worn patches. He looks about Dad's age and smells of something I can't quite place. He's much too close for comfort and I wish he'd go away. If only Jackson would leave him alone.

The man takes a bottle from his pocket and lifts it to his lips. I see from the label it's sherry. That's the smell. Like Christmas. He wipes the bottleneck on the sleeve of his mud-caked jacket and offers it to me.

"No thanks. It's a bit early," I say politely. I take a step backwards. He looks at me closely for a moment. Jackson won't stop sniffing and rubbing himself against the man's trousers, but he doesn't seem to mind. He's too busy staring at me. He leans towards me for a better look and I take another step back, yanking at Jackson's lead.

"Well I'll be darned. You're one of 'em, aren't you? That's wunnerful." He looks genuinely moved and tears well up in his eyes. "Thought the line would die out with Mary."

I've no idea what he's talking about.

"I think you're confusing me with someone else."

"You've got the eyes. And the lovely fair hair. No need to be afraid of Robert here, I won't tell no one."

I feel really uncomfortable.

"I don't understand, sorry." I wonder if I should run to the church. Why do people round here keep thinking they recognize me?

"So what's Joseph Pengelly to you then?"

He's read the memorial stone before. He must know this graveyard well. Maybe he sleeps here? I can almost feel the cold of the graveyard creeping into my body just thinking about it.

"He was my grandfather. But I never met him."

"I knew it! You're a relative of Mary's!" He tips his bottle in his excitement, and a glug of sherry splats onto the ground.

"No. I definitely don't know a Mary."

He doesn't seem to hear me. "Of course, I've gone daft. She must be your mother. I never knew. My, how the time goes…"

This is too weird. I feel a bit sick.

"My mother's name's not Mary. It's Erin."

"That's her! Mary Erin! Haven't seen her in so many years… Well blessed be. How is she?"

My heart starts pounding. He *is* talking about Mum.

"She's not well. She's in Bodmin Hospital."

I've no idea why I told him that. He's a total stranger.

He looks at me carefully, steadying himself on a gravestone. I notice his eyes are an unusual turquoisey blue, like the sea.

"I'm truly sorry to hear that, girl. You give her Robert's warmest regards, won't you?"

There's no point in telling him my mother doesn't even recognize me right now.

"Okay," I mumble.

The man sways slightly. He's drunk. I should get away from him, but Dad will be out any minute and I want to ask this man what he knows.

"So how do you know Mum?"

"We were friends, way back when. Haven't seen her since what happened, mind."

I'm not sure what he means. I want to ask him more questions but suddenly I can't say anything because I know talking will make me cry. It seems there's so much about her I don't know.

"'Course, it was all a long time ago." He sighs and I catch a waft of sherry. The smell of wet leaves rises from his clothing when he moves.

"Tragedy, it was. Things was never the same after." He stares at the ground and neither of us says anything for a minute. I guess he's talking about when her father drowned. I concentrate on not crying. Then he reaches down to stroke Jackson.

"You look so sad, girl. Maybes I can help. Here, take this charm from old Robert, but don't tell no one. And I won't tell no one about you."

He reaches out to hand me a strip of blue material he's pulled from his jacket pocket. It looks like a piece of old tent canvas, with three knots tied in it. I'm not sure if I should touch it, let alone take it off him.

"Listen well. When things aren't going too good, untie one of these here knots. The wind'll change for yer. The last knot, he's the strongest. That's for when youse in real trouble."

"Thanks," I say. I hesitate for a second, then snatch the thing quickly and shove it in my pocket. It might make him go away. He's obviously either mad or drunk.

"Folk don't appreciate the old ways these days." He grins at me and I notice a few gaps in his teeth. "But I've always had a soft spot for your kind. Especially Mary Erin."

His cheeks go pink. I wonder what he means, but don't like to ask.

"Maybes see you again, girl."

It's all so strange, I don't know what to say. I just nod and smile. He touches his hand to his battered trilby and turns to go. Jackson strains at the leash, wanting to follow.

I watch him dodge round the gravestones and walk unsteadily out through the lychgate. He doesn't turn round again. Maybe he needs another bottle of sherry already. I touch the knotted canvas in my pocket and pull it out to have another look. The knots look surprisingly complicated.

It's only when he's completely out of sight that it dawns on me. If he knew Mum, he must know where she lived. He probably knows her mother's name too. How could I be so stupid? I stuff the charm back in my pocket and start to run after him. At that moment, Dad and Michelle come out of the church.

"Won't be a minute," I blurt, racing towards the gate. Jackson's more than happy to run with me. When I get there, the lane is totally empty in both directions.

"Which way did he go, Jackson?"

Jackson looks at me and wags his tail. Stupid bloody dog. Michelle comes running up to us.

"What's wrong, Danni? Are you okay?"

She looks worried. I ruffle her curly red hair. My little half-sister is great. We don't know each other that well, seeing as I've hardly ever been able to come to Cornwall before, but I think she really likes me. She smiles whenever I look at her and she keeps offering me her sweets.

"It's nothing, Shell. There was some bloke in the graveyard. I wanted to ask him something."

"About the memorial?"

"I thought he might know more about it…"

Dad comes ambling over, oblivious to what's gone on.

"Danni, there's a notice in the church you might find interesting. Do you want to see it?"

"Yeah maybe," I mutter, not really listening. I still wish I'd managed to catch up with Robert.

"It's about the memorial – something about your grandfather."

"What? What exactly does it say?" Suddenly I'm interested.

"Not much. Take a look – it's on a church information sheet pinned to a board by the door."

"Thanks, Dad!" I thrust Jackson's lead at him and run back to take a look for myself.

The church has a massive arch-shaped oak door and I have to use both hands to turn the circular iron handle and lift the latch. The door creaks loudly as I go in. It swings shut behind me with a bang.

It takes my eyes a moment to adjust to the gloom. The place smells of damp and candlewax. I hear footsteps outside and the door opens again. A shaft of grey light pierces the gloom. It's Michelle. She points to the information board.

"There it is, Danni. Dad's right, it really doesn't say much."

"Thanks, Shell, you're a star." I scan the sheet of information about the church. It's just a couple of sentences.

Some gravestones in the churchyard are also of interest, including the memorial to Joseph Pengelly, a fisherman from the village here at Ancrows who was lost at sea. Sadly, like so many drowned seamen, his body was never found.

That's it. After that it's just waffle about how many lives are lost at sea along this coast.

But now I know. Mum's father came from Ancrows. I'm guessing she and her mother must have lived here too. We drove right up the main street to the Chill Out in that big chapel on Saturday night. It's not a huge place.

We probably drove past Mum's childhood home without even knowing.

chapter 12

Of course I want to go down into Ancrows immediately, but Dad just wants to get back to the shop.

As we drive along the road heading back to Cararth Crystals, I go over the strange encounter with the homeless man in my head. I realize there's one thing I can check without having to go anywhere.

"Dad, is it true Mum's first name is Mary?"

"Yes it is. She never uses it though. Why do you ask?"

"There was a man in the churchyard who asked if I knew Mary. I didn't even know it was her name."

Dad clenches the steering wheel.

"What man? I didn't see anyone – who was he?

Why was he talking to you?"

I glare at Dad and don't bother to answer. What does it matter who the man was? The point is, how come I didn't know my own mother's name?

Michelle understands why I'm upset though.

"Maybe your mum just hated her real name and so never told you about it? Isn't that why people change them? Like if you're called Smelly or Bottom or something." She giggles. Smelly is very funny when you're eight.

I try to smile back. "Yeah, maybe you're right, Shell."

"You don't want to encourage strange men," mutters Dad.

"You didn't see him, Dad. Jackson liked him. I think he was okay and he said he knew Mum years ago."

Naturally I don't mention the fact he was homeless and smelled of sherry.

"I don't think you realize how attractive young teenage girls like you are, Danni. Just be careful, that's all I'm saying."

I feel my anger melting slightly. Maybe Dad does worry about me after all. And it's not his fault I didn't know Mum's name. Mum should have told me herself. I even asked her once why her bank statements were addressed to M E Lancaster, and she lied to me. She told me it was a mistake and it should be Mrs E Lancaster.

Michelle's right. She obviously hated the name Mary.

* * *

Elliot looks up from the delivery note he's checking as we come in through the shop door. His eyes light up when he smiles. I smile back. It's the first time I've seen him since Saturday.

"Shop busy?" asks Dad.

"Nah, hardly anyone's been in. I've priced the new incense burners. I'm putting them up here." He points a shelf next to the incense display. "What do you think?"

"They look great. Thanks, Elliot. I'll come down in a minute so you can get off home."

Dad and Michelle go upstairs to make themselves a hot drink. I linger in the shop a moment. Elliot grins at me.

"Nigel said you were going to look for your grandfather's memorial this morning. Did you find it?"

"Yep. It was at a church just outside Ancrows."

"Oh I know it – the little one at the top of the hill?"

"Yes that's it! And guess what? It turns out he lived in Ancrows – so it's probably where Mum came from too."

"Seriously?"

"Think so. As far as we could make out from the notice in the church. It seems likely…"

Elliot's stopped smiling and he's staring at me as if he's suddenly noticed something. I brush my hand over my face self-consciously.

"What is it?"

"Danni, I know it's a weird thing to ask, but do you look at all like your mum?"

"I suppose so. People keep telling me I do."

"My mother's family came from Ancrows too. She moved here to Cararth when she married Dad. But Aunty Bea still lives there."

Suddenly I make the connection. "You mean my mum and your Aunty Bea might have known each other?"

"Almost certainly, it's a small place."

"Wow." For a moment I let the information sink in.

"I wondered why Aunty Bea was so rude to you the other night. At the time I thought her problem was with Levi. But it was you, wasn't it? It was like she sort of recognized you."

I think back to my brief encounter with his aunt.

"Elliot, even if you're right and she knew Mum before, why take it out on me?"

Elliot's laugh sounds bitter. "Who can say? Aunty Bea seems to dislike practically everybody."

I feel uneasy. From the way she reacted to me, Aunty Bea must have hated Mum with a vengeance. But why?

I want to talk about it more, but Dad comes back down to the shop with a cup of coffee in one hand and a large box under his other arm. I move to take the coffee before he spills it.

"Thanks, love." He smiles at me. "While I remember,

I've promised to take Michelle to a party tomorrow afternoon. Will you be okay staying here?"

"Of course I will, Dad," I say. But I can't help thinking how nice it must be to have friends round here. Elliot's the only person I know, and I'm beginning to really miss my friends in Graymouth. For a moment I feel slightly envious of Michelle.

"Do you think you could help Elliot with some pricing while we're out? I don't like to ask, but I've got a lot of stock in suddenly."

My stupid envy vanishes immediately. Dad is actually giving me a perfect reason to spend time alone with Elliot. I even manage a smile.

Levi phones when I'm back upstairs making myself a sandwich.

"Everything okay? How's your mum?"

My elation at the prospect of being left alone with Elliot vanishes.

"No change. But I found out where she comes from when we went to visit my grandfather's memorial."

"So tell me."

"Ancrows – that village we went to for the Chill Out club."

Levi is silent for a moment. "Are you sure? That's a bit weird."

"Yeah, really. I had no idea she was from round here."

"Why on earth didn't she tell you…? I don't understand. What's the big deal?"

"Who knows? I don't understand either. Mum's never talked about her family. But if she came from round here it might explain why she got so difficult with Dad when he moved to this area. Maybe she didn't want to see people she knew? Anyway, now I want to find out whether my grandmother is still alive – and if she still lives there."

"Guess it's possible. Definitely worth looking since your mum's been asking for her. And it shouldn't be too hard to find someone in a small village. Maybe I can help you start looking at the weekend? It means waiting a couple of days, I know, but I can't come sooner because of minding Cheryl and Syrus while Mum's at work."

"That would be great, Levi. Thanks. Dad's next to useless because of the shop, and he doesn't like the idea of me asking around Ancrows on my own."

"Fine. I want to come down and see Sarah again anyway, if it's okay for me to stay at yours?"

I should have realized Levi would have his own agenda. Still, it would be brilliant if he could help me.

"Just sort out the trains and I'll get Dad to collect you. Shouldn't be a problem, even if Michelle's still here."

"Ace. I'll call you back tomorrow. Meanwhile, why not

ask Elliot if he can find out anything for you? He lives in the area, so he probably knows a lot of people there."

"Okay." I decide not to tell him about my conversation with Elliot earlier. I still feel uneasy about it.

We say goodbye and I put the phone down.

I start thinking about Levi's suggestion and realize I don't want to ask Elliot. I try to work out why. It's not as though I don't like him, and he'd probably be really helpful. The problem is I'm worried he might ask his Aunty Bea. After all, she does live in Ancrows and she probably knew Mum, so it would be a logical step. But I don't want that woman to even know I'm looking. I can't think about her without shuddering.

I'd rather just wait for Levi to come down and help. Dad should be fine about me looking if I've got Levi with me. I just wish he could make it sooner.

On Thursday morning, Dad drives me to the hospital to see Mum.

"Can I come in with you, Danni?" asks Michelle.

I'm touched she wants to be with me, but I can't believe she wants to come inside the hospital.

"It's horrible in there, Shell. Mum doesn't really talk or anything. I'm just going to say hello. She won't even know I'm there." I already feel depressed at the prospect.

"That's okay, I don't mind."

She obviously means it. She's being so open and lovely with me, I could cry. I look at Dad. I think he's pleased Michelle and I are getting closer. I am too. Before staying at Dad's this week I could probably count the number of times I've spent more than an hour with Michelle on one hand.

"If she wants to go with you, Danni, it's okay with me."

"You're not coming in with us?"

"No, I'm picking up an order of Peruvian shaman rattles from my supplier – I'll come up and find you when I've got them."

I reckon he's probably just made that up as an excuse not to visit Mum with us, but I don't mind. It'll be nice to have Michelle along, and Dad would probably just get in the way.

Mum's room smells a bit better. More like soap. Someone's opened the window a little too, so there's some air.

Mum just sits in her chair, staring straight ahead. She's not showing any real improvement since I last saw her, but she does seem a bit calmer. Less fidgety somehow. Maybe it's simply because Michelle is talking to her normally, as if there's nothing wrong.

"I'm going to a party later," says Michelle. "I've got a new dress. My mum made it for me because I wanted wings on it. Like fairy wings, you know?"

Mum doesn't look at her but strokes the arm of her chair distractedly. It breaks my heart to see Mum completely ignoring us, but Michelle just keeps chatting.

"I wanted to put glitter on the wings, but my mum said it wouldn't go in the wash, so she actually sewed sequins on instead."

I think back to when I was little. Parties were so important. Mum was never much good at sewing, but Marlene, Levi's mum, used to make dressing-up clothes for me sometimes. I remember Levi insisting she made him a lobster outfit once and I smile at the memory of him waving his pincers at everyone.

Michelle starts telling Mum about the present she's bought for her friend. It's a complicated new game and Michelle chatters away about how you play it. Mum just stares into the distance.

I glance at my photo on top of Mum's cupboard. There's a vase of flowers next to it. They're lovely. I wonder where they came from? I feel bad that I didn't think of bringing any. I open Mum's cupboard while Michelle's still talking to her.

"Just going to sort your laundry, Mum," I say. She doesn't look at me. The vase of flowers on her cupboard wobbles and I reach out to stop it spilling. There's a beautiful heart-shaped stone next to the vase.

"Wow, look at this, Shell!"

I hold up the stone. It's a glittery white rock of some kind.

"Oh, that's beautiful!" says Michelle. "What a nice present."

"Who gave you this, Mum?"

Mum doesn't answer me of course.

I look at the flowers again. Someone else must have visited Mum. But who?

Dad doesn't show up for ages, so in the end Michelle and I decide to go and wait for him outside. On the way out of the ward, I say hello to the male nurse. He's the same one as last time.

"How's your mum today?" he asks.

"Not much different. Nice flowers. Do you know who put them there?"

"Yes, it was the old lady earlier. She was in a hurry so I didn't get a chance to ask her much. Said she was a relative. They really cheer the room up, don't they?"

My head reels in shock. I can't think what to say, and before I find my tongue, a patient starts shouting and screaming from a room down the corridor.

The nurse runs towards the sound.

Michelle and I get in the lift.

"Why didn't you tell me your mum had relatives round here?" she asks.

"I didn't know, Shell. Mum's always been very secretive. She told Dad she hadn't any family."

"But you're looking for your grandmother, so you think she was lying."

I smile at her.

"You catch on fast, sister!"

"Wow. Wouldn't it be amazing if it was your grandmother who left the flowers?"

"Nice idea – but I doubt it. Even if she's alive, how would she know Mum was here?"

"I don't know. But it might have been her! There were flowers in the graveyard too – the same kind. Maybe she left those as well?"

I stare at Michelle in astonishment. It's the first time it's occurred to me that it might not have been Mum who left the flowers in the graveyard. It was the anniversary of my grandfather's death. Maybe it was my grandmother?

chapter 13

Michelle is all dressed up in her new pink party dress with sparkly wings. She looks angelic but she's scowling at Dad.

"Do you have to come too?"

"Yes, I'm invited to stay along with the other parents. I'm looking forward to it. What's the problem?"

Dad is wearing a well-worn Glastonbury T-shirt, which is far too short for him. When he raises his arms, it exposes his beer gut. It's the pride of his vintage T-shirt collection, so I guess it's his equivalent of Michelle's pink party dress. He's stuck some beads in his dreads too. No wonder Michelle doesn't want him there.

"Are you sure you'll be okay here, Danni? You can come with us if you want?"

He has to be joking.

"Nah, you're all right, Dad. I'll be fine."

I wink at Michelle and she grins at me.

"Come on, Dad," she says. "Put your coat on. We'd better get going."

A few minutes later, I see Dad's car driving past the shop. Michelle waves at me from the back seat as they go by and points at Dad's hair, pulling a face. I have to laugh.

Dad's left me a load of dreamcatchers to price while they're out, so I sit on the floor next to the counter and gradually unpack the box. The feathers keep getting tangled and they're really annoying to sort and price. I don't care though. I'm in the shop with Elliot.

I can't help watching him when he's serving customers. He has this habit of pushing his hair back off his forehead, and the dark fringe constantly flops back again when he takes his hand away. His hands are beautiful. When he catches me watching him, I look away quickly and pretend I'm concentrating on untying some feathers.

A shadow crosses the window and I look up. There's an old man outside the shop staring in. I smile in an effort to be friendly but he just glares at me.

Suddenly he does this really weird thing, flicking his hand in front of his face three times, kind of slowly and deliberately. He glares at me again, then spits on the pavement before he walks off. It's horrible and quite disturbing. I glance at Elliot to see if he noticed, but he's too busy hanging up the dreamcatchers. Maybe the man just had some kind of dementia, but I feel unsettled. It looked like it was personal.

I stand up to stretch my legs and try to shake off the feeling. I wander over to the window and spot the newspaper boy coming towards the shop. He smiles at me as he comes in, and leaves a paper folded on the counter. He winks at me on his way out again and I smile back, relieved not everyone's unfriendly to me round here.

Elliot's busy showing a customer some crystal skulls in a glass cabinet, so I sneak a quick look at the paper. It's the *Cornish Guardian*. The word *Porthenys* instantly catches my eye on the front page. Porthenys is a small place. Even before I start reading, anxiety gnaws at my stomach. I pick it up and open it out.

TRAGEDY OF WOMAN AT PORTHENYS

Police have revealed the identity of the mystery woman found in Porthenys last week as Mrs Erin Lancaster.

It's about Mum. I knew it. My heart twists.

...found unclothed, soaking wet and unconscious on the beach by a man out walking his dog.

Unclothed? I immediately think of the priest on the beach saying he covered her with his coat. Does unclothed mean naked? Mum would hate to be seen naked by someone like him, I'm sure of it. Thank goodness she was unconscious. But why the hell had she taken her clothes off? This time of year, it's crazy to go swimming without a wetsuit.

Local people believe this sad event may possibly have been an attempted suicide.

What? Attempted suicide? No way. No bloody way! They're wrong. They're so totally wrong! Tears sting my eyes. I hardly notice the shop bell ringing as the customer leaves.

...Mrs Lancaster is the only daughter of tragic local fisherman Joseph Pengelly. Mrs Lancaster was found on the anniversary of the sinking of her father's fishing boat, the *Eva Marie*, twenty-two years ago. The boat went down just off the very same treacherous stretch of coastline.

The tears start spilling down my face. It can't be true. Surely it isn't true? Was she really trying to kill herself?

Elliot comes over to me quickly from behind the counter. He puts his arm round me.

"What's up, Danni? Tell me what's wrong."

I can't speak. I bury my face in his shirt and sob. I don't care that I look awful when I've been crying. I don't care about anything. I feel Elliot's steady heartbeat through his shirt. He keeps holding me. Gradually I calm down. I breathe in the smell of fresh laundry and start to feel embarrassed. I hope I haven't just messed up his clean shirt by blubbing onto it. I break away slowly, trying to hide my blotchy face as I wipe a sleeve across my eyes.

Elliot reaches over and gets me a tissue from a box under the counter. When I've blown my nose, I hand him the newspaper.

"Elliot, why didn't anyone tell me?"

"Tell you what?" He looks at the article and we don't speak for a few minutes while he reads.

"I just can't believe…" I pause while I try to think of a way of saying it without crying again. "That she was, you know, that unhappy, she'd try to…" My eyes fill up again.

Elliot doesn't say anything. I can't read his expression so I blink and look away. It must have been what everyone was thinking except me. How come I'm so stupid? I'm the one that was living with her, seeing her every day.

Why didn't I notice she was depressed?

I feel Elliot touch my arm, obviously trying to reach out to me again.

"It's just what some people have been saying, Danni. You know, because of the date she was found and everything. But it doesn't make it true."

"I wish someone had mentioned it to me before now. I'm so angry with Dad for not warning me." I can't help the tears welling up again.

"Do you think he knew?" Elliot asks quietly. "I mean, you didn't realize and you're the one they spoke to at the hospital."

"He must have done. And Dr Murphy. I hate them both."

"That's a bit harsh. It just says 'local people'. Your dad and that doctor might not think anything of the kind. Newspapers always try to make things more sensational."

I hope he's right. I try to remember what they said in the hospital in case I missed something. The consultant did say Mum might need more radical treatment. Dr Murphy said it was a treatment for depression, but not to worry about it. I didn't ask why they thought she was depressed. Now I want to know more.

"I'm going to phone the hospital."

Elliot looks worried, but doesn't try to stop me. I leave the tangle of dreamcatchers on the floor and run upstairs.

"Can I speak to Dr Murphy, please? It's Danni Lancaster."

"I'll put you through."

There's silence for a moment and then a series of clicks.

"Hello, Dr Murphy speaking."

"Dr Murphy, it's Danni, Danni Lancaster – my mother is…"

"Oh yes, Danni – is there a problem?"

I'm faltering already. I was angry before, but now I don't know where to begin.

"Um, have you seen the *Cornish Guardian*?"

"No, I don't usually read the local paper. Why?"

"Mum's on the front page. It says she was attempting suicide."

My voice cracks on the last word and I almost start crying again.

There's another moment of silence.

"So where did the reporter get that idea?" She sounds annoyed.

"The day they found her on the beach… It was the anniversary of the date my grandfather drowned." As I'm telling her, I realize it sounds more and more likely that everyone must think the same thing. "And it was the same bit of coast where the boat went down."

"I'm very sorry to hear that, Danni. I didn't know. I suppose you can see why the newspaper has jumped to that conclusion. However, in my opinion, that's not the case."

I breathe a sigh of relief.

"So what do you think she was doing on that beach?"

"I've no idea, but from her symptoms I'd say she's suffering from shock, not depression. Mr Albright's diagnosis may be different however. I wonder, have you found out any more about her mother yet?"

"No, why?"

She doesn't say anything for a minute.

"I think finding your grandmother could help. Call it a hunch."

I get the strange feeling we're talking in riddles. I've never liked puzzles. I like things clear.

"But you don't think Mum was trying to kill herself?"

"I don't believe she was, no. But I'm aware other people may consider it a possibility when they read the article. I'm sorry, I have to go now, Danni, but you can talk to me next time you visit the hospital."

"Okay. Thanks. Thanks a lot."

I put the phone down. I wish I could have asked her more questions, but I'm glad I called.

I start wondering about Dad instead. He must have heard people in the village talking, surely? But then Dad's oblivious to most things. On reflection I think it's likely he hasn't a clue. In which case I'd better warn him about the newspaper as soon as he gets back.

I feel a lot better about things by the time I head back downstairs. Elliot untangles all the dreamcatchers ready for me to price. I find myself staring at his hands, amazed at how quickly he does it. I want to talk to him more, but unfortunately there's a customer in the shop who doesn't stop asking about crystals and takes all Elliot's attention.

The rest of the afternoon goes quickly. We're so busy, I don't even get much time to think about the newspaper article again. Every so often I look over and Elliot catches my eye. It's stupid, but I get butterflies every time he smiles at me.

When the last customer leaves the shop, Elliot shuts the door and turns the sign round to CLOSED. Dad and Michelle aren't back yet.

"Do you need to wait for Dad so he can pay you?"

"No, it's okay, I can call by tomorrow."

I feel a pang of disappointment, but I can't think of anything to say.

"I could kill for a can of Coke though. Do you want one? I'll go up to the corner shop."

"Oh, um, is that, er – do you mind? Yes, please."

Now we're finally alone, I can't even speak properly. I wish I didn't sound like such an idiot.

He just smiles.

"Back in a minute."

When he's gone, I wonder why I still haven't told him I don't really like Coke.

A few minutes later, Elliot reappears. He hands me a can, and we grab ourselves a couple of chairs from behind the counter. We sit down and drink in silence for a moment. I feel so awkward. I try and think of something to say. Elliot shifts on his seat.

"Would you…"

"Do you…"

We both start speaking at the same time and then laugh.

"After you," I say.

"No, you first."

We're sitting so close that whatever I was going to ask him goes completely from my mind. He reaches out and moves a wisp of hair out of my eyes.

"I love your hair," he says.

The air seems to crackle between us. I wonder if he feels it too. He moves closer and I can feel his warm breath on my cheek. I close my eyes, a part of me secretly glad I reapplied my mascara after I stopped crying earlier. Then I sense him hesitate.

"Danni, I was going to tell you earlier…"

At that moment the shop door opens and the shop

bell clamours. My eyes snap open and Elliot jumps up off his chair as Dad, Michelle and Jackson burst into the shop together.

"Oh great, glad I caught you," says Dad.

I feel myself go red and take a swig of Coke to hide my expression. I can still feel the spot where Elliot was breathing against my cheek.

Fortunately for me, Jackson is so excited he starts jumping up at everyone, and Dad tries frantically to stop him knocking anything over. Finally Jackson calms down and Dad turns to Elliot again.

"Elliot, I must pay you for today. Sorry we're a bit late."

"That's fine, me and Danni have just have been chatting. The shop's been really busy this afternoon."

Dad looks pleased and he and Elliot start talking about the day's takings. Dad spends a lot of time worrying about money.

"Come upstairs with me, Danni, you can share my party bag," says Michelle.

I'm touched. Having Dad and Michelle around is beginning to make me feel like I'm part of a proper family. I guess I always have been, but I've never really felt it before. Up to now, it mostly seemed like there was only me and Mum.

I'm beginning to realize Mum must have preferred it that way.

chapter 14

There's a door in front of me. Faded blue with peeling paint. The knocker is old and blackened, shaped like a dolphin. The door creaks open. In the darkness, someone is watching, waiting for me. I want to know who it is, but I'm afraid. The door opens enough to step into the dark and unknown. I try to force myself through. The fear is too great. My heart starts beating faster. I have to wake up.

The bed is damp and my hands feel prickly. I want to switch the light on to look at them, but it's not even dawn yet and I don't want to disturb Michelle, fast asleep in the twin bed next to mine. I know the water has been coming through my hands again. Where does it all come from? There's no way it's just sweat. I'm sure it's not normal.

Panicking makes my heart race, and I'm even more awake. I would go to the front room, but Levi arrived yesterday so he's in there. He'll be really grumpy if I wake him up too early, especially since it's Saturday and he's been looking after Cheryl and Syrus all week. Instead I lie on my back and stare at the pattern the street light makes on the pink, fairy-covered ceiling. Eventually I close my eyes.

I'm underwater. Diving in the deep green light. I can swim so fast, it's exhilarating. I belong here.

Someone else is here, keeping to the shadows. I swim quickly upwards to get away.

On the surface, a splashing sound. I turn in panic. An old woman floats on the waves, her eyes dark, unblinking. Watching me.

Floundering, spluttering in salt water, I start to sink.

I sit up in bed, coughing and rubbing my arms. My dreams feel so real, it scares me. I never used to dream like this. Since Mum went missing, it happens every night.

Michelle stirs. She's about to wake up. I run to the bathroom and load my toothbrush with toothpaste to get rid of the taste of brine.

* * *

Dad is taking Michelle back to her mum's before he opens Cararth Crystals, so it's still early when we pull up in Ancrows. Levi and I scramble out of the car while Dad keeps the engine running. He winds down the car window to say goodbye.

"Good luck with the search, Danni. Just call me if you've got any problems. I'll come back to collect you at about midday."

"Thanks, Dad. We'll make sure we're back in time."

I try to smile at him, but I'm feeling queasy. I'm not sure where to start the search for my grandmother and I wish he had time to help. I already checked the phone book before we set out, but couldn't find anyone with the name Pengelly listed in Ancrows.

Levi waves to Michelle in the back of the car as Dad drives off. She's blowing kisses at me, so I blow one back. I'll miss her. She's been here all week for the half-term break, but she's heading home today.

"See you next weekend, Shell!" I shout. I hope she heard me. I'm guessing I'll still be around unless Mum makes a miraculous recovery.

Levi looks at me. He obviously realizes I'm stressed about the search.

"Don't worry so much, Danni. This place isn't that big. And we know your grandmother's surname even if we don't know her first name. How many Mrs Pengellys can there be? We'll just ask around in all the shops. If she still lives here, someone's bound to know her."

As we walk, I can't shake off the image of the blue door in my dream. The peeling layers of paint. The black iron dolphin knocker. My head starts to throb. I check my hands quickly, just in case, but at the moment they're fine. We cross the road and head towards the harbour where the cafes are. The vision keeps flashing into my mind and I wonder if I'm getting ill. Everything feels unreal and dreamlike.

We decide to go into all the little gift shops we come to on the way down to the harbour. Ancrows is only a small place, but because of the tourist trade there are quite a few. We ask in every shop to see if anyone knows of a Mrs Pengelly in the area. No one's heard of her, though it turns out most of the traders are outsiders who've only moved here in recent years. Even so I can't help feeling disappointed.

Along the path by the river, we come to a small cafe. Levi studies the menu up on display in the window and his stomach rumbles loudly. I'm not hungry, but I've agreed to stop for brunch because I know Levi's useless without food inside him. I still don't feel right though. I try to stay calm and focus on nice things, like going to the Chill Out again with Elliot later, but it's no use. I feel too anxious.

"Looks good," says Levi. "And we've got enough to cover it. Shall we go in?"

I nod.

"You don't look too sure, Danni – do you want to check out the other options first?"

"No, you're all right." I smile as brightly as I can. Trailing round looking at other cafes isn't going to help me feel better. We may as well sit in this one.

Levi orders a full cooked breakfast. I settle on just toast and marmalade.

As we sit waiting for the order to arrive, I try not to think about the smell of greasy fried food that pervades the entire place.

Levi's eyes light up at the sight of his breakfast when it arrives, and he tucks in straight away. I try to force myself to eat some toast and drink a sip of tea.

When he's finished, he looks up at me. "Danni, you've got to try to calm down a bit. You look really pale. I know you're worried about your mum, but you're doing your best. Let yourself off the hook a bit why don't you? I'm sure we'll find your gran soon. Don't you want to eat your toast before we go?"

"Nah, I'm fine. Can we leave now?"

Without waiting for an answer I grab my rucksack and go outside. I stand on the pavement waiting for Levi, feeling so strange, I'm worried I'm going to faint. Levi comes out and joins me.

"Just going up here a minute." I point at a narrow

alleyway between the cafe and the shop next door. I start walking, not giving Levi enough time to protest. My head feels like it's on fire. My hands are itching and my vision is starting to blur.

"Where are we going? There's no shops up there!" Levi says plaintively behind me. I ignore him. There's something about this place. I can't explain why, but I have to keep walking.

I stumble up the cobbled path, trying to concentrate on breathing. At the top of the narrow alley there's a short row of cottages. They're hidden behind the cafe and shops on the river front. I stop dead. Waves of nausea bring the taste of bile to my mouth. I gaze at a blue front door with peeling paintwork and an old dolphin knocker in the centre. As I watch, it starts to open slowly.

"What's going on, you're acting really weird," moans Levi, catching up with me. He glares at me, then his expression changes. "Hey, are you all right? You look a bit green."

"That's the house, I know it." I point at the blue door. It's exactly the same as the one in my dream.

"Eh?"

I understand why he's confused. I am too. The door opens wider.

"It's my grandmother's house." I'm not just guessing. I *know* it. My hands are prickling and I'm breaking out in a cold sweat.

"How do you know? You've never been here before…" An old woman pops her head out of the doorway and stares across at us. Levi stops talking. I don't know exactly what happens next because everything goes black.

I open my eyes. I'm lying on my back on the cobbles. Levi is leaning over me, supporting my head and looking really worried.

"Danni? Are you okay? You hit the ground so hard. Tell you what, blink twice so I know you haven't gone mental."

I smile and blink twice.

"I'm fine."

It's not true. I stay lying on my back. My head is throbbing.

The woman from the house has come over. She bends down to look at me. Her eyes are dark, velvet brown. Just like Mum's. Just like mine.

"You're Danni, aren't you? My granddaughter?"

I nod at her, speechless. No wonder I passed out. It's the woman from my dream. The one floating on the waves. Yet I'm wide awake and she's here, looking at me. It's all too weird. I sit up with Levi's help and have to put my head between my knees for a moment so I don't pass out again.

"Danni? Are you okay? You're so pale! Should I call an ambulance?" Levi sounds really worried.

"No, I'm all right, really." I say it as firmly as I can, though actually it feels like the world is crashing down on me. An ambulance is the last thing I want right now. I might end up in the psychiatric ward with Mum.

I lift my head carefully, and struggle to get to my feet. Levi gives me a hand. I feel very wobbly standing up.

"Don't worry, it's only like this at the beginning." The old woman gently holds my arm to steady me. "You'd better both come into the warm and have some tea."

"Thank you, you're very kind. Are you Mrs Pengelly?" Levi looks at her and then at me like he's comparing us.

"Yes. But call me Mamwyn. It's easier," she says.

"Mamwyn? I've never heard that name before," I say. My voice sounds distant to me, like it's coming from the bottom of a well.

"It's an old Cornish word," she says. "It just means grandmother."

Mamwyn leads us into her tiny cottage.

"Danni needs a glass of water," she says to Levi. "Stay by the fire and make yourself comfortable. We won't be a minute. I'll put the kettle on."

She guides me straight through to the kitchen at the back of the house. Daylight filtering through the tiny leaded glass windowpanes makes the room glow faintly green. I sit down shakily on a wooden chair by an old pine table. Mamwyn fills a kettle and puts it on an ancient kitchen range to boil. The range smells of burning driftwood, which is warm and comforting.

Mamwyn gives me a glass of water then takes a chocolate cake out of a tin, cuts a big slice and puts it on a plate.

"I'll just take this through to your friend. What's his name?"

"Levi."

"He looks nice."

Mamwyn disappears with Levi's slice of cake. If only my head would stop throbbing, I could concentrate. She said it's always like this at the beginning. What did she mean? The beginning of what?

I have to find out more, but I'm afraid I won't like what I'm about to hear.

Mamwyn bustles back into the kitchen, puts a teapot on a tray and adds three mugs.

Suddenly she grabs my wrist and I nearly jump out of my skin. She stares into my eyes.

"Have you started getting the dreams?" Her voice has fallen to a whisper. I get the impression she doesn't want Levi to hear. I nod dumbly. There's no point pretending I don't know what she's talking about. I'm shaking so much I make the tray of china rattle on the table.

"And the seawater?"

"Seawater?"

"Coming through your hands."

So I wasn't imagining it. I feel the room start to spin.

"What does it mean?"

"Your mother hasn't told you?" She sighs. "It's nothing to worry about. It's just the way it starts. Once you've been through the changing it all stops – except the foretelling. That's part of the gift."

Her words aren't making a lot of sense, but I try to keep up.

"Changing?" Something about the way she said the word resonates with me. I sense it's the key to everything that's been happening.

"It's your time," she says. "Come back here on your own, soon. I can help you understand what's happening to you."

She stops whispering and starts humming as she slices some more cake.

"Now we'd better join your friend, if you're up to it?"

I nod, but she notices I'm still shaking.

"I'll carry the tray. You bring the cake," she says. "And try not to worry."

I attempt a smile. But my head is full of questions. What does this "changing" involve? It must be something serious, since she won't talk about it with Levi around.

"Hey, Danni, this place is *awesome*!"

Levi is staring at a pair of garishly painted wooden breasts on a massive mermaid. He's transfixed. He hasn't even wolfed down all his cake yet. The mermaid is a ship's figurehead and it dominates the whole corner of the room.

I look round, and for a moment I forget my headache and everything else. I've never seen anything like it.

There's no paint or wallpaper on the walls. Instead, thousands of pebbles and shells have been set into the plaster to make mosaic pictures of the sea, the harbour and fishing boats. Black pebble dolphins jump in and out of cockleshell waves and seals made from mussel shells search the seabed. Shoals of fish swim in every direction, all made out of tiny winkle shells and bits of mother of pearl.

Every shelf and piece of furniture in the room has been carefully constructed from nets and lobster pots and pieces of wood washed up by the sea. The green sofa by the fire looks like the only thing that she's bought from a shop, but it's very old and battered.

"Do you both want tea?" Mamwyn puts the tray down on an old orange crate.

Levi flashes his special smile, the one he uses when he wants something.

"Lovely, thank you so much."

I notice he's now stuffed the last bit of his cake into his mouth. I bet he's hoping for more.

Mamwyn sits down on the sofa in front of the fire, and Levi and I find a couple of lobster-pot stools. She takes the plate of cake from me and hands him another slice without even asking. She gives me a piece too. It smells delicious.

As I take a bite, Mamwyn looks at me. She sighs deeply.

"I guess you've come to tell me about Mary. Or Erin as she calls herself these days."

Her eyes go dark with tears and her voice wavers. "I don't know what to do."

I put my plate down. I can't eat the cake. For a moment I want to cry too.

"Was it you who took in the flowers? Why didn't you tell the staff who you were?"

For a moment it seems she's too upset to speak, then she pulls a cotton hanky from her apron pocket and blows her nose.

"Yes, I took flowers. Robert told me she was in there."

"Robert?"

"Said he saw you in the graveyard. You told him she was in hospital."

"You know Robert?" I realize immediately it's a stupid question.

"He keeps out of the village mostly these days. Sleeps in a shed up near the little church. Came in specially to tell me. He and my Mary were close once." Mamwyn dabs her eyes with the hanky. "Of course she won't get better in that place. It's not a place for people like us."

"Are you sure? I thought she seemed a little better when I last saw her," I say. "Maybe she knew you'd been to see her? She was asking for you all the time before."

Mamwyn sighs. "That's because even in the state she's in, she knows you and I are the only ones who can help."

From the look on her face, I'm sure she wants to tell me something. She glances at Levi then at me. I understand. She won't tell me while he's here. It's exasperating because my brain is practically exploding with questions.

I've got to come back and see her alone as soon as I can. I want her to tell me about Mum, and what happened between them that made Mum avoid coming here. Mum had way too many secrets and I'd really like some answers. Why didn't Mum tell me about Mamwyn, and how come she never brought me here to meet her? Most of all, I want to know what this *changing* thing she mentioned is about.

I need time to think. All the weirdness that's happened since Mum went missing is way too much to take on board. My head is throbbing again.

Suddenly I remember we have to meet Dad. "What's the time, Levi?"

He looks at his watch. "We've got ten minutes to get to the car park. Good thing you asked." He smiles at Mamwyn.

"This has been awesome! Thank you so much for the tea and everything."

I smile despite my worries. Levi is so easy to please. All it takes to make him happy is a couple of slices of home-made chocolate cake.

Mamwyn comes with us to the car park. It's a bit awkward, as Dad's never met her, even though he was once married to Mum.

"Nice to meet you," he says, shaking her hand. He looks uncomfortable. "My name's Nigel, by the way. Shame we haven't met before…"

"Yes, I'm sorry too," says Mamwyn simply. "But it's lovely to meet you and my granddaughter at last! I hope you'll let her visit me again."

"Yes of course." Dad glances at his watch. "Look, I have to get back to my shop now – it's called Cararth Crystals if you'd like to drop by any time. The number's in the phone book and I've got a website…"

"Thank you, Nigel. And I hope to see you soon, Danni. We have so much catching up to do."

I smile nervously. Mamwyn is clever. She's just skilfully made sure it'll be much easier for me to come back and see her on my own. The thought makes my stomach knot with nervous tension.

Levi and I climb into the car. I wave at Mamwyn

through the window as Dad drives us away, thinking how weird it was finding her today. Yet somehow she already feels familiar, like someone I should have known all my life. I wonder again why Mum went to so much trouble to keep us apart. I have to find out. And soon.

chapter 15

It's evening. Levi and I vie for the bathroom mirror as we get ready to go out. Levi grins at his reflection so he can inspect his teeth. I elbow him so I can get a look in too and check my eye make-up.

"Making a bit of an effort, aren't we? Who's all the slap for?" He turns his stupid grin towards me.

"What about you? Is that meant to be a dazzling smile? You look like a donkey."

My head's still aching from landing on the cobbles outside Mamwyn's earlier, but we'd already arranged to go to the Chill Out tonight, and I'm looking forward to seeing Elliot so much that I don't care. I'm hoping it'll take my mind off everything else.

I hear a car horn outside and run to the front room. I look out of the window.

"Levi? Elliot's waiting outside," I shout. I watch Levi take a last look at himself in the bathroom mirror on his way out, and we grab our coats and head for the stairs.

Elliot is sitting in the front seat next to his dad. Levi and I climb into the back. I'm too nervous to say anything, but as we drive towards Ancrows, Levi chats to Elliot about football and the Champions League. Elliot's dad joins in. I'm glad I don't have to say anything. Football's not really my thing.

We wave goodbye to Elliot's dad. Elliot catches my arm on the way into the chapel building.

"You're very quiet, Danni, are you okay?"

"I'm fine." I smile at him.

Elliot knows about us meeting Mamwyn earlier today because he was in the shop when we got back. But I only gave him an outline.

"I'm amazed you wanted to come out after going through all that today. It must have been so emotional finally getting to meet your grandmother!"

"Levi wanted to see Sarah again. I couldn't let him down." I don't tell him how much I wanted to see him too.

"I'm glad you came." He smiles and my legs feel like

jelly. He strokes my hair gently with his fingers. "You've got a lot of stuff to deal with right now."

I make an "urmph" sound and start blushing. I'd like to say something intelligent, but my tongue feels like it just got too big for my mouth.

When we get inside, the minister, Mrs Goodwin, comes over. "Can you help me with the table tennis tables, Elliot?"

I offer to give them both a hand. Mrs Goodwin looks at me.

"Hello, Danni. I'm glad you've come back again. Thought Elliot might have put you off telling you about our gruesome history."

"What gruesome history?"

She laughs. "Ah. That explains why you're here – he didn't tell you. Well it's nice to see you again anyway."

As soon as I get a chance, I ask Elliot.

"What did she mean?"

"Who?"

"Mrs Goodwin. The history."

"Oh that. I meant to tell you after the club last week but then everything went haywire when the police found your mum."

"So tell me now, I'm curious."

Elliot looks so serious, I almost wish I hadn't asked.

"It all happened a long time ago, okay, Danni? But it

affected everyone here and local people still won't talk about it much, especially the older ones."

"So tell me. I really want to know." I smile, but Elliot doesn't smile back. He hesitates a moment as if he's weighing up whether or not to go on, then takes a swig of Coke before he starts talking.

"The minister back then was a man called Crawford. Cyril Crawford. He was mad."

"Mad in what way?" I probably sound a bit defensive. People might describe Mum like that right now.

"As in crazy. But powerful. He became a sort of cult leader. And he killed a child."

The room temperature drops. I feel the chill in my bones.

"Cult leader?"

"Sort of."

"How did he kill the child?"

"Exorcism."

"That's not funny, Elliot."

"No, really, it's true. Ask Mrs Goodwin. She probably knows more than me."

"Ask Mrs Goodwin what?" The minister comes over with a large bag of crisps in one hand.

"About Crawford."

"Oh him." Her eyes shift to the Latin Bible text on the wall. It still hasn't been painted over. "It all happened before your time, back when I was a girl. I remember everyone talking about it. It was in the headlines for weeks."

"But he actually killed someone?"

"Yes. A young boy. Dreadful business."

"Why did he do it?"

"Crawford was obsessed with ridding the village of evil – evil as he saw it anyway. Apparently he believed the boy was possessed. He and his followers, the so-called *Chosen*, decided to exorcise the boy and took it much too far. Please don't think that kind of behaviour is condoned by our church. It definitely isn't."

I shiver as Mrs Goodwin wanders off to put out the evening drinks and snacks on a side table.

"Are you okay, Danni? You look upset." Elliot puts his arm round me. It's amazing having him so close and I want to be able to enjoy being with him. But I can't stop thinking about the boy.

"How did Crawford kill him?"

"I'm not sure, but I heard he shook him too hard."

I try to picture the scene. "How old was the boy?"

"Eight. Does it matter? It was a terrible thing to do, however old he was."

"He was only eight? That's how old Michelle is!"

"Like Mrs Goodwin said, it was a long time ago, Danni. And Crawford went to jail for manslaughter."

"I should hope so."

"Try and let it go. I told you, people round here are still sensitive about it and it's too late to change anything. Come on, let's get some food."

I follow Elliot over to the snack table. I try to think about something other than the tragedy, but I can't. Why would anyone shake a young boy to death? I know Elliot doesn't want to talk about it, but I have to find out more.

"What had the boy done?"

"Nothing. I told you, the man was mad."

"So why did Crawford think he was possessed?"

"Oh that. Ancrows had a reputation back then." Elliot looks uncomfortable. I don't really understand why.

"What sort of reputation?"

"Witchcraft, that kind of thing. Crawford was determined to stamp it out."

"Witchcraft? That's stupid! No one's been killed for being a witch for hundreds of years, have they? Anyway, the boy was only eight!"

"Yes, I know. And his family were just wind sellers too. Totally harmless." He bites his lip as though he thinks he's said too much.

"Wind sellers? What are wind sellers?"

"They used to sell weather charms to fishermen. It's a gift that runs in families. Supposedly."

"You mean like the dreamcatchers Dad sells in the shop?"

"Probably about as much use, yes." Elliot smiles. "But not so tangly and easier to put in your pocket."

The word *pocket* triggers something in my memory. Suddenly I think of the homeless man, Robert, in the graveyard.

"Elliot, what do weather charms look like exactly?"

"Not sure. I heard they were just bits of knotted rope or sailcloth."

I don't say anything. But I know exactly what a weather charm looks like. I've got one in my coat pocket. No wonder Robert was cautious when he gave it to me. A boy in the village was killed for making things like that.

"Penny for them." Elliot is watching me.

"Eh?"

"Penny for your thoughts. That's what my mother used to say when she was alive."

For a moment I can't think of anything to say. I've been so wrapped up in my own worries that I'd almost forgotten he told me his mother was dead.

"You must really miss her."

He says nothing and just stares at the floor for a while. I want to hug him to make the pain go away. Instead I reach out and squeeze his arm gently.

"What happened – or is it too difficult to talk about?"

"Accident."

"That's awful. How old were you?"

"It was two years ago."

Elliot looks at me. He's fighting back tears. I'm overwhelmed with sadness too.

"We make a right pair, don't we?" he says softly. "Let's go outside a minute."

Out in front of the chapel, I link my arm through Elliot's.

"I thought things were difficult for me with Mum being in hospital at the moment. But I guess I'm really lucky she's alive."

"Even better, you don't have to put up with someone like Aunty Bea all the time." Elliot manages a faint smile as he mentions his aunt.

"Is she your mum's sister?" I shiver involuntarily at the thought of his Aunty Bea.

"Yes. But just because they were family doesn't mean they had anything in common. They hardly spoke when Mum was alive. Mum couldn't stand her either."

"I'm not surprised!" I say it without thinking. "Sorry, didn't mean to be rude."

"No, don't worry. You're right. She's a nightmare." He brushes my cheek with his fingers and looks deep into my eyes. "Still, good things come out of bad situations sometimes."

He rests his hands on my shoulders and we're so close I can feel his breath on my face. He looks into my eyes.

"I've never met anyone like you before," he says quietly.

"Neither have I. Um, I mean, met anyone like you before." My heart's fluttering so much I'm finding it hard to string a sentence together, but somehow it doesn't seem to matter.

He traces a line across my bottom lip with his thumb, and I hardly dare to breathe.

He pulls me gently closer, then looks at me questioningly to check I'm okay with that. I smile. I forget about everything else going on in my life as he kisses me, softly, gently. It feels amazing.

I start to kiss him back, unthinking of the cold or where we're standing right in front of the chapel, or anything else at all.

A loud rattling signals someone trying to open the heavy chapel door. We pull apart slightly, but Elliot grabs hold of my hand. He obviously doesn't care if other people see we're together. I feel like I'm glowing, despite being out here in the cold and dark.

Levi sticks his head round the door, light from the chapel flooding out behind him.

"What are you two doing? I need someone to slaughter at table tennis. Danni? It's your lucky day!"

chapter 16

Levi has to get back to Graymouth. It's Sunday lunchtime and term starts again tomorrow. After we've waved him off at the station, Dad gives me a serious look.

"Danni, we have to talk about you going back to school. It's important you keep up with everything."

I hadn't given school much thought until now. I wonder what he wants me to do about it.

"Do you think I should stay at Mum's or something?" I ask.

"Not on your own!"

I pull a face. He's right. I don't want to stay there by

myself. "I guess it's too far for you to drive me there every morning?"

Dad looks worried. "I could manage it once or twice a week, but not every day."

"If Mum gets better, it won't be a problem."

Dad sighs. "Danni, you may have to face up to the fact that it could take a long time. You might be better transferring to a school over here for a while."

I'm getting close to tears.

"Pity Levi's place is so small. Otherwise I could stay with him." My bottom lip starts wobbling. I bite it quickly, but Dad notices anyway and gives me a hug. I know he means well, but the stupid beads in his dreads slap against my face and a faint smell of burned sage wafts up my nose.

He sighs. "I'll tell you what, love. We'll go over to the school tomorrow and pick up some schoolwork for you. I'll talk to the head to see if you can spend the rest of the week here. In the circumstances, I'm sure they can make allowances."

I wonder briefly what the headmaster will make of Dad. But it seems like the best solution for now, and if we're going into Graymouth, I'll get the chance to pick up some more of my things from home. When I left, I didn't think I'd be staying at Dad's for so long.

There's also the diary page I found in Mum's drawer. Since I read it, I've been dying to search through her stuff to see if the rest of the diary's there somewhere. I feel bad about nosing into her personal things, but it might hold some more clues to her past. And I have this weird feeling that if I can understand what she's been trying to hide, I can help her to get well again.

Mamwyn said we're the only ones who can help. Whenever I think about going back to see my grandmother, my pulse rate shoots up and I feel really anxious. But even so, if I didn't have to go to Graymouth tomorrow, I'd be back there like a shot.

Dad drops me at the hospital in the afternoon. I spend the next couple of hours with Mum. Her condition hasn't improved at all. She just scratches at the arms of her chair and whimpers all the time. It's so sad, and I feel terrible. I know she'd hate it if she was aware of the state she's in. Mum's usually so overprotective of me and spends her time fussing round and nagging me to make sure I get to swimming events on time and stuff like that. Now I feel guilty that I found it so irritating.

I try really hard to stay upbeat and keep talking to her. I tell her about what happened when I met Mamwyn and ask her lots of questions. Of course there's no point. She doesn't answer. I even tell her about Elliot, but there's no response.

Normally she'd be asking me loads of questions about him, trying to find out if he's the kind of person she'd want me to spend time with, and generally being really annoying. But so much better than this. This is awful.

I give up. She doesn't even know I'm in the room. It's far worse than last time, when Michelle was with me. I start crying, and once I've started, it's hard to stop. No one comes in the whole time I'm there.

When it's time to leave, I can't seem to shift the smell of disinfectant in my nose. My eyes feel sore and puffy.

Things don't get any better when I get back to Cararth. I want to go to Mamwyn's but Dad says it's too late to just turn up unannounced.

I cheer up a bit when I get a message from Elliot wanting to meet up later in the week, but I still feel edgy and restless. After tea, I spend the evening with Dad, watching a sci-fi film I've already seen on TV.

The evening seems to drag on for ever.

Dad and I spend half of Monday morning at my school. I have to go and see all my teachers individually to get work from them to do at home. It's great to see a few friends, and I get a chance to catch up on some of the school gossip at break time while Dad's in with the headmaster. Everyone's really nice to me about Mum.

I know Dad wants to get back to the shop before lunchtime if we can, so I say goodbye to everyone at the end of break and go to find him.

He's waiting for me outside the headmaster's office.

"Everything okay, Danni?" Dad looks relieved to see me.

"Think so, Dad. Have you finished with Mr Sutton?"

He nods. "Let's go then, shall we?"

We drive straight to my house from the school. Dad decides to wait outside in the car again, but I take Jackson in with me this time. No point worrying about dog hair now I know Mum's not coming back anytime soon.

It smells damp and it's so cold without the heating on. Upstairs in my room, I check my shelves for school books. When Dad saw the head, he got permission for me to work from home for a couple of weeks, but I have to keep in touch with my teachers and send homework when I've finished it.

Jackson rolls on my carpet while I search through my drawers for one of my favourite tops. After a few minutes he jumps up and sneezes a couple of times. He wanders out onto the landing.

When I've got everything I need, I can't resist it any longer. I walk into Mum's room. It smells very faintly of her perfume. Jackson has already made himself at home and curled up in the middle of her bed. He glances up to see if I'm leaving. When he realizes I'm not, he yawns and puts his head back down on his paws.

I open the top drawer where Mum keeps her underwear. I want to find the rest of her diary if it's in there. I search through, pulling out the remaining socks and tights and dumping them on the bed. Nothing. I stare at the empty drawer, which is lined with shiny red paper. It doesn't seem to fit in the drawer properly, so I skim the surface with my fingers. I can feel the outline of something underneath. My pulse is racing as I lift the paper.

I find an old school exercise book and a couple of faded postcards. I pick up the postcards. They're of fishing boats. I turn them over, but there's nothing on the back. I look at them again. I can just make out the name of one of the fishing boats. *Eva Marie*. My grandfather's boat. Looking more carefully, I see the same boat is in the other picture too. My eyes sting with tears. Poor Mum. This must be all she has to remind her of her father.

I put them back and pull out the exercise book. I flip through a few pages, my hands now shaking with anticipation. It's obviously the rest of the diary. The inside cover says *Private*, and Mum's proper name, *Mary Pengelly*. No wonder she kept it hidden from me.

Looks like she didn't write in it that regularly. Months go by when she writes nothing.

Mam and Dad were rowing AGAIN last night...

Doesn't look that interesting. I flip through to the next year.

I think Beryl's in love with the minister...

Lots more about what a cow Beryl is. I turn to the middle of the diary. She's fourteen now, nearly as old as me. I'm drawn in immediately.

March 21st

The dreams have begun. Mam says it always starts like this. It gets stronger and stronger until the changing. Soon the water will come through too.

I was hoping maybe I was like Dad and not her, but Mam says it's a wonderful gift and I'll understand that soon.

I don't want the bloody gift. I just want to be normal. Everyone hates the way we are and they're scared of us. Even Beryl pretends to be scared of me since she started going to the chapel. It's not like it was in Mam's day.

I feel a prickling sensation in my hands and glance down at them quickly. My heart plummets. The water is seeping out of my palms again. I feel dizzy suddenly, like I might faint. I drop the book and sit on the bed staring at my hands. The water pools and starts to drip onto my jeans. I can't hold back the tears any more. Jackson jumps up and tries to sit on my lap. He knows I'm upset. I stroke him and his fur becomes all wet. I look at my hands again but I can't see properly because the tears have made my vision blurry. I wipe my eyes on Mum's duvet cover, leaving a smudge of mascara.

The water's stopped but Jackson's fur is still damp. I run back to my room to pick up my things. I just want to get out of here.

Back in the car, I dump my stuff on the back seat. I didn't bring anything from Mum's room. In fact now I realize I've left her diary on the floor. I can't face going back for it.

"Are you okay, Danni?"

I nod and attempt a smile.

I wonder if I should tell Dad about what's happening to me, but I can't. He'd worry too much. If I told Levi, he'd just say I was imagining things. There's only one person I know would understand.

"Dad, is it okay for me to cycle to Mamwyn's this afternoon?" I ask.

chapter 17

I wave at Dad standing in the shop doorway. It's three o'clock already and I want to get to Mamwyn's and back in daylight.

"Go carefully!" says Dad.

As I wobble off, I'm not sure if he's more worried about me or Michelle's bike. I gather speed and ride as fast as I can along the high street towards the coast road. Unfortunately it isn't fast enough.

"Hey, Danni! Where are you off to in such a hurry?"

Elliot. My heart leaps. He must be back from school early. Of course I'm delighted to see him, but my hands have started to tingle again. I begin to panic. I pull the brakes sharply and the bike shudders to a halt.

"Nice bike." He grins.

Michelle's bike is several sizes too small for me and it's got a pink flowery basket strapped to the front. Things are bad enough as it is without having to look ridiculous too. The tingling in my hands is getting stronger. I can't think straight.

"I'm going to see my grandmother." Even as I blurt it out, I can feel the water seeping out through my palms. Again. Second time today.

He looks concerned. "In Ancrows? It's a bit of a way if you're riding that thing. Couldn't your dad take you?"

"Michelle's mum is dropping her round after school with a friend. And he has to be in the shop."

"Would you like to come over to mine when you get back later? I'd love to see you."

"No thanks, I can't, sorry. Um, I have to go now." I feel the water starting to drip down my fingers and I have to get away before Elliot sees. I need to get to Mamwyn's. I just know she's the only one who can help me stop it happening.

Elliot stares down at the pavement. When he looks up, I see the hurt in his eyes and I feel like my heart's been squeezed in a vice. He must think I'm giving him the cold shoulder, trying to get rid of him.

"Well be careful on that bike," he says. "There's a storm coming."

More than anything, I want to jump off the bike and give him a massive, reassuring hug. But a drop of water falls from my hand and hits the pavement by my foot. I have to go.

I push away from the kerb and start to pedal off, swerving along the road until I get my balance. "Thanks," I shout back as I ride off, not daring to turn round to look at him.

I'm scared and really upset. It feels horrible leaving Elliot like that. And what the hell is wrong with me? The water coming through my hands is making it difficult to grip the handlebars.

At the edge of the village, the road comes out on the clifftop. The strong wind catches my jacket and blows the bike across the dotted white line to the wrong side of the road. A car approaches fast from the opposite direction, and I'm terrified it's going to hit me. I hear the car brakes squeal, and for a second I don't think I can get out of the way in time.

Adrenalin pumps through my veins and I pedal with all my strength against the wind. I manage to wobble the bike back across the road in the nick of time. The driver honks his car horn and hurls abuse at me out of his window. I'm glad he doesn't stop to lecture me. I'm already shaking from the shock of such a close brush with death.

Elliot was right about the storm. There's a sudden downpour of icy cold rain and within minutes I'm completely soaked through. It's incredibly dangerous cycling up here in this weather. I jump off the bike and start pushing it along the grass verge next to the road, hands freezing in the wind and rain.

After a few paces, I try holding the bike with one hand and putting the other hand in my pocket to warm it up. I feel something in my pocket. I pull it out to see what it is. The knotted blue canvas flaps in my fingers.

What was it that homeless man – Robert – said? Something about when you want the wind to change. The knots are intricate and my hands are wet and cold, but I've still got a couple of miles to go and the sky is threatening another downpour. I duck behind a gorse bush to try to escape the weather. I sit on the grass and lay the bike down beside me.

It takes me several minutes. I keep telling myself I don't know why I'm bothering. I'm probably just wasting time and being stupid. But something about the strange things that have been happening to me recently makes me think it's worth trying. Anyway I'm curious. Gradually I manage to loosen the first of the three knots with my freezing fingers.

At first I don't notice the wind dying down. I'm too cold to think. Then as I finally undo the very last part of the knot, the wind drops. I stand up shakily. There's no more than a light breeze blowing. The rain's stopped completely. A feeble ray of sun breaks through the clouds and lights up the tufted grass at my feet.

Did that really happen?

I think back to what Robert said in the graveyard. *Folk don't appreciate the old ways.* Surely the charm can't really have made the weather change?

I stuff it back into my pocket and climb on the bike again. I'm still soaked through and shivering. I feel very wary about cycling again at first, but soon realize I can control the bike now there isn't a gale blowing.

As I pedal along the cliff road, I keep going over it in my mind. The wind turned from gale force to a breeze in minutes. I didn't imagine it. Only a few weeks ago I'd have said it was coincidence. But some part of me sensed the power in that knot as I was undoing it. I think it was the charm. It actually worked.

I get to the downhill stretch of the cliff road leading to Ancrows. I could freewheel down this hill in minutes. My pulse quickens now I'm getting close to seeing Mamwyn. I have no idea what's happening to me, but I need answers. And soon.

By the time I reach the bottom of the hill, I'm travelling at speed. Suddenly a woman steps out into the road in front of me.

"Look out!" I shout.

The brakes squeal as my fingers squeeze the levers as hard as they can. I swerve the bike to avoid her and nearly go over the handlebars as I screech to a halt.

"Watch where you're going, you idiot!" The woman is really shouting at me.

We recognize each other at exactly the same moment. It's Elliot's Aunty Bea.

"You! I might have known. Your sort are nothing but trouble. Always were, always will be. Just keep away from me."

I stare at her blankly. It was her fault she nearly got run over, but there's no point in saying so. She pushes her face closer to mine.

"And you can keep away from Elliot too, or I'll make you sorry you ever met. I won't have him mixing with the devil's own." She spits at me. "A curse on you sea people."

I'm so shocked and upset, I don't say anything back to her. She turns and quickly disappears down a path between the houses. I sit astride Michelle's bike with my feet on the ground, shaken by what just happened. I breathe deeply in the cold air, fighting back the tears and trying to recover myself. The devil's own? What's that about?

And what did she mean by "sea people"?

chapter 18

I struggle along the narrow lane leading to the harbour, still reeling from the encounter with Aunty Bea. I try to calm myself down as I push the bike up the narrow passage to Mamwyn's house.

The blue door opens before I reach it. Mamwyn looks delighted to see me.

"Danni! I was expecting you. It's turned out to be a perfect evening for it."

"A perfect evening for what?" I ask.

"The stormy weather might have made things difficult but that seems to have passed over now. Come in. Let me find you something dry to wear, you look half drowned!"

I chain Michelle's bike to the railings and follow Mamwyn into her front room. I'd almost forgotten how incredible her house is. The mosaic dolphins and fish dance in the flickering light of the fire, making the walls look alive.

I'm not sure why, but I immediately feel safe. Almost as if I've come home.

I sit on Mamwyn's sofa, wearing a threadbare purple velour dressing gown. It's meant to be floor length but it only comes down to my calves because she's shorter than me. My clothes are hanging by the range in the kitchen to dry.

Mamwyn pokes the fire. It's all so homely, I can't understand why Mum never brought me here.

"Why didn't Mum ever tell me about you? I didn't even know you existed."

"She wanted to protect you." Mamwyn's voice is steady, but she looks sad.

"That's crazy. Protect me from what?"

"It was very difficult for her growing up in Ancrows. She didn't want you to suffer the way she did."

"Why? I don't get it. What made it so bad?"

Mamwyn is quiet for a moment. She stares into the fire as she answers. "It was when the new minister came. He and his followers shunned people like us."

"You mean Crawford? The one who killed a boy?"

"Crawford." Mamwyn almost hisses the name. "Such a nasty piece of work. Though there are those who would still disagree. Most of the village were in his congregation at one time."

A thought occurs to me. "Did you know the boy – the one he killed?"

Mamwyn's voice softens. "Oh yes. He was called Billy. Such a sweet child." Her eyes fill with tears.

"Did Mum know him too?"

"Of course. He was her Robert's little brother."

Her Robert? For a moment I'm speechless.

"You mean Mum went out with that homeless man?"

"Up to that time, Mary – your mother – and Robert were always together." Mamwyn's tears fall and she wipes them on her sleeve. "When Billy died, that was the end of it. Robert nearly went mad with the grief. Started living rough. Mary moved away after she testified at Crawford's trial. Changed her name and everything. She didn't want to come back again and she doesn't to this day. Only when she has to."

"What do you mean, *has to*?"

"She needs to return to the sea sometimes. It's our way."

"But if she hates coming here so much, why not go to the sea somewhere else? Even Graymouth's by the sea!"

Mamwyn smiles. "It wouldn't be the same. She needs to come here."

I still don't get it and I feel annoyed.

"So why didn't she bring me? She could at least have told me about you!"

"But if she'd told you, you'd have wanted to visit. She thought it would be dangerous for you."

"Why?"

"You don't know how it was after Crawford came. Before that it wasn't a problem. Sea people were just accepted as part of the community."

"What does 'sea people' mean anyway?"

"Sea people means us, Danni. Our family. We are special. But some people just don't understand. They fear what they don't know. Even now there are some round here that would prefer us dead."

A chill runs down my spine. "Like Elliot's Aunty Bea," I mutter.

Mamwyn picks up on what I said immediately. "Bea? You mean Beryl? Her that went to school with my Mary? She's evil, that one. What's she said to you?"

I'm taken aback. So Aunty Bea is the Beryl in Mum's diary. The one she hates. That explains a lot.

"I just saw her in the village. She cursed and spat at me."

"Keep away from her, Danni. And her family. They're poppet makers. Always been trouble."

"Poppet makers?" It sounds harmless enough to me but it's obvious Mamwyn doesn't think so.

"Little figures for putting curses on people. They call 'em poppets, though I don't know why. There's nothing nice about them. Before Crawford's time, people would pay her family to make them. It takes a family like Beryl's to make a poppet. It's in their blood. Cursing is all they're good for."

I don't say anything. Elliot comes from a family of curse makers. That's not what I want to hear. He's the only friend I've got round here.

"So who's this Elliot?"

Mamwyn doesn't miss a trick.

"He works in Dad's shop. Bea – Beryl is his aunt. But he doesn't like her either."

She looks at me steadily for a moment.

"Well you be careful around them. Remember, it's in their blood. That's all I'm saying."

She stands up and pokes the fire again, then turns to me and smiles. "Anyway, that's more than enough about the past, girl. This is your time now. The moon is still waxing, and that's a good time for new beginnings. Come through to the kitchen and we'll start to prepare for tonight."

My heart starts pounding in my chest like a hammer.

"Actually I can't stay that long. I haven't got any lights on the bike. I just popped over to see you, that's all…"

She looks directly into my eyes. "Danni, you're afraid because you know something is happening to you, don't you? Think about it. The water. The dreams. You can't just ignore it. It won't go away."

"So what am I supposed to do?" I'm angry and close to tears. She's right – I am scared.

"You need to understand what's happening so you can stop fearing it, but I can't do anything to help unless you let me."

"Does it have to be this evening?" I feel like everything's slipping out of my control and I want to take it back.

"There won't be a better time, but you can put it off if you want."

I finger the wind charm in my pocket for a few seconds and don't say anything. I didn't ask for any of this and I'm afraid. I'd much rather go home and pretend everything's normal. But deep down, I know she's right. I have no choice. I need to know what's happening to me.

"Okay," I say.

She smiles. "So call your father and tell him you're staying."

I reach in my bag for my phone.

As the light outside fades in the early evening, Mamwyn bustles round the kitchen. She went upstairs earlier and changed, and she's now wearing a very odd-looking flowery garment that's somewhere between a baggy dress and a dressing gown. I've seen them before in vintage shops. It looks a bit like it's made of curtain material and has big pockets. I'm amazed anyone would actually choose to wear one.

She catches me staring. "What's the matter? This is my favourite housecoat. It's very practical."

I smile sheepishly, and watch as she scrabbles in a drawer in the kitchen table and pulls out a box of matches. She pops it in her pocket. She hums softly as she takes some drying herbs off a hook and shoves them in the other pocket. Then she looks up at me.

"We're almost ready. Just need to find you some dry shoes."

She disappears into the front room and I hear her going back up the stairs. A minute later she comes back with a pair of hideous orange Crocs and hands them to me.

"You expect me to wear *them*?"

"What's wrong with them?" She looks puzzled.

"Er, nothing. Just not a big fan of orange." I slip them on my feet and wiggle my toes. They're surprisingly comfortable, but I'm so glad none of my friends can see me.

"Ready?" She smiles encouragingly.

Suddenly I'm nervous again. My mouth goes dry and my pulse starts racing in anticipation.

"I guess. So what exactly are we going to do?"

"It's best we just get on with it and you ask me questions

later. Don't look so worried. You'll be fine! Just follow me."

She pulls back a rush mat from the flagstone floor. One of the stones underneath has an iron ring set in it, which has been carefully recessed into the slate so the mat will lie flat and cover it.

Mamwyn bends down and pulls the heavy ring. The slate slides back easily, revealing a yawning pit below. A stone stairwell leads down into total blackness. It looks ancient. There are dents in the centre of each step where the stone has been worn away by use. My heart feels like it's beating so loudly Mamwyn must be able to hear it.

"We're not going down there, are we? It looks seriously creepy."

"It's just a passage. You won't come to any harm. Best not to think about it too much." I guess she's trying to reassure me, but I'm not happy about going down into the dark. I go to get my phone from my rucksack.

"Just leave your stuff on the table," she says. "You won't need it where we're going."

Great. So I can't even take my phone in case of emergencies. I hesitate, then realize there's probably no signal down there anyway. I may as well leave it.

"There's no need to be afraid, girl. This is a special time. You've inherited the family gift. And it's wonderful!" She smiles so broadly, I know she means it. But I've seen the page in Mum's diary.

I don't want the bloody gift. I just want to be normal.

I try to put it out of my mind.

Mamwyn takes down a couple of candle lanterns from a kitchen shelf and lights the candles inside. The smell of sulphur from the matches hangs in the air as she passes a lantern to me.

"Before we set out, you must swear an oath never to tell anyone about what happens in the ceremony. Otherwise the gift will be lost to us."

"Okay," I say.

She looks at me hard.

"If you don't hold to the promise, you'll put all our lives in danger. People may think they know about us, and some of what they believe may be true. But no one must ever witness the changing, and you can't talk about it. Ever. Not even to your life partner."

I look her in the eye. She's deadly serious.

I nod.

"Okay. I swear."

I'm hoping it won't be a difficult secret to keep.

Mamwyn smiles.

"Always remember, it's a gift," she says. "You go first, I have to close the doorway after us." She holds her lantern high and points down the steep stone stairs.

Doorway? I suppose she means she's moving the flagstone back into place when we've gone down. I feel the panic rising as I take the first step. The smell of ancient stone and earth rises from below, along with a hint of something else I can't quite place. A bit like a bonfire a few days after it's burned out. The closeness of the stone surrounding me is oppressive.

"Keep going!" says Mamwyn.

I go down a few more steps and the stairs start to spiral. The sound of our footfall echoes down into the well of darkness below. I'm glad I've got a lantern so I can see where to put my feet. It's like going down inside a lighthouse, the steps going round and round so you can't see the bottom until you get there. I don't know how many I've gone down already but it seems a lot. Suddenly they come to an abrupt end and my foot lands on a floor of packed earth and bedrock. I'm in a dark, low tunnel.

Mamwyn comes down the steps right behind me and brushes past so she can lead the way.

"Come along!" she says. She sounds so happy and ordinary, as if we're just heading to the kitchen for a cup of tea and a slice of cake. I almost want to laugh. Stuck in a dark tunnel with some mad old woman, and no one even knows where I am.

"Come along, it's not far," Mamwyn calls cheerfully. She's shorter than me, but even she has to bend low to avoid hitting her head on the tunnel ceiling. It must have been made by dwarves or something. I remember Mum once telling me that people were shorter in the past. I have to bend almost double to avoid injuring myself, and even then I scrape my arm on the rough-hewn walls a few times. The sleeves on the dressing gown I'm wearing are way too short to offer much protection.

Just when I start wondering if the tunnel stretches on for ever, the air becomes fresher and the tunnel widens. I can just make out a massive stone blocking the way in front of us. I'm about to say something to Mamwyn when she suddenly disappears. There's only the stone in front of me, shaped and rounded to fit the space. I start to panic. It feels like the walls are closing in on me. There's no way forward, yet she hasn't gone back past me. She's vanished into thin air.

"Just walk round it." Mamwyn's voice is muffled and deadened by the emptiness of the tunnel and the stone blocking my way. I reach out and feel it. It's the kind of cold, hard granite you find on the moors. A hand reaches out of the blackness at the side of the rock and I jump.

"What are you doing, girl? Take my hand!"

I hold up my lantern and see Mamwyn's face peering round the side of the rock, her arm stretched out towards me.

"Oh, there you are," I say relieved. I squeeze myself

through the narrow gap, following her into the darkness beyond.

The cave arches above us, almost perfectly rounded like the inside of half a gigantic grapefruit. Now we're here, there's no visible way in or out. The cave walls are uneven, but there are no chisel marks like I saw in the tunnel. I think it must be a natural cave, not man-made. It's obvious people have been here before though. The cave surface is covered with spots of dark red, forming beautiful patterns and spirals over the walls.

"It's not blood, is it?" I immediately think of documentaries I've seen about tribal ceremonies. Sometimes they involve ritual cutting or bloodletting, and it looks horribly painful.

"Not human, don't worry." Mamwyn picks up a dark red stone from the cave floor and hands it to me. The rock is strangely soft, like densely packed sand.

"It's ochre." Her tone is suddenly serious. "The ancestors believed it was the blood of the earth."

I wonder how long ago that was.

"Ours is a gift from the dawn of time," she says.

I get the uncomfortable feeling she can sense what I'm thinking.

"So how long has this cave been here?"

"Quite a while. The sea people found this one when sea levels rose and they had to move. Or so my mam told me and her mam told her and so on, back to when we first came."

I shiver. The way she talks about these things, it's like it was yesterday. But surely that must have been thousands of years ago?

"Best not to think about it too much."

That's the second time she's said that. I only wish I could stop myself thinking.

"The moon will be up soon. It's time for us to begin." She smiles at me contentedly. "Sit here and I'll start the preparations." She points to a flat stone, like some ancient altar, rising slightly from the cave floor.

As I move towards the stone, I wonder whether to run out of here while I still can.

But deep down, I know it's too late to turn back now.

chapter 19

Mamwyn places her candle on a rock by the cave wall and takes down a clay bowl from a ledge above it. She hands the bowl to me. It's old and heavy and the inside is blackened by fire.

Pulling a handful of the dried leaves from her housecoat pocket, she places them in the bowl. She doesn't say a word. I notice her face looks different in the flickering candlelight. She could be almost any age if it wasn't for the white hair.

Reaching into her pocket again, she brings out the box of matches and strikes one. For a second the ochre patterns on the cave walls are lit by the flare. She places the lighted match in the bowl. As soon as the leaves catch fire, she blows out the flames and a cloud of smoke wafts up in my face, practically blinding me.

"Don't drop the bowl, just close your eyes."

I close them, then start coughing. The pungent smoke reminds me of Dad burning his sage, but it's much stronger.

"Try not to cough. Keep breathing, breathing in the smoke."

Since I'm holding the bowl for her, I don't have much choice. The smoke billows up my nostrils and into my lungs. I swallow hard, trying not to choke. I open my streaming eyes to catch a glimpse of what's going on, just as Mamwyn reaches out and takes the bowl from me. I watch as she dips a hand in the bowl and covers her fingers in ash. She puts the bowl down.

For a second I think Mamwyn's saying something, then I realize she's chanting, mumbling a load of words I can't quite catch. She moves towards me and I focus on the chanting. The words aren't English. I don't recognize the language at all. Some of it sounds more like clicking and whistling noises than actual words.

I feel her fingers tracing the ash in spiralling patterns down my face and neck. I'm hypnotized by her voice and the strange ceremony. In the smoke and darkness of the ancient cave I see spots of light appearing. At first I think my eyes are playing tricks on me.

"Let go of all thoughts and concentrate on the lights." Mamwyn reaches back up to the ledge and gently lifts something down.

It looks like a living thing, some kind of animal. But when she holds it up in front of me, I see it's not alive – it's an animal skin, dark grey with swirling patterns and spots of silver, about as big as a hearthrug. The markings on the pelt dance like the lights at the edges of my vision. It's the most beautiful thing I've ever seen. It changes subtly in the candlelight, the patterns moving like liquid mercury, and I want to bury myself deep in the magically soft fur.

"Take off your gown and your shoes and I'll give you this gift from our ancestors." The word *ancestors* echoes round the cave walls. "It will be yours for the rest of your lifetime."

Just for a second I feel self-conscious and I hesitate. At the swimming pool I find changing excruciating, and try to cover myself with a towel as quickly as possible. I look up at Mamwyn and see she's already taken her housecoat off. She's standing like a marble statue, waiting for me, holding the pelt as though it's a sacred offering. She looks surreally beautiful. My awkwardness drains away and I take off my borrowed things.

In the flickering candlelight we look like the ghosts of cave dwellers from long ago, our shadows dancing on the cave walls. There is something ancient about this ceremony, and I feel elated as I take the skin from Mamwyn. As soon as I touch it, I get a sense of countless others who have gone through this before me. I hold it up to my body, feeling the warmth, wanting to bury myself in this amazing thing.

"Push yourself into it. Don't think about it, just do it." Mamwyn's voice now comes from the dark of the cave.

I bring the shimmering pelt up to my face and press it against my skin. Even when I close my eyes I can still see the swirling patterns of silver and the points of light ahead of me in the darkness.

"Keep following the lights," says Mamwyn. "Push your way towards them."

I think of nothing but reaching the light spots, wanting to get closer to find out if they're real. Gradually I start to feel patches of light and warmth on my skin. The spots become brighter and brighter, until they sparkle on the edges of my vision like stars around a tunnel of velvet darkness.

"Now go into the tunnel."

I wonder how she expects me to go into a tunnel that isn't really there.

"Think yourself into it." Her voice sounds closer now.

I try to push myself into the tunnel with my mind and somehow my body just follows. It's as if I have no choice. The sensation is dreamlike, but I know it's real. I feel as though my entire life has been leading up to this point and I've only just realized it. As I enter the tunnel, I have the sensation of falling, dropping through starlit space. The spots of light spiral round me, then zoom ahead, pooling together to form one bright, dazzling circle. The light is so intense I can see it with my eyes closed.

Toc!

The sound is like someone clicking two large pebbles together. Everything shifts. I'm through.

I'm face down on a hard, lumpy surface. I lift my head to see where I am. My chest is flat against the stones on a rocky beach. It's dusk. The half-moon hangs in the darkening blue sky of early evening. Somehow the way I'm seeing things is completely different, as if there's a faint rainbow around everything, even the silver moon above. I'm filled with wonder.

The smell of the sea is more intense than anything I've ever experienced, a profusion of salt and seaweed and a thousand other things I can't begin to identify and have never even noticed before. Every pebble has a different scent.

I try to turn around and I fall flat on my nose. Suddenly I'm afraid. Why can't I move properly? I raise my head again. A grey seal is looking straight back at me with dark brown eyes. I start to panic, but the seal pushes her face towards mine, slowly and deliberately, until I can feel her whiskers and the reassuring warmth of her breath. I see the spots on her pelt shimmer and swirl, a magical, living thing, and I realize she is Mamwyn.

At last I make the connection.

Sea people. Seal people.

Mamwyn turns and moves across the rocky beach towards the water. She keeps looking back at me until I understand she wants me to follow her. It takes several painful minutes and all my concentration to get to the shoreline, even though it's only a few metres away. It's difficult to move in this new form and I start to feel anxious. What if I'm stuck like this? I have to use my elbows to drag my heavy body forward and I keep losing my balance, nosediving onto the rocks.

It becomes much easier the moment we get to the water's edge, and I calm down slightly. The sea starts to support my weight. It's still so early in the year but it doesn't feel cold. I slide towards the open water. Once I'm in deep enough, I dive under the waves to the world beneath.

Part of me thinks I must be dreaming, yet I know I'm not. I'm underwater, able to see clearly in the dusky early evening light filtering down from the surface. The lumbering awkwardness I experienced moving across the beach is gone. I glide through the water with ease, using only the power of my legs. Or rather, the part of me that was legs before the changing.

Within seconds I realize how perfectly this body is adapted for life in the sea. The water is still winter cold, but I'm warm, warmer than if I was wearing the most expensive wetsuit. I sense a sharp outcrop of rock looming in front of me even before I see it, and quickly swerve away. Somehow the whiskers on my face are sending signals directly to my body, helping me avoid obstacles without even thinking. I can hear a thousand clicks and noises from all the creatures that live and move in the sea, and I know exactly what direction each sound is coming from. It's so exhilarating that I feel no fear at all.

I can see as clearly as if I was wearing a diving mask, but with a far wider field of vision. From the tiniest prawns walking along the bottom to the shoals of glittering sand eels, everything looks totally amazing. I feel like I've just been born. How could anyone not want to experience this?

Mamwyn stays close by, and I know precisely where she is at any one time without even turning to look. It doesn't seem odd that we're in this form, not even for a moment. She circles around me a few times until I understand that I should follow her. Then together we swim for what must be miles around the rocks and gullies offshore, chasing fish through the seaweed and over stretches of tide-rippled sand.

Lobsters raise their claws menacingly from rocky crevices as we dart past. Shoals of sand-speckled flatfish flutter across the seabed when we get too close. Out in the open water, we circle a swarm of ghostly jellyfish with cauliflower-like tentacles that have somehow survived the winter, drifting along on some invisible current. I swim through the darkening water, somersaulting round and round in sheer joy at the sensation and the freedom.

We stay under for such a long time, only needing to surface every so often to breathe. Each time we come up, I notice the sky is getting darker and more stars are beginning to appear.

A distant rumbling sound gets much louder. I look round in alarm. The noise becomes deafening, confusing me by blocking out all other sensation. Sound waves judder right through my body. Mamwyn swims away but the vibrations are holding me to the spot. The clunking of the engine is almost overhead before I understand it's a boat.

I dive down deep to get away, then panic, knowing I have to take a breath soon. I swim until I can hear other sounds in the sea again. Lungs bursting, I surface and see the silhouette of the fishing boat against the deepening indigo sky. It's so much further away than I thought. Sound is different underwater.

Mamwyn surfaces beside me, and then dives again, expecting me to follow. I sense it's important we leave now. We swim fast, following the shoreline. I know immediately when we're getting close to the rocky beach we started from. Usually I have no sense of direction at all.

As we approach the shore, I'm distracted by a shoal of mackerel that swishes in front of us out of nowhere. Swimming close together, they move as one, underbellies flashing silver in the twilight. I smell the oiliness of their iridescent skin and I'm compelled to try to catch one. I chase them backwards and forwards, up and down until I manage to single one out of the shoal and snap it up in my jaws. I surface and swallow it whole, no problem. Then I dive down again and follow Mamwyn, heading into the beach by the cave.

We heave ourselves out of the water and immediately I feel the weight and awkwardness of this body on land. The last tip of the half-moon sinks below the horizon, and as I look up at the stars they start to move and spiral together. Time stands still. I spin through a vortex of intense pain, aware of every cell in my body, shifting, changing. I can't breathe for several long seconds. It feels as though the life is being squeezed out of me, yet I'm strangely unafraid. At the last moment, I manage to will myself through, into the circle of light.

Toc!

I hear the sound again, like the clicking of pebbles.

And I'm back.

I lie on the beach in the dark. I feel really sick and start to shiver uncontrollably. I try to get up. My legs are shaking. Then I lean over the stony beach, retching and heaving until finally I throw up. It's horribly painful. When I look down, I realize I've thrown up a mackerel, whole, just a few bite marks on its body.

"Good thing it was a small one," said Mamwyn. "I forgot to tell you not to eat while you're out there."

chapter 20

Mamwyn points to the sealskin lying on the barnacled rock next to me.

"Pick it up quickly – we need to get off the beach."

My stomach is still churning from throwing up the mackerel but I realize we have to get out of view of any passing boats as soon as possible. I wrap my sealskin round my body like a towel and stumble across the rocky beach, following Mamwyn back towards the cave. I'm amazed how fast she climbs over the massive boulders at the entrance, despite her age. I guess she's had plenty of practice.

I look down at the floor of the cave, unable to see where I'm putting my feet in the semi-dark. The place smells of damp rock and rotting seaweed. By the time I look up again, Mamwyn is nowhere to be seen. A voice calls to me from somewhere above my head.

"Come on, don't hang about!"

I look up and can just make out Mamwyn's face peering through a fissure in the cave roof. We must have come through it on the way out, but I have no memory of it at all. I scramble up onto a massive boulder, slimy from all the algae growing on it. When I reach the top, I have to lean forward to avoid hitting my head on the rough surface of the cave roof. I push my way up through the incredibly narrow opening to reach the cavern above, clutching my sealskin round me more tightly so I don't get scratched.

The candles we left earlier have burned down low in the lanterns, but the ochre spots on the cave walls still dance in the flickering light. As soon as I'm through, Mamwyn moves a slate slab over the crack in the floor. The slab is worn and old and has been made to fit perfectly. I guess sea people have been using it for many generations to keep the upper cave hidden from anyone entering the sea cave below. Not that many would. The coast is treacherous and the beach has too many sharp rocks and boulders to make a good landing place for boats.

I'm cold and wet and exhausted. But I feel exhilarated. Crazy as it is after what's just happened, I feel normal for the first time in weeks. Suddenly everything has become clear.

The weird dreams I've been having, the seawater seeping through my hands – it was all part of this. I wasn't going mad. I've inherited the family legacy, and I believe Mamwyn is right.

It's a gift.

My elation holds, despite being freezing and having only an old, threadbare dressing gown to wear. Mamwyn puts our sealskins away on the ledge.

"That was a great start, Danni. Everything went very well." Her wrinkled face glows in the candlelight. It's reassuring the way she talks about things. Almost as if turning into an animal is a perfectly normal thing to do. I can't help smiling. Levi would probably laugh his head off if I told him, though of course he wouldn't believe a word of it. Anyway, I can't tell him. I've taken the oath. Thinking about it sobers my buoyant mood a little.

I'm going to have to deal with everyday life and the people around me exactly the same as I did before this happened. Yet my world is now a completely different place.

"Looks like you're thinking too much again, Danni. Just enjoy this time. It's more precious than diamonds."

I swear that woman's a mind-reader.

Back up in the house, Mamwyn goes straight through to the front room and builds up the fire.

"I'll show you your room upstairs," she says. "It used to be your mother's. I've just felt your clothes by the stove and they're not dry yet, so I'll find you something else to wear. You're still shivering and that dressing gown isn't warm enough for you."

I follow her up the tiny spiral staircase next to the enormous painted wooden mermaid. Mamwyn bustles into her room and I stand on the landing for a moment, staring at a picture carved into a whale's tooth that's hanging on the wall. It's dated 1709 and the picture is of a sailing ship.

"Here you are, put these on." Mamwyn has reappeared to hand me a garishly patterned jumper and large pair of navy-blue cotton trousers with an elasticated waist. I try to keep my face free from expression. I just hope my own clothes are dry by the morning. There's no way I'm wearing this stuff back home. What if I bumped into Elliot again?

She shows me into Mum's old room.

"You may as well keep the dressing gown up here for now since you haven't any night things with you," she says. She leaves the room and closes the door behind her.

The room is painted green. The faded curtains have a repeat pattern of a fleet of yachts racing past a red and white striped lighthouse, and the leaded window looks out onto a tiny yard at the back. The headland rises steeply behind it, so the house isn't overlooked by anyone. The furniture consists of a bed, and a lamp on an old sea chest beside it. The room is almost as compact as a ship's cabin. An extra door in the wall leads into a cupboard space where there's a rail to hang clothes. It's completely empty. I'm a bit disappointed. Mum hasn't left anything here at all. I shut the cupboard and get changed quickly into the dry clothes.

A delicious smell of cooking drifts upstairs as I head down to the kitchen.

"Fancy some soup? It's leek and potato." Mamwyn is stirring a large pan on the range. The yeasty aroma of warm bread escapes into the room when she opens an iron door in the front.

Despite my recent experience of throwing up the mackerel, I'm starving. I'm practically dribbling as I sit down at the table.

"I'd love some, please. It smells wonderful."

Mamwyn puts out two bowls for us. The bowls are different sizes and have different patterns. They look old, and I start wondering where she gets all the unusual things in her house. I guess they're probably all finds from the sea, or debris washed up by the tide.

She brings the bread out of the oven and puts it in the centre of the table on a breadboard, then reaches into a drawer and hands me an alarming-looking knife with a bone handle.

"Cut the bread, could you? I'll serve the soup."

As I cut the bread, I think back to the day at Dad's when the water first started coming through my hands. It feels so long ago, but it's hardly any time at all. Since then, my life has been turned on its head.

Mamwyn puts a bowl of soup in front of me and I stop thinking about everything and tuck in immediately. It's the best soup I've ever tasted. Everything feels so homely. Although I realize things went badly wrong for Mum when she lived here in Ancrows, I still can't understand why she doesn't visit.

"Does Mum really never come back to see you?" I ask.

"Like I said, she comes back because she has to, and I see her in passing. But she usually arrives when she knows I'll be out. Often on the anniversary of my Joseph's death when I'm up at the graveyard."

I put my spoon down and stare at her.

"Why? That's so mean!" I feel upset on Mamwyn's behalf. She's old and she looks so sad now she's talking about it.

"She's never forgiven me. She thinks I could have saved my Joseph."

"My grandfather? How?"

"Fishermen don't just marry sea people like us for love, you know."

I stare at her, dismayed.

She smiles. "Don't get me wrong, Danni. Love's the most important ingredient in any marriage, and of course me and my Joseph did love each other. But in fishing villages like Ancrows, they've also heard tales of how we can help them get to land if anything happens at sea. How we're supposed to be lucky for them."

Tears well up in her eyes as she speaks. "Mary never understood what happened that night. I really couldn't save him. And I wanted to, believe me. I wanted to so much." A tear spills down her cheek and she wipes it away quickly with her apron.

My heart goes out to her. I feel bad, as I've obviously opened an old wound. I try to bring the subject back to Mum.

"If Mum blames you and doesn't want to see you, why does she come back at all?"

"She has no choice. She has to go through the changing from time to time. If she doesn't, the problems return." Mamwyn catches my mystified expression. "You know, the seawater coming through your hands, the dreams – it all comes back if you leave it too long. Water is part of what we are. The gift is meant to be used."

I get a sudden image of the pool of water on the work surface the day Mum disappeared. The wet chair in her room. So that's what happened. She avoided going back. She left it too long.

"How long is too long, Mamwyn?"

"I'm not sure. She comes here about once a year, so probably no longer than that."

It begins to dawn on me why Mum might see the family gift as a curse. She can't get away from it. She has to return here whether she wants to or not. And that means I will too. Right now it doesn't seem such a hardship, but what if it becomes a problem, like it is for Mum?

I start to think about Elliot. Would I ever be able to tell him? How would he react?

"Mamwyn, how much did you tell your husband – did he know about the changing?"

"Like I said, you should never talk about it, even with those you're closest to. And they must never, ever witness any part of the transformation."

"But what about the cave and everything? He lived in the same house as you, didn't he ever go down there?"

"I said it was an old smuggler's tunnel. I told him it was dangerous. I only went down myself when I knew it was safe because he was out at sea. But of course he'd heard about sea people. The whole village knew the legends."

"So didn't he ask you about it? Or try to follow you?"

She hesitates, just for a second, but long enough for me to notice.

"He knew more than he should. But it was all right before Crawford came, people respected the old ways. They knew better than to ask too many questions."

"I can't imagine anyone I know not being curious enough to want to go down there and take a look."

Mamwyn looks thoughtful. "Maybe. And maybe not. But there's no point you worrying about it – keeping the cave hidden isn't a problem for you while I'm the only one living here."

She smiles at me.

I attempt a smile back. She's right. I'm jumping ahead of myself. But I still get the feeling that there's something she's not telling me.

By the time we finish our soup, I've practically fallen asleep.

"You need to go upstairs and get a good night's rest," she says.

I want to ask so many more questions, but I'm exhausted and I figure they'll keep until morning. She's right. It's time for bed.

I wake to the smell of frying bacon. I feel fantastic. It's the first night I haven't been woken by nightmares since Mum left. I jump up and reach for my dry clothes, which

Mamwyn put on the chest next to the bed last night.

Now it's daylight, I notice how badly the sea chest is damaged. There's a big chunk hacked out of the front, as if someone had to cut the lock out. It's a shame because the chest looks valuable. It's made of very dark wood, carved in patterns around the edges, and is obviously very old. Whoever cut the lock out must have been really clumsy, as there are gouges in the surrounding wood. I can't resist gently lifting the lid to see if it opens. It does. The chest is empty and smells of dust and wood. There are a couple of dead woodlice at the bottom. I shut it again quickly and pull my clothes on.

"Morning, Danni – would you like some breakfast?"

I nod enthusiastically. Mamwyn looks delighted to see me. I wonder how much time she has to spend on her own, and feel angry with Mum all of a sudden. Keeping me from Mamwyn seems so selfish. Whatever happened to her in the past in Ancrows, there's no excuse. I had to grow up with only Mum for company most of the time and now I feel like I've really missed out. She's even been difficult about me seeing Dad, especially since he moved here.

Suddenly I picture Mum as she is now, lying in hospital, and I feel terrible. I wonder how long it will be before they try some new treatment on her. Then I remember something Mamwyn said when I first met her.

"Mamwyn, you said only you and I could help Mum. How come? Surely the hospital can do something?"

Mamwyn puts a delicious plate of cooked breakfast in front of each of us and sits down. She looks at me across the kitchen table.

"You don't know what's wrong with her, do you?" she says.

"No. I have no idea."

The old woman's eyes fill with sadness again. "She's lost her sealskin. I've been worried out of my mind for over a week. I found her clothes in the cave so I knew she'd been here." Her voice drops to a whisper. "But her sealskin is missing. It's no longer on the ledge."

I sit with my fork poised in the air a moment, while the enormity of what she's just said slowly sinks in.

"Can we get her another skin?" I whisper.

But I already know the answer. I feel the connection with my sealskin, even now. A bond. It's a part of me.

Mamwyn shakes her head. "That's like asking if we can get her a new soul. Of course not. She needs her own. When I gave you your skin last night, I told you it was yours for your lifetime."

"So where did it come from? I don't understand."

"The skins were given to us by the seals at the beginning of time, back when animals and men still spoke to each other."

203

I laugh. "Really? And when was that supposed to be?"

She doesn't smile. "I'm only telling you what was told to me. I don't know, because I wasn't there. But I believe it to be true."

My mind is whirring, trying to tell me it's just a story. It's too far-fetched, impossible. But I already know there is truth in the legends about sea people.

"Does this mean others have had my skin in the past?" I shiver slightly at the thought, remembering how I felt a sense of other people going through the same experience when I first touched my sealskin.

"Of course! Many, many sea people will have owned it over the centuries. The skins have been passed down from generation to generation. They're our legacy. Our gift."

"Are we the only sea people?"

"I was told there were once many of us, a whole tribe – and there may still be others out there. I don't know. I've never seen any and neither did my mother, but before that I'm not sure. What I do know is that when I die, my skin will be put back on the ledge until the next youngster is ready to take it on. That's when it comes alive again."

"Are there other skins in the cave besides ours?"

"Yes, but they're all lying dormant now. They wait for their next owner to be born. In a sense, the skin chooses you."

The significance of what she's saying sinks in. "So there's no way Mum's skin can be replaced?"

"Never. And worse. The way she's behaving, it's as if her skin's no longer in this world."

"What do you mean?"

"Just think about your sealskin, Danni. Close your eyes. Picture it in your mind for a moment."

I do as she says. Suddenly I can visualize the skin clearly, sparkling slightly in the dark of the cave, waiting until I return. Even just imagining that makes me feel good.

"I can tell you see it from your expression. Now think about your poor mother."

I feel myself welling up as I realize the truth. "She can't see hers, can she, Mamwyn?"

"No, I'm afraid she can't."

The tears spill down my face. "So how on earth are we supposed to find it?"

chapter 21

I have to get back to Dad's so he doesn't start worrying about me. But as I unchain my bike from the railings, Mamwyn and I are still trying to think of something we can do to help Mum. We've been going round in circles talking about it for the past half-hour.

Mamwyn tells me she's already searched the beach at Porthenys and didn't find any sign of the lost sealskin.

"I can carry on looking across all the other local beaches, in case it washes up somewhere," she says, watching me put the bike chain in my rucksack.

"But what if someone sees you? Be careful, won't you, Mamwyn?"

"They won't see me, don't worry. There are ways to manage these things. No one really notices us in seal form, anyway."

"Maybe I can keep checking the beach at Cararth while I'm at Dad's. Save you looking there."

"Good idea. We may as well keep looking. It's the best we can do for now, even though…"

"Even though what?"

"Nothing. Just that feeling…something's not right. Can't put my finger on it."

I give her a hug. "Try not to worry. I'll come back as soon as I can get away from Dad and the shop. We can go over it again, and see if you've figured it out."

I wheel the bike down the narrow alley back to the harbour road, waving as I go round the corner.

The minute I leave Mamwyn's I start to dread what it's going to be like when I get home. Thank goodness Dad's usually so oblivious to what's going on. I've no idea how I'll manage to pretend everything's normal.

I keep a sharp lookout for Elliot's Aunty Bea as I reach the main street in Ancrows. I decide to take the longer way out of the village, avoiding the very steep hill where I ran into her yesterday. The cottages in Ancrows are old, all painted in muted colours and most with grey slate roofs. Many have tiny gardens at the front, where primroses and daffodils are out. It looks like a picture postcard of the perfect Cornish village, yet I now know there are things going on here that people couldn't begin to guess at.

As I walk up the winding road out of Ancrows, I notice a tiny lane leading off to my left. There are no houses along it, just an old, boarded-up petrol garage on one side. The rusting petrol pumps look like something from another era. Elder bushes and buddleia have sprouted out of the cracked concrete forecourt. I catch sight of something glinting in the shrubbery and look more closely. My heart suddenly skips a beat when I realize what I'm looking at. Mum's car. Parked in amongst the buddleia, tucked against the wall. No wonder the police couldn't find it.

I look behind me to see if anyone's watching, but the road is empty. It's still early. I push the bike down the lane so I can check the car. Mum obviously parked it here to keep it hidden. It seems she didn't want anyone to know she was in the village. If Mum hadn't lost her sealskin, Mamwyn might not have known she'd been to Ancrows at all.

The car doors are locked. Mamwyn didn't say anything about finding Mum's car keys with her clothes, so I reckon they must be here. I rest the bike against the wall and kneel on the cold concrete so I can feel under the wheel arches. I fumble round and finally touch cold metal on top of one of the tyres at the back. Thought so. I've known her to hide the keys like this before.

I grab the key and open the car. She didn't leave anything inside, not even under the seats. I get out and open the boot to see if I can find something there.

Mum's handbag is hidden under the coat she wears to work. A quick rummage reveals her house keys, her purse and her make-up. The bag smells of damp leather.

I can't decide whether to take it with me or not. I don't want to draw attention to the fact that Mum left her car here in case people start asking questions about how she got to Porthenys. In the end, I just take her purse, make-up and house keys, and shove it all into the flowery basket on the front of Michelle's bike. I leave the bag where I found it in the boot. I put the car key back on the tyre, carefully checking to make sure no one's watching me.

I can take her make-up into the hospital next time I visit. I feel a wave of sadness when I think about it. She doesn't need it. She won't even be aware that I've brought it in. One of the nurses would have to put it on for her and they probably don't have time. Worse, her condition won't change, whatever treatment they give her, until I can find her sealskin.

I get on Michelle's bike and head back to Cararth with a heavy heart.

"Hi, Danni, guess what? The drains flooded at school! There was poo floating over the playground so Dad had to bring us back." Michelle has her party dress on and is playing some elaborate fairy game.

Pink netting stretches all around the front room. I'm not sure, but I think it's meant to be fairyland. I'm so glad she's here. It means I haven't been immediately bombarded with questions by Dad about why I stayed at Mamwyn's last night.

I smile at Michelle. "Who's this?" I point to a girl in a silver-sequinned outfit who's staring at me shyly from behind the netting.

"That's Sasha. She's my friend."

"Hi, Sasha, Shell's friend," I say. I notice Jackson is sparkling slightly too, and a closer inspection reveals a light covering of pink glitter in his fur. He's also wearing silver tinsel round his collar. Poor Jackson.

"Do you want to play with us, Danni?"

"Thanks for the offer, Shell, but I'd better do some schoolwork." I grin at them both and back out of the room.

It's true, I probably should do some schoolwork, but I feel too restless. I wish I could go and see Elliot straight away to try and make up for cycling off in such a hurry yesterday, but I can't. He'll be at school.

I decide to take Jackson down to the beach before I attempt anything else. I want a chance to look for Mum's sealskin before I have to be at the shop with Dad answering loads of his stupid questions, or worse, trying to do a project for school.

My headmaster made it clear that I'd have to start attending the school nearest Cararth if I don't keep up with the work they send me. Right now, the last thing I need is to have to start at a new school on top of everything else going on.

When I reach Cararth Strand, the tide is out and the beach is empty. Rock pools glisten in the morning light and gulls wheel overhead, busy building nests high above me on the cliff face. The tang of salt in the air brings back all the joy I felt swimming with Mamwyn underwater, and for a moment I feel the same exhilaration.

Concentrating on my search for the sealskin brings me back to earth. I wish things had been different for Mum. From what Mamwyn's told me, it sounds as if she found no joy in the gift at all, and I find that incredibly sad.

Following the line of flotsam left by the tide, I kick at debris and scan the beach for any sign of the skin. I poke through a stinking mound of seaweed with a stick, disturbing hundreds of sandhoppers and tiny flies, but find nothing except lumps of driftwood, plastic bottles and discarded lighters. I reach the end of the tideline and clamber over the rocks, trying to avoid getting my trainers wet in the myriad rock pools.

Suddenly I spot something wedged in a cleft in the rocks, and my heart leaps. Could it be? But when I get closer, I see it more clearly. It's just a big piece of ship's rope, frayed by the sea and stuck there. I can't resist pulling at it, even though I know it's not what I'm looking for. It's cold and slimy and it smells rank. I let it go. I hope it didn't come off a sunken ship. I think of my grandfather's fishing boat smashed on the rocks, and shiver slightly.

Jackson barks to get my attention and I turn round. He's on the beach, proudly holding a massive piece of driftwood in his mouth. I climb back down onto the sand and spend a while throwing the stick for him, amazed he finds the game so endlessly entertaining. Eventually I decide I can't put off my work any longer, and head slowly back up the winding cliff path. Jackson bounces along excitedly in front of me, still carrying his precious stick.

I'll have to come back and search for the skin again later. At the moment it seems like the only useful thing I can do to help Mum. Meanwhile it's time to face up to Dad and the dreaded pile of books.

Back at the flat, I find it impossible to concentrate on anything. After a couple of hours, I realize I haven't taken in a single word I've been reading, so I give up and go down to help Dad out in the shop.

I was right. He wants to ask questions.

"How was it last night, Danni? Did you have a good evening?"

"Yes, thanks. It was great spending time with Mamwyn. Really tiring though."

"Tiring? But she's an old woman. Don't tell me you went out clubbing all night or something!"

That's Dad's idea of a joke.

I sigh. "No, we went for a long swim round the bay."

Of course he thinks I'm not serious and he laughs.

"Actually, Dad, getting to know people can be tiring."

Dad nods. "So did you find out why Mum never sees her?"

"Yes. As it turns out, I was right about that. Mum blames her for what happened to my grandfather."

He shakes his head. "Strange, isn't it? You'd think your mother would have stopped blaming her after all this time. It can't possibly have been her fault that his boat went down."

Dad asks lots more questions about Mamwyn's house and what we did all evening. It seems like it's the first time he's been really interested in what I've been up to for ages, and I can't believe how much he keeps going back to it. He's like a dog with a bone. I tell him as much as I can, which of course isn't much.

The afternoon seems to drag by. My head aches with the effort of behaving as though nothing has happened. Part of me wants to go straight back to Mamwyn's so I can talk about it freely. I want to connect with my sealskin again, feel the sensation of gliding underwater. It's difficult acting as though everything's still the same.

At three, Michelle's mum comes and picks up both the girls. She and Dad have a brief conversation about what they're going to do if the school drains aren't fixed, and Michelle's mum agrees to look after her tomorrow.

When they've gone, Dad announces that he has to go into Bodmin.

"I've got a new consignment of crystals just shipped over from China," he says. "They're waiting for collection in the courier's depot – do you fancy coming with me, Danni?"

"I could look after the shop for you instead, if you like," I suggest, secretly hoping Elliot might call in on his way home from school.

"No, you may as well come with me. I'll shut the shop early – it's so quiet in here today. We can go to the big supermarket on the way back."

I can't think of any excuse not to go with him, and anyway, after yesterday I doubt Elliot will show up. Plus anything has to be better than sitting here, thinking too much about the changing and how I can help Mamwyn find Mum's sealskin.

Dad is studying the supermarket bill.

"It's much cheaper than shopping in Cararth – we should come here more often!" He looks really happy.

"Great," I say, not really understanding how anyone can get that excited about shopping in a supermarket.

"Tell you what, love – I'll put this lot in the car and you go and order us both a cup of tea in the cafe." He gives me some money and trundles off with the trolley.

The supermarket cafe is crowded. It seems a lot of people shop at this time. I pick up a tray and join a long queue. While I'm waiting, I look round to see if there are any tables free.

Suddenly I freeze. Elliot's Aunty Bea is sitting at a table by the window, deep in conversation with someone. When he turns slightly, I recognize him. It's the minister I saw on the beach in Porthenys that day. The one with the horrible dog.

They haven't seen me yet but they're bound to spot me in a minute. I have to get out. At the same time I can't stop staring at them, hypnotized by the air of intensity surrounding them. Whatever they're talking about is completely engaging their attention. I edge carefully out of the queue, keeping my head down in case they look up – but they're far too involved in their conversation to notice me. Heads bent close together, the minister gesticulates wildly as he talks.

Above the hubbub I only hear the odd phrase.

"Completely sealed…darkness…how long?" I think that's what he said.

"Burning…consecrated ground…spring tide." That's Aunty Bea. They're making my skin crawl. I get the strangest feeling they're talking about something to do with me, which is crazy. They can't be. I'm getting paranoid. Even so, I edge carefully towards the exit and put my tray back on the rack. I keep my face turned away from them and leave the cafe as fast as I can. I hope they didn't see me. My heart's thumping.

I catch Dad just as he's taking his empty trolley back. I hope I don't look too flustered.

"It's really full in there, Dad. We'd have to wait ages. I'll make us a cup of tea when we get home, okay?"

One of the brilliant things about Dad is he doesn't notice much.

"Okay," he says. "We can have fun unpacking the crystals too."

Sometimes Dad's idea of fun and mine simply don't coincide at all.

chapter 22

I can't stop thinking about the encounter on the drive home. I think back to the time Levi and I first saw the minister that day on the beach. There was something so creepy and horrible about him. Even Jackson didn't like him. And now it turns out he knows Aunty Bea. The way they were hunched together makes me shudder.

I need to find out more about that man. I bet he's the minister at whatever church Aunty Bea goes to. I'd like to ask Elliot about it, if he's still speaking to me. Thinking about Elliot makes me feel anxious about yesterday again. I'm desperate to see him so I can try to explain why I rushed off like that.

By the time we get back to the shop, I've tied myself in knots worrying about the minister. Deep down I know I should really talk to Mamwyn about all this, but I want to see Elliot so much. Can I get close to anyone now I know what it really means to be one of the sea people? I certainly hope so. The last thing I want is to end up like Mum, finding the gift is more of a curse.

Dad carries the box of crystals into the shop and I bring in some of the shopping.

"Dad, my head's aching a bit. Can I take Jackson for a walk round the block when we've got all the stuff in from the car?"

"Okay – but I thought you were making a cup of tea?"

He looks so hopeful that I feel obliged to put the kettle on while I unpack the shopping. I make us both a cup, and take them downstairs. I spend the next half-hour admiring the crystals as Dad pulls them out of the box and trying not to get too impatient. When I've agreed with him for the thousandth time that the crystals are excellent quality and how amazing it is that they've arrived in one piece all the way from China, I finally find an opportunity to escape without drawing too much attention to myself.

"Think I'll pop out now, Dad. I was thinking of calling by Elliot's place for a bit. I won't be late."

I can feel myself blushing while I'm telling him, and try

to work out why I feel so awkward. Probably because it's the first time I've felt like this about anyone, and he happens to work in Dad's shop.

"Really? That's nice. It's great that you've found a friend round here."

I breathe a sigh of relief. Dad's back to his usual oblivious self.

I dawdle on the street outside Elliot's house, wondering whether to go up and ring the bell. While I'm trying to build up the courage, the door opens and light floods out from the hall. It's darker out here than I thought. I hold my breath in case it's Elliot and he's seen me. But it isn't.

A woman steps out onto the street, still talking to someone behind her in the hall. I catch a few words of what she's saying.

"Nothing but trouble...stay away."

Aunty Bea again. I can't believe my bad luck.

I panic and duck quickly out of sight behind a car. I watch Aunty Bea stride off towards Cararth car park. I keep absolutely still. The last thing I want today is another encounter with that awful woman.

As soon as the coast is clear, I walk off quickly in the opposite direction, heading up the hill towards Cararth Castle. I can't stick around. I'm too worried Aunty Bea might turn back to Elliot's. I hear footsteps behind me and start to panic. It's her, I'm certain. My heart's thumping. I try to speed up, but I hear someone cough right behind me.

"It's only me, girl, don't youse worry."

Robert. I recognize his voice and hesitate. As I turn round, I catch a faint waft of sherry in the air.

"You frightened me!" I'm annoyed with myself for being scared, but he shouldn't have followed me like that.

"I'm sorry, girl. Didn't mean to make you jump." He scratches his head distractedly. "Jus' wondered howse your mother's getting on? She was in a sorry state when I went to see her."

"You visited the hospital?" I can hardly hide my amazement. In fact I'm surprised they even let him in. He must have cleaned himself up a bit first, or somehow managed to avoid any hospital staff seeing him.

"After I saw youse in the graveyard." He smiles shyly. "I knows Mary from way back, see."

"Yes, I heard." I soften a little. I find it hard to believe Mum ever went out with him though. I guess he looked different back then.

"Now listen to me a minute, girl. You needs to take proper care."

I stare at him. "What do you mean?"

"You was right to hide from that Beryl jus' now."

I'm speechless. Is everyone round here keeping tabs

on me or something? He leans closer and whispers conspiratorially.

"She's bad news. Her family's all bad news. Always have been. She knows too much about the old ways, girl. Makes her dangerous. You need to keep away from them for your own good."

I know he's right about Aunty Bea, but I'm getting the distinct impression that both he and Mamwyn are warning me off Elliot too. I feel angry.

"Thanks for the advice, but I can look after myself," I say defiantly.

"Tha's good then. Was only sayin'. I'd best be off now, girl. I hears the bus coming."

I hear the rumble of the bus engine too. It's so quiet round here. I remember what Mamwyn told me about Robert going mad with grief, and I feel mean. I guess he was trying to be nice.

"Don't worry about me," I say. "I'll keep out of her way. I know you're right about her anyway. She's horrible."

He smiles at me and I see the gaps in his teeth.

"Tha's good, girl. Just make sure she never gets any of your hair. They use your hairs or nails to do their craft, see. You take care, now." He turns and lumbers off towards the bus stop.

I watch him vanish into the darkness, then take a deep breath and walk back down to the village.

chapter 23

Back outside Elliot's, I still can't decide whether or not to ring the bell. I stare up at the old, three-storey terrace from the other side of the road while I think about it. The lights are on in the upper two floors, and I see a shadow pass the window on the top floor. Suddenly Elliot's face appears. He sees me and waves. I raise my hand to wave back, embarrassed that he caught me gazing up at his window. He disappears from view. He must be coming down to open the door, so I cross over quickly. As I do so, I'm sure I see someone duck into a doorway a few doors down.

The door opens and Elliot comes straight out onto the doorstep to give me a hug. I'm so nervous I can hardly breathe. At least he doesn't seem upset about the last time I saw him, or if he is, he's hiding it well.

"Great to see you, Danni. Wasn't the bell working?"

"No – I mean yes, probably it is – I was just checking I'd got the right house." Even as I'm saying it, it sounds like the feeblest excuse in the world. I feel my cheeks colour.

Elliot looks serious. "You were worried Aunty Bea was here, weren't you?"

I nod. "Actually, I did just see someone duck into a doorway down the road – I wondered if it was her."

Elliot's expression darkens. "Right, we're going to check. I'm not having this." He puts the door on the latch and pulls me out into the street. "Which doorway was it?"

"Think it was the pasty shop."

He puts his arm round me and we walk past a few houses to the pasty shop.

"Nobody here. Maybe you imagined it?"

But someone has been here recently. I detect a scent of leaf mould, and a faint hint of sherry.

"Probably. Sorry about that." I don't want to admit that I know who it was. I just wonder how long he's going to keep watching me. He obviously didn't catch that bus after all.

We go back to Elliot's house and he shows me up to his room. It's a large attic room on the top floor.

He smiles at me. "Grab a seat, and I'll get us a couple of Cokes from the fridge."

"Thanks." I smile back. I'm beginning to like drinking Coke when I'm with him. I sit on the chair by his desk and look round the room while he's gone.

It's a nice room, big enough to have a couple of chairs as well as a bed, a desk, and other bedroom furniture. It smells cedary, like Elliot. The walls are covered in peeling wallpaper with a repeated pattern of racing cars. Elliot's tried to cover up as much of the wallpaper as he can, mostly with posters of bands and football teams. On one wall is a massive map of the world.

I hear Elliot coming back up the stairs. He appears round the door and smiles as he hands me a can.

"I'm so glad you've come over tonight, Danni. We need to talk about what's going on."

"What do you mean?"

"Something's wrong. Aunty Bea is worse than I've ever known her. And she's obsessed with keeping us apart." He looks at me with a worried expression. "Of course I'm ignoring her completely, but it's getting out of hand. That's why I had to check the doorway just now. I honestly wouldn't put it past her to be watching to try to stop me seeing you."

I take a deep breath. "Actually it wasn't her. I know who it was. It was Robert."

"Robert? The homeless guy?"

I nod.

"Are you sure? How do you know?"

"I could smell sherry. And he was out here earlier when I went past. I know it sounds mad, but I think he's sort of looking out for me."

Elliot doesn't look as surprised as I expected.

"He's probably worried about you because of Aunty Bea. Robert used to live in Ancrows, too, you know. Our family had a bad reputation back then. Mum told me."

He looks sad when he mentions his mother. I reach out and squeeze his arm.

"What did your mum say, exactly? I don't like to ask, but it could be important. Both Robert and my grandmother have warned me to keep away." I pull a face. "Probably too late though. Your Aunty Bea cursed me already."

Elliot looks horrified. "Why didn't you tell me before?"

"I haven't had a chance. It was in Ancrows when I went to visit my grandmother. I nearly ran into her on Michelle's bike. She cursed me and spat at me and told me to keep away from you."

Elliot groans. "I'm so sorry, Danni. That's awful." He hesitates a moment.

"What is it?"

"Look, you don't need to worry, okay? A binding curse involves more than just shouting and spitting."

Elliot obviously knows a lot more about cursing than I thought. For some reason this makes me uneasy.

"So can you tell me what your mum said about it?" My voice is practically a whisper. It's just occurred to me that Elliot looks more like his Aunty Bea than his father. The resemblance is very slight, but he has her colouring.

He looks down at the floor. "I've never talked about this to anyone before. It's too horrible."

"That's not your fault."

"I guess not, but it's about my family." He hesitates a moment. "Okay. So this is what my mother told me. We were known in Ancrows for making curses and binding spells, using little figures we formed from wax or clay for the purpose, called poppets. People would buy them from us."

"That's what my grandmother said too." My skin comes up in goosebumps at the thought. "Why would anyone want to buy stuff like that?"

"All kinds of reasons. If they wanted to make sure their husband or wife stayed faithful, they'd ask for a binding spell. Or if they wanted revenge on someone, they'd want a curse – that kind of thing. Poppets are made for a particular reason…" He catches my expression. "Look, it's probably all just superstition, don't worry."

I think about the wind charm Robert gave me. "I'm not

so sure, Elliot. I reckon that sort of thing can actually work."

"Well don't worry. I've no intention of trying it. I'm not like that."

"Promise?"

"Promise."

I hope he means it. He seems to know a lot about it, and both Mamwyn and Robert have told me the ability to make curses runs in his family.

I realize he's looking at me oddly.

"What's wrong?" I ask, feeling a bit self-conscious.

"My family aren't the only ones with a reputation, Danni. Your family's got one too. That's what I wanted to say. It's what Aunty Bea's been creating all this fuss about."

"You mean about us being sea people?"

"You know?" He looks relieved. "I was worried it would be really hard to explain to you if you didn't. Honestly, whenever Aunty Bea says 'sea people', she looks like she's swallowed a wasp."

I smile. "Hey, don't worry about it. We sea people may be different..." I pause while I think how to avoid saying too much. "But compared to your lot, we're definitely harmless."

Elliot smiles and reaches out to stroke my hair gently with his fingers.

"The things she's said about you are plain crazy! I

honestly don't see how anyone could believe it. Anyway, it doesn't matter what our families think, does it? I still don't really understand why there's so much bad feeling between them."

"When I was at my grandmother's, she gave me the impression that it all goes back to when Crawford came to Ancrows. Apparently everything changed back then. Mamwyn didn't say that much about it, but I found out that the boy who was killed in the exorcism was Robert's brother. That's why Robert's like he is now. The grief sent him a bit mad."

"Yes, I heard that too. You can imagine. The poor man."

"Mamwyn also said Mum used to go out with Robert before it happened. I think she even had to testify at Crawford's trial."

Elliot freezes for a moment and stares at me.

"What's wrong?"

"She testified at his trial? Do you realize what that means?"

I'm starting to feel anxious. "No, what does it mean?"

"If she had to testify, it's possible she witnessed what happened."

I'm horrified. Surely that can't be true? "You think she was there? She can't have been! Where did it happen?"

Elliot looks at me carefully. "In the chapel at Ancrows. I thought you realized that."

The room feels colder suddenly.

"But I read Mum's diary, Elliot – she wasn't even allowed in the chapel." I hesitate, wondering if I've said too much.

"So how come she testified at the trial?"

"I've no idea. How can I find out? Do you think my grandmother would tell me?"

Elliot stands up and goes over to his desk. He flicks his computer into life.

"Let's see what there is about it online. After all, the exorcism must have been big news back then."

He brings another chair over to his desk for me and types *Crawford* and *Ancrows* into the search engine.

chapter 24

There's a lot about Crawford on the internet. A list of links pops up straight away, with headings like *Cult Minister is Child Killer* and *Exorcist Cult Leader Found Guilty of Manslaughter*. Elliot clicks on the Wikipedia link and we skim through the details of the trial in silence for a minute. The last paragraph confirms my fears.

A key witness at the trial was a 16-year-old girl seized by Crawford's followers along with Billy Tregorra. She told the court how Crawford shook 8-year-old Billy for at least 20 minutes until he fell unconscious. She was unable to help the boy because she was held down by members of the congregation, who apparently believed Crawford was saving the boy's soul. Billy died before the ambulance arrived.

"Oh, Danni, your poor mother. That's the most shocking thing I've ever read." Elliot puts his arm round me to try to comfort me. But the image of Mum held down by force and witnessing the murder of a boy she probably knew well is too much. I burst into tears. Elliot holds me tighter.

"No wonder your mother didn't want you to know where she came from," he says gently.

"Have you got a tissue?" I ask. My nose is running. I hate to think what I look like, and try to hide my face behind my sleeve.

"Of course, I'll just find you one. There's a box here somewhere." Elliot jumps up to look round the room.

While he's searching, I skim a few other links to Crawford, then go back to the original page again. The grainy photograph of him looks strangely familiar.

I feel the blood drain from my face. I didn't think things could get any worse, but they just have.

"Danni? Are you okay? Here, have these." Elliot hands me the tissues. "You're so pale. Do you want a glass of water?"

"Elliot, it's him!"

"Who?"

"Crawford."

Elliot doesn't understand. "Have you seen this picture before or something?"

"No. But I've seen *him*. Crawford."

"Surely not! Isn't he locked up somewhere?"

"No, it was only manslaughter. See this headline here?" I point to one that says *Chosen Minister Gets 10 Years.* "He must have been out for ages. He looks much older now – but I'm positive it's the same man. He lives in Porthenys."

"Porthenys? He can't! That's really close. Why would he even think about coming back to this area after what happened?"

I sit down, covering my face with my hands.

"I've no idea. But he's the man who found Mum on the beach."

Elliot looks stunned.

"Are you sure? How do you know?"

"Levi and I ran into him. It was after the first time we went to see Mum in hospital. I wanted to know what she was doing in Porthenys that day – so we went to the beach to look for clues. We ran into Crawford with his horrible dog."

"You mean you actually *spoke* to him?"

"Yes, I had to get Jackson away from his Rottweiler. He was really weird with me, just like your Aunty Bea. Now I know why. He recognized me, the same way she did. Because I look like Mum."

"You probably scared him. Your mum wouldn't have been much older than you when it happened. Maybe seeing you reminded him?"

"Perhaps. Mostly I just got the feeling he hated me – which is probably exactly how he felt about Mum if she testified against him in court. Anyway there's something else you should know – Crawford's a friend of your Aunty Bea."

"No way!" Elliot looks so shocked, I realize I should probably have been a bit more sensitive about telling him.

"Afraid so – sorry, I didn't mean to blurt it out like that."

"That's okay – but I can't quite get my head round the idea. How do you know?"

"I saw Crawford again in Bodmin when I went with Dad to the supermarket earlier today. He was sitting in a cafe with her. The way they were talking, it looked like they knew each other well. In fact I was going to ask you about it – I thought you might know who he was."

Elliot shakes his head. "We didn't think Aunty Bea had any friends. That's why Dad won't tell her to get lost – he feels sorry for her. So why does she have to be friends with him, of all people?"

My mind is reeling. Mum's diary flashes into my mind.

I think Beryl's in love with the minister...

Of course. The minister must have been Crawford.

"Elliot, think about it. She knew him before. She went to the chapel. I just saw a link online that said half his congregation thought Crawford shouldn't have gone to prison at all. They thought he was a good man, and killing Billy was a terrible accident. Your Aunty Bea must have thought so too."

Elliot looks deep in thought.

"No wonder your grandmother and Robert warned you to stay away from my family," he says eventually. "They have every reason to hate us."

"But none of this is your fault," I say, reaching up and gently touching his face.

He puts his arms around me and we hold each other close for a few moments, not saying anything. I think we're both exhausted. I rest my head on his shoulder.

"I should go back home," I say in his ear.

"I'll walk with you."

"Thanks."

When we pull apart, I notice a couple of pale blonde hairs on his jumper. Mine. I feel a bit wary still. He seemed to know a lot about making curses. I pluck them off carefully, feeling slightly guilty that I don't tell him why.

We hold hands as he walks me back to the shop.

Standing outside the back door, Elliot pulls me into his arms again. I close my eyes. I feel his lips brush mine, then we kiss, his mouth soft and warm and gentle. I feel like I've just melted. When I open my eyes, I notice how brightly the stars are shining over his shoulder. We hold each other for a moment, breathing in the crisp, clear night air.

"Do you want to see me again?" he asks.

"Why wouldn't I?"

"Let me see now – maybe because I have a seriously dodgy background? Oh, and an aunt who hangs out with a known killer."

I laugh. "Of course I want to see you."

"I'll call you."

"Sounds good."

"And next time let me know you're coming round and I'll pick you up. There's no way I'm letting you run into Aunty Bea again by yourself – not if I can help it."

The light above the back door comes on and I hear Dad coming down the stairs. We kiss again briefly and Elliot says goodbye.

Lying in bed later, I can't sleep. I'm haunted by the thought of Mum in the chapel. I go over everything Elliot and I talked about. Something nags at me. Suddenly it hits me and I sit bolt upright in bed.

Mum wasn't allowed in the chapel. She said so in her

diary. Which means Crawford must have dragged her in, along with Billy, for a reason. So what was it?

Elliot said Billy's family were just wind sellers. But Crawford saw any of the so-called "old ways" as evil. He must have heard the stories about sea people around the village too – Elliot's Aunty Bea would have made sure of that. She hated Mum. Which means it's more than possible Crawford forced Mum into the chapel because he intended to do one of his exorcisms on her – but Billy's death put a stop to everything.

Mum couldn't have been more unlucky that it was Crawford who found her on Porthenys beach. I bet she was unconscious. There's no way she'd have let him near her otherwise.

I remember how shifty he looked when I asked him if Mum had anything with her when he found her. I was sure he was lying. Mum's sealskin could have been close by her on the beach. If he saw it, I'm positive he'd have taken it.

I reckon Crawford has got her sealskin.

I groan out loud in the dark. If I'm right, how on earth are Mamwyn and I going to get it back?

chapter 25

I look at my phone. It's only 5 a.m. I've hardly slept. Everything keeps turning over and over in my mind, and I'm unable to come up with a solution. I have to see Mamwyn, but can't think how I'm going to persuade Dad to let me go over to her place until I've done some schoolwork. I can't tell him why it's so important I see her. I can't tell anyone.

I'm so restless, I decide I may as well get out of bed. Up at the bedroom window, I peer out onto the street. It's still pitch dark outside. My heart starts beating faster as an idea forms in my head. I could get to Mamwyn's and back before Dad's even awake if I set out now.

I quickly pull on my jeans and a sweater, not bothering to wash or clean my teeth in case the noise wakes Dad. Jackson looks at me hopefully from his basket on the landing as I put my jacket on, but I whisper at him to stay. The last thing I need is a dog barking his head off when I get the bike out. Jackson loves chasing bikes. It's one of his most annoying habits.

It's so dark outside, I almost have second thoughts. The sun won't be up for a couple of hours. I fix the lights onto Michelle's bike as quietly as I can before closing the back door, then push the bike along the path and round to the front of the shop before I dare switch them on. Thank goodness it's a calm, clear night and the stars are still out. Even so, it's scary out alone in the dark.

By the time I've pedalled up to the cliff road, I can feel the dawn is getting closer. A blackbird sounds its alarm call in a hawthorn tree next to me, and as I cycle along towards Mamwyn's, the sky gradually turns from black to dark grey.

When I reach Ancrows, I avoid the lane where I nearly ran into Aunty Bea last time. Instead I cycle down the other road, past the old cottages and the lane where Mum's car is parked, down to the harbour. The silence of the village is suddenly broken by a few gulls, screaming at each other to greet the start of the day.

I get off the bike by the cafe at the bottom, relieved

there's no one else about. The last thing I need is any gossip getting back to Dad when I'm not supposed to be here.

Mamwyn is waiting for me in her doorway as I push the bike round the corner to her house.

"I knew you were coming," she says, giving me a quick hug. "I dreamed about you. Come inside and get warm. I'll put the kettle on." She pulls her woollen shawl closer to her body to fend off the chilly morning air and goes inside. I chain the bike to the fence and follow her, closing the door behind me.

I stand in front of the fireplace warming my freezing hands. The fire's already blazing, so I reckon Mamwyn must have been up a while. She comes out of the kitchen carrying two mugs of tea and hands one to me.

"I'm guessing the news you bring isn't good?"

"No, it's not. It's about Crawford."

She stares at me, her dark eyes reflecting the light from the fire. She doesn't say anything for a minute, but picks up a poker and pushes a log further in. Sparks fly up the chimney.

"I knew something was up. That's why I was awake so early. All the signs pointed to it. What about him?"

"He's back in the area, and—"

"Back in the area? How do you know?" She asks the questions quick as a flash, before I've had time to explain.

I take a deep breath. "I went round to Elliot's. We were talking about Ancrows in the old days and looking stuff up online. Crawford's picture came up." My voice starts shaking. "Mamwyn, I've seen him before. On Porthenys beach, where Mum was found."

She turns to me, her eyes filled with dismay.

"Are you sure?"

"Positive. Crawford is the one who found her. I think he lives there."

Mamwyn seems older suddenly, almost as though she's shrunk into herself. She looks desolate. "Crawford at Porthenys. How can he possibly move back near here after what happened?"

"I don't know, but it seems he has."

"He can't have been back long – it's a small place and word travels. Oh, if only your mother hadn't gone up onto that beach…" Mamwyn sounds as anguished as I feel.

"At the hospital they said she had some bruising round her temple. It's possible she was knocked unconscious, or simply got confused and came ashore there by mistake. Mum's not usually the type of person to take risks."

Mamwyn picks up more driftwood to put on the fire. "You may be right – it would certainly help to explain how she got there. But Crawford finding her is the worst kind of luck. He knows more than he should about sea people. He made it his business to find out anything he could about the old ways. He was determined to stamp us all out. If he saw a sealskin, he'd have taken it."

"That's exactly what I was afraid of."

Her voice sinks to a whisper and she sounds like she's close to tears. "Of all the people who could have taken it. If he destroys it, she's as good as lost to us for ever. She won't get better."

I feel like crying. Mamwyn's confirmed all my worst fears.

"We have to get it back off him, Mamwyn. As soon as possible."

She doesn't say anything for a moment and seems deep in contemplation. Then she looks at me.

"Porthenys is difficult to get to without a car. There's no bus goes there, you know – too far off the beaten track."

"We can use the gift, Mamwyn, I've already worked that out. We can swim there easily, can't we?"

She rubs her arms, thoughtfully.

"It's dangerous, that coast. It's where my Joseph drowned, you know. The currents are strong and you're too unpractised yet."

"But you'll be with me. Won't you?"

"You can't go, Danni. It's too difficult for you. I'll go alone."

"No way. If we can find out where Crawford lives, we might need to break in or something. What if you ran into him on your own? He hates us and he's dangerous. I'm coming with you and you can't stop me."

We glare at each other for a moment. She looks quite fierce when she's angry. Suddenly she smiles and her face transforms.

"You're so like my Mary when she was your age."

Right now, I'm not sure I like the comparison.

"No I'm not. I'm nothing like her."

"Well, maybe not quite the same. But you have her determination, and that's no bad thing."

I smile at her. "So how soon can we go?"

"Can you come back this evening? We need to prepare. I'll have to make sure things are ready for us when we get there, so it's safe."

"What do you mean, *prepare*?"

"Think about it, Danni. We're going to look for Crawford's house. We need clothes."

Until she said it, I hadn't even considered how we'd manage when we got to Porthenys.

"Can't we carry them with us tonight somehow?" I ask.

"It's safer if I go first, by myself – I know what I'm doing. I'll take the things we need over at high tide when the current's not so strong. They should still be there when we go back this evening."

"You mean we'll have to get dressed on the beach? What if someone sees us?"

"They won't, don't worry. There's an old slate miner's cave in the cliff at the end of the beach – I'll leave our bag in there. It's mostly cut off from the beach except at low tide. We'll have to time our visit so we can walk round from the cave before the tide cuts it off again."

I don't say anything. It still sounds risky to me, but we have no choice.

"Come on, let's sort out what we need while you're here."

"But I didn't bring any spare clothes with me!"

"That's okay, you can have some of mine. Stay here by the fire. I'll pop upstairs and see what I can find."

A few moments later, Mamwyn comes back downstairs with an armful of clothes and dumps them on the floor by the fire. For herself, she's chosen an old green woollen dress with a massive red reindeer on the front and a pair of turquoise leggings.

"I never wear these things, so they don't matter," she says, by way of explanation. Frankly I'm surprised she bought them in the first place, but I don't say so.

For me, she's picked the hideous navy trousers with the elasticated waist I borrowed the other night, an old-lady style woollen vest, and a strange garment made of nylon. It's beige.

"What on earth's that?" I ask.

"A cagoule. Should keep the draught out and it's got some handy pockets."

I pull a face. I can't help it.

"I've got a nicer one, but I don't want to lose it – and we'll most likely have to leave our clothes there," she says. "Have you got any money with you?"

"I'm not sure, why?"

"It might come in handy. You never know what's going to happen. If we get stuck, having a few pounds can be useful. You can put it in the pocket of that cagoule."

I feel in my jacket for my purse. "I've only got a five-pound note – will that do?"

"Plenty. We don't want to take more – and I hope we don't need it."

As I pull the money out of my jacket, the weather charm Robert made comes out too and falls on the floor. Mamwyn is busy folding the clothes and doesn't notice.

"We're going to need a strong, waterproof plastic bag," she says thoughtfully. "I'll see if I can find one."

She wanders out to the kitchen and I hear her opening drawers and rummaging about. While she's out of the room, I pick up the charm and stuff it in the cagoule pocket with the money. We may need all the luck we can get and it can't do any harm.

Mamwyn comes back with a green plastic bag with

"bag for life" written on the front. "This should be strong enough, I reckon. I'll get us some flip-flops."

"Flip-flops? Won't that be a bit cold?"

"We'll be fine. They're nice and light."

Mamwyn adds a couple of pairs of old flip-flops to the pile, then squashes everything as far down in the bag as she can. She ties a knot in the top and pulls it tight. "Need to keep them dry if possible," she mutters.

I feel for my phone in my jacket to check the time. It's six-thirty.

"I need to go home, Mamwyn. Dad will be getting up soon. What time should I come back?"

"Low tide is about six this afternoon. We need to get there an hour before if we can, to give us time to search round Porthenys and avoid the stronger currents."

"I'll aim for four o'clock. Is that early enough?"

She smiles at me. "That'll be perfect. Meanwhile I'll take this bag over."

I wonder how she'll manage to pull the bag through the water when she's in seal form. "Will you be all right by yourself?"

"I'll be fine. I'm used to it. It won't take too long and I can get some rest before this evening. I'd advise you to do the same if you can. Crawford's clever as well as dangerous. My feeling is he hasn't destroyed your mother's sealskin yet – but getting it back isn't going to be easy."

Her words send a chill up my spine. We can't afford to fail. We have to get it back, whatever it takes.

There's no sound from upstairs when I get to Dad's. I inch the bike carefully in through the back door and lean it against the wall in the downstairs passage. I tread lightly up the stairs, standing on the edge of each step trying not to make any creaking noises. But the second I open the door at the top that leads into Dad's flat, Jackson ruins the whole thing. He makes a massive fuss of me, whining and jumping up and licking me as though I've been gone for months.

"Is that you, Danni? What's up with Jackson? Are you taking him out for a walk?"

"Yes, I'm just getting his lead," I say. Brilliant. Dad has just presented me with the perfect excuse for being up and dressed. I grab Jackson's lead and he bounces down the stairs barking with excitement and runs to the back door, tail wagging furiously.

The lack of sleep and early morning activity starts to catch up with me as I walk Jackson down the high street towards the castle. There are a few people up and about now, and suddenly I spot Elliot heading for the bus stop to catch the school bus.

"Elliot! Hi!" I run across the road towards him.

"Danni! Do you make a habit of getting up this early?"

I smile. "No, not if I can help it."

He goes to hug me, then pulls back suddenly. "Ouch!"

He looks like he's in pain. "What's wrong?"

"Dunno – got sudden heartburn – must have eaten breakfast too quickly."

The school bus swings round the corner and for a moment everything is drowned by the noise of the driver hooting the horn to let all the local kids know he's there.

"Better run – I'll call you later, okay?"

I try to tell him I'm going to Mamwyn's but the noise of the bus drowns out my words. Elliot turns round and mimes making a phone call and grins. I grin back, and wave as he climbs on board. I don't bother to wait around for the bus to leave. I head off to take Jackson for a run in the grounds up by the castle.

The day drags and I find it impossible to complete any schoolwork. Dad's busy in the shop, so I take the opportunity to try to get some rest after lunch. It's hard to sleep because I can't stop thinking about Crawford. When I finally manage to catch a quick nap, I dream I'm swimming through forests of dark seaweed, unable to see the nightmare creatures I know are hidden there.

I wake up with a start, still gripped by a residual feeling of terror. I fumble for my phone to look at the time. It's nearly three. Time to leave.

I run downstairs to remind Dad that I'm going to Mamwyn's.

"Remember to take the lights for the bike, Danni. You've got schoolwork to do again tomorrow, so I'd rather you didn't stay over. I can come and collect you later if you like?"

"It's okay, Dad. Don't fuss! I'm sure I'll be fine."

I give him a quick grin and go to get my rucksack. I try not to worry about the fact I just lied to Dad. I've no intention of coming back tonight. I set out on Michelle's bike, deliberately leaving the lights in the hall.

Mamwyn wants us to leave as soon as we can. It's already gone four and the light will be fading soon. We need to be able to see our surroundings when we get there.

"We have to go carefully, remember. You must stick with me. No going off chasing mackerel, okay?" she says.

"Of course not. Once was enough. I'm not that stupid."

"The currents are strongest and most dangerous around the Pig Stacks. That's the outcrop of rocks rising from the seabed where my Joseph's shipwreck is."

A thought strikes me.

"Is that what Mum was doing that day? Looking at the wreck?"

"Must have been. It's the only reason I can think of that she'd have ended up on that beach. Which all goes to show

how dangerous it is. She probably got swept into the rocks by the current."

I think of Mum diving down to the wreck of her father's boat and shiver.

"Why on earth would she want to go there?"

"The wreck always haunted her. She couldn't understand why her father went out in the storm, or what he was doing so close to the rocks. I think she goes to look for reasons. But it's a bleak place and there's nothing to find."

I get a sudden flashback to my dream about a chain spiralling in the water. "Mamwyn, can I show you something?"

I fumble round the bottom of my rucksack to find the chain with the crucifix, still stuffed down there since Dr Murphy gave it to me. With everything else going on, I'd totally forgotten about it. I hand it to Mamwyn. She gasps and goes pale. She twists it round in her fingers to see it from every angle. When she looks up at me, I see tears of shock in her eyes.

"Where did you get this?"

"Mum was holding it when she got to the hospital. She was holding it so tight, they had to prise it off her."

Her voice has gone down to a whisper. "It's my Joseph's."

"Are you sure?"

"Certain. He always wore it after he got involved with Crawford. When he became one of them."

"One of what?"

"The Chosen. Crawford persuaded many people in the village to join him back then. That's when Joseph started wearing that crucifix."

I hear the bitterness in her tone, and think back to Mum's diary.

Mam and Dad were rowing AGAIN last night...

Poor Mamwyn. No wonder she and Joseph were arguing. I take the crucifix back and stare at it.

"He was wearing it the night he was lost," Mamwyn whispers.

"So maybe she found it in the wreck – before she somehow ended up on the beach."

For a moment neither of us says anything. I can't stop thinking about Joseph's body, trapped down in his fishing boat all those years ago. She probably can't either.

Mamwyn sighs. "No time to dwell on it now. Best leave it here on the table. It's getting late and we need to set out. Are you sure you still want to come?"

I don't bother to answer. I pull back the mat and uncover the flagstone with the iron ring. Mamwyn glances at me and pulls the stone back. "You're so stubborn. I just hope you're not sorry when we get there."

So do I. But of course I don't tell her that.

chapter 26

"We could be a while," says Mamwyn, taking a couple of extra candles from the drawer and shoving them into her pocket. "We may need these if the ones in the lanterns go out before we get back."

She doesn't need to explain why she thinks we might be a long time. We both know we have to keep searching until we find out where Crawford lives. Once we've done that, our plans are a bit hazy. We can't really decide what to do next until we know if he's at home or not. Whatever happens, we're bound to be away from the cave for a few hours.

We head down the dank stone stairs into the darkness. I hold my lantern low so I can see where I'm putting my feet, and try to quell my rising anxiety about what could happen to us when we get to Porthenys. We wind through the narrow tunnels, breathing in the damp, earthy air until we reach the rock in front of the cave entrance. Mamwyn turns back to me.

"No need for all the ceremony this time. Now you've been through the changing once, it gets easier." She disappears from view as she slips behind the boulder into the cave beyond. I take a deep breath, then push my way round the rock to follow her.

"Last chance to change your mind, Danni. Are you sure you want to come? Like I said, it won't be easy."

"I'll be fine." I try to sound confident, but my legs are wobbling. I look round at the swirling patterns of ochre on the cave walls to distract myself. The whole experience of the changing took on such a dreamlike quality afterwards, I'd almost started wondering if it really happened. Now I'm here again, with the faint smell of burning herbs still lingering in the salt air, and every part of me knows it was real.

Mamwyn takes down the heavy clay bowl.

"I thought you said we didn't need the ceremony this time?"

"We don't. But you must always burn the mixture before you set out. I'll teach you how to make it later. The smoke helps you remember your way home."

"Do you think Mum forgot to do it?"

"No, she wouldn't forget something she's done all her life. But it wouldn't protect her from strong currents – or from someone like Crawford." She hesitates for a moment. "Listen, Danni, just in case anything happens to me, I've written the recipe down. It's in the kitchen table drawer if you should need it."

Her words drive home the terrible reality of the situation. Crawford is ruthless and he hates sea people. He would probably prefer us dead. And we're about to set off to find him.

I watch Mamwyn pull the herb mixture from her housecoat pocket and arrange it carefully in the bottom of the bowl. I seize the opportunity to ask more questions while I can.

"What is it that makes him hate people like us so much, Mamwyn? I don't understand. When I went to the chapel with Elliot before I knew about any of this, Mrs Goodwin, the minister, was really nice. Is that because she doesn't know about sea people?"

"Crawford is one of a kind. We were always welcome at the chapel before he came. But he was different. He said God called him to save the village from evil. In the end it turned out the only thing the village needed saving from was him."

"But why did anyone listen to him?"

"He had a way with people. And he was a handsome man in his day."

I think about the Crawford I've met. I don't see it at all.

"I don't get it. He's so creepy." My skin crawls at the thought of him.

"No, I never understood it either, but it's true. Even my Joseph sided with Crawford against us."

"But why did Crawford stop you and Mum going to the chapel? You'd think he'd encourage you to go."

"He said he couldn't allow us in God's house until we'd had the devil cast out of us. It was his answer to anything he didn't really understand. He said it was in the Bible, but I can't believe that's true. When poor Joseph drowned, he still wouldn't let us in. We had to hold his memorial service at the little church outside the village, just so Mary and I could attend."

She strikes a match and sets the herb mixture alight. It burns brightly for a moment before she pushes at the mix with her fingers to smother the flames. As the fire goes out, thick, pungent smoke rises from the bowl.

I fidget nervously. "So how come—?"

"No more questions now, girl. It's time we started. Let it go and make yourself ready."

I try to stop thinking about it but I can't. As I take the purple dressing gown off again ready for the changing, my mind is reeling with everything she's just told me. Then the smoke fills my nostrils, and I know I must focus. I need to help Mum and I have to concentrate. The lights start to flash in front of me as Mamwyn hands me my sealskin.

The smell of the skin is immediately familiar. A mix of brine and cave wall. Earth and sea. I push myself into the pelt and the air crackles around me. The lights dance and spiral together. This time I'm more aware of the pain. The lengthening and fusing of bone, the skin hissing and fizzing as it becomes a part of me. The lights combine into one bright disc right before my eyes, and I am blind to everything else. I reach towards the shining, dancing light.

Toc!

The sound of clacking pebbles is loud in my ears.

I'm on the beach again. I am changed.

We lumber across the stones until we reach the water's edge. Mamwyn turns to look at me, the darkness of her seal eyes reflecting the evening sky. As the sun sinks briefly below the thick cumulus clouds, for a moment it looks as though the sea has caught fire.

We slide into the water and move quickly from the shallows. From under the waves the sun's rays filter down, transforming the water into vast cathedrals of light. I glide through the liquid gold, and feel a sudden stab of intense sadness about Mum. Because of what happened to her, she was too afraid to tell me anything about this.

We swim through a shoal of shiny bronze-coloured pollock, eyes shimmering like liquid glass as they turn backwards and forwards in the light. Beyond them the darkness of the deeper water spreads like a vast blanket beneath us. The clicks and calls of other marine life bombard us from all directions. I see shoals of cod, sounding to each other as they swim open-mouthed towards us, then turning away as one when they see us approach.

Suddenly the cod are back again, swimming so fast that they're gone in an instant. Something bigger must be out there. Fear of the unknown spreads cold fingers up my spine. I swim faster to keep close to Mamwyn. I think she senses my fear, as she immediately turns back towards the shallower water. Soon I can see the seabed again, and I feel safer knowing we're closer to the shoreline. Brightly coloured cuckoo wrasse scatter into the kelp as we swim overhead.

All at once I feel the current. Mamwyn circles round me to signal the coming danger. Ahead, vast rocks pinnacle up from the seabed, reaching towards the canopy of light above. The rocks are pale flesh colour. Nothing seems to be growing on them, only patches of dark algae like moles on skin. Blood red sea anemones cling in the crevices like boils. I can see why they're called the Pig Stacks. They look like animal carcasses, piled up in mounds nine or ten metres high. Down in the gloom close to these rocky outcrops, my grandfather's boat lies rotting on the seabed.

As I stare down, I notice a dark shadow moving below us. It's getting closer, snaking up from the depths where the shipwreck lies, heading straight for us. I'm almost paralysed with fear. Mamwyn doesn't move from my side. I sense she's waiting for the creature to reach us. As the shadow comes into focus, my heart is hammering. Conger eel. I've heard tales of them attacking divers. Its dark grey skin glistens like wet slate. It must be three metres long, with a girth as big as my waist. I see the sharp, backward-pointing teeth in its ugly open mouth as it gets close, and feel the movement in the water as it pushes in between us. I watch in horror as it coils and twists its way round Mamwyn, moving fast as lightning.

It takes a moment to realize. The eel isn't attacking her. It's curious. The way it snakes around her body is almost like a form of greeting. All at once, I see the dark glimmer of intelligence in its eyes as it looks straight at me. I try to suppress my terror as it starts coiling around me, checking me out, just like it did with Mamwyn. I've no idea what it all means, but after turning for one final look at us, it glides back down into the gloom.

Gradually my heartbeat steadies. I feel the pull of the water surging past us towards the rock towers of the Pig Stacks. It's getting stronger. I watch a shoal of silver whiting as they swim against the flow, fighting their way out of the current. The tide is still racing out. Mamwyn circles round me to let me know I should follow her closely. She gives the treacherous rocks a wide berth and I stick to her like a shadow.

As soon as we're safely past, the seabed starts to rise sharply as we approach the shoreline. Mamwyn heads for a mound of slate boulders just off the beach. We surface for air.

Heads bobbing in the swell and keeping close to the rocks, we scan the beach for any sign of movement. A flock of sandpipers peck at the flotsam and seaweed on the tideline. Apart from that, nothing. Mamwyn dives back under and glides through the water towards a crevice in the cliff face at the sea end of the beach. I follow, heart pumping faster. I try not to think what would happen to us if anyone sees us transforming. At least there are two of us, and we've planned to do this. Not like when Mum came.

After a final check to make sure there's nobody about, we haul ourselves out of the waves, as close to the cliff cave as we can get. As soon as I feel land under my body, the lights flash and dance on the edge of my vision. For a moment I'm held in the web of pain as bones and muscles contract, stretch, change. I keep pushing through the spiralling lights to the circle of brightness.

Toc!

The pain stops. I struggle to get myself upright and off the cold, damp sand, holding my sealskin around my body. We both head straight into the cave, shivering in the freezing offshore wind.

"Oh good – the bag's still in one piece!" says Mamwyn, picking up the green plastic bag from behind a boulder. She carefully undoes the knot and opens it, taking out all the clothes and handing me the things I'm going to wear.

I put them on as fast as I can, but it's really hard to get dressed quickly when your body's still wet. I struggle into the scratchy woollen granny vest and awful navy trousers, carefully holding my sealskin in front of me like a towel. I feel far more exposed and self-conscious here. Now the tide's out, someone could walk past the cave entrance at any minute. I grab the cagoule and pull it over my head. It's not nearly warm enough, but it helps to keep the wind chill out a little.

When I look at Mamwyn, I almost laugh out loud. The combination of her Christmas jumper dress and leggings with the flip-flops is extraordinary. But I guess I probably don't look much better.

Mamwyn rolls up our sealskins and squashes them into the carrier bag. Even though she manages to push them far enough into the bag to hide them, I swear I can see them shimmering through the green plastic in the dusk.

I shiver. Just now I thought the conger eel coming

up from the wreck was some kind of monster. But I was wrong. The real monster lives here. And we've come to find him. Even so, I don't want to encounter anyone while we've got our skins with us.

"Hope we don't meet anyone while we're carrying that bag," I say. "Can't we leave it in the cave?"

I'm worried the bag will attract attention, and the strange way we're dressed doesn't help either. We're much too vulnerable.

"We don't know how long we'll be, and the tide could cut us off," says Mamwyn. "We don't want to be stranded. Quick, let's get off the beach, out of this breeze."

She must be as cold as I am. Flip-flops aren't exactly ideal footwear for a chilly evening so early in the year, and we could both use a few extra layers of clothing.

We head round the bottom of the cliff and across the beach towards the holiday cottages. The season hasn't really started yet and they look empty. No lights, no smoking chimneys. A pair of crows on a rooftop chatter loudly and one of them takes off, gliding in the wind. It circles and flies up the lane, cawing to its mate.

"We should go that way. Crows always know."

"Let's hide the skins first, Mamwyn. There's a ruined cottage up here that might be good."

I lead her to the hidden ruin that Levi found when we first came. We duck under the ivy and step inside. It's even bleaker in here in the fading light. Mamwyn isn't happy.

"I don't like this. It'll be dark soon. It's not right to leave them."

Something tells me it would be worse to take them with us. I follow my instinct and take the bag from her.

"They'll be okay up here under the ivy. I can find them for us later."

Even in this light, I catch a glimpse of Mamwyn's expression as I push the bag out of sight on the top of the crumbling back wall. I try to reassure her.

"I can't explain why, but I think we have to leave them."

She stares at me intently for a moment and then nods. We peer through the overhanging foliage and check the lane carefully, before ducking back out.

Mamwyn looks up at the sky. The crows are circling. As soon as they see us, they fly off up the lane. Mamwyn starts walking in the same direction.

"This is the way. The crows know."

I don't say anything. As far as I can see, there's only one road so we don't have any choice. It smells of damp earth and the musky scent of fox. My anxiety has increased tenfold.

"I hope he doesn't attack us." I'm thinking about the Rottweiler.

"Don't be silly. There's two of us, remember. And Crawford's no spring chicken."

But his dog looks big enough to eat people. I don't mention it because I've told her about Gabriel already. But I've seen him and she hasn't.

The car park is deserted. One of the crows lands on the broken tarmac and pecks at it with his beak. As soon as we're level with the entrance, it flies off again up the lane.

"We'd better hurry. We don't want to lose our guide," says Mamwyn.

Her crow stuff is making me irritable. Or maybe it's fear.

"This is the only road, for goodness' sake."

"It forks in a minute." She points up ahead.

I fight the urge to be sarcastic and ask if the crow told her.

"Have you been up here before?"

"Bits of your grandfather's boat washed up here. I thought the body might too."

Now I feel bad. Of course, that was probably the last time she came to this village. And in the end, the body didn't wash up anywhere. I shiver. Poor Mamwyn.

We come to the fork. The road out of Porthenys goes straight up the hill. The lane to the right looks like it leads to the houses higher up the cliff. The crow is sitting on a hedge by the lane. He looks at us with beady black eyes and caws loudly, beak open, black head tipped back. Soon his mate is wheeling above him, carrying a large twig.

He takes off clumsily and Mamwyn and I watch in silence. They fly together for a few hundred metres, then we see them both land in a pine tree at the top of the hill.

"Do you think that's the place?" I'm not convinced the crows know anything. They're just nesting there.

"No harm in looking."

We walk as quietly as we can in the flip-flops. There's no one around, but we don't want to be noticed.

A sudden rustling and I freeze and breathe in sharply.

"It's just a rabbit. You don't need to be so jumpy. I'm here with you."

I look down at her. She's an old woman and she only comes up to my shoulder. I can't help smiling.

"That's better." She smiles back, and her brown eyes twinkle in the half-light. "He can't eat you, you know."

"Yes, but what about the dog?"

It's getting darker and I wish we had a torch with us. It's okay now, but I'm already worrying about the journey back.

"The moon should be up soon," she says, almost as though she read my mind.

I wonder what the sea is like in the dark. And what were the cod so afraid of? I don't think I want to find out. Especially not at night.

The road climbs steeply. Soon the scent of pine fills our nostrils. We reach the tree and listen to the crows making settling noises in the branches high above. A gloomy

Victorian house squats in the garden behind a stone wall. A strip of yellowing lawn surrounds the house, flanked by dense laurel and hydrangea bushes. It could be a holiday let property, but somehow it doesn't feel like one. People try to make holiday lets more welcoming. We look at each other.

"Do you think this is the place?" I ask.

She nods. "It has to be."

We study the house in silence for a moment, then Mamwyn points to a faint patch of light on the hydrangeas, coming from a room at the back.

"Someone's left that light on. Doesn't mean he's home, of course – in fact my feeling is he's gone out. But we may as well ring the bell to double-check before we start snooping."

My heart's really thumping now. I'm finding it hard to breathe.

"Are you sure? Why draw attention…"

Too late. Mamwyn's already gone through the gate and is walking up to the porch. I scurry up behind her in time to hear the jangling of an old-fashioned door pull echoing through the house. No barking. Thank goodness. We wait a moment. No one answers. I breathe a sigh of relief.

"He's not in." I'm stating the obvious. If he was, that dog would probably be trying to knock the front door off its hinges to get us by now.

"Let's have a quick look round while he's out." Mamwyn turns and heads out of the porch.

"What if he comes back?" For someone so old, she walks really fast. It's all I can do to keep up with her.

"We'll tell him we thought he must be round the back because we saw a light on."

"But how do we explain what we're doing here? We'd hardly be making a social call!"

"We'll think of something."

Mamwyn seems far less worried about running into Crawford than I am. I wish I found it reassuring, but I don't. I feel very uneasy.

We skirt round the damp lawn, keeping our distance from the house, until we can see the room with the light on. We stand half hidden in the dark laurels and stare across into what looks like a study, with bookshelves round the walls, and an old desk and chair. Someone's left a reading lamp. It's the only light on in the whole place, and it's not very bright. There are things on the shelves I can't make out.

"I'm going closer to get a better look." Mamwyn's stage whisper is so loud it makes me jump. I watch her tread carefully over the lawn to the window and push her face up to the glass. She turns and beckons, her short frame silhouetted against the dim light. I realize it's getting darker. I check round quickly before I run up to join her.

I feel the hairs on the back of my neck rising as I stare at the shelves. They're full of animals. A raven looks as though it's about to fly off a branch in its glass cage, but the movement is frozen. Two hares are caught for ever in a boxing pose. A pair of crows stand by their nest, watching a clutch of eggs that will never hatch.

On top of an old wooden chest, a half-finished deer head lies surrounded by wads of stuffing and reels of thread. The lamp is pointed towards it, which makes it look like someone's been working on it recently. The glass eyes are so lifelike, I can almost feel its sadness.

"He must be keeping her sealskin in that chest." Mamwyn is more focused on our mission than me. "It doesn't feel right."

"Doesn't feel right? That's an understatement. What kind of person stuffs animals for a hobby?"

"Ignore the poor creatures, they're past our help. Concentrate on the chest a minute. Can you feel it too?"

"Feel what?"

"Just try it."

I look at the chest. I'm about to ask her what she's talking about, when suddenly I feel it. A cold, dead sensation. Mamwyn must have noticed my expression.

"That's what lead feels like," she says. "The chest must be lined with it."

"Does everyone feel it like that?" I'm surprised I've

never noticed it before, but then I probably haven't had much contact with it.

"No, they don't. But anyone who works with the old ways would know the properties of lead. It forms a barrier, even better than iron. You can't sense anything through it. But Crawford would only know that if someone told him. That Beryl has a lot to answer for, I reckon…"

She doesn't have time to say any more. The crows croak out a harsh alarm. I clutch Mamwyn's arm. A low growl comes from the growing darkness behind us.

chapter 27

"Well, well. What have we here, Gabriel? A nest of vipers it seems."

I'm determined not to let myself give in to the terror, but it's a real effort. My legs are shaking.

"That's rich coming from you," I squeak.

Gabriel growls like he wants to rip my throat out and Mamwyn nudges me hard in the ribs to keep quiet. My mouth is dry with fear. I never thought I'd be so scared of a dog, but I can see Gabriel's teeth glistening in the dim light from the study window. He looks like he wants to kill us.

"We saw the light on, Crawford. We've come here to

speak with you. I'm sure you know why." Mamwyn maintains her stature and dignity in a way that puts me to shame. Gabriel stops growling, and even Crawford's smug expression drops a little.

"I have no idea what you want to talk about, Mrs Pengelly. Or why you would wish to come all this way to do so."

Despite my fear, I feel a flash of anger. He's such a liar. Of course he knows why we're here. I'm about to tell him so when Mamwyn nudges me again. I shut up and let her do the talking.

"I believe you have something of my daughter's. You must realize how important it is that you return it. Keeping it from her is making her life a living hell."

Crawford can't resist the temptation. "Better a living hell now, than eternal damnation." His smile is sinister. "Believe me, Mrs Pengelly, I know more about these things than you. My mission to save her is a direct command from God."

"I thought your God allowed us personal choice. What right have you to choose for her?"

I have to hand it to Mamwyn. I want to shout and scream in his face, but her quiet words seem to have more impact. It doesn't do us any good though.

"I assure you I have nothing that belongs to you or your family. You are here on a false errand. Now I'd thank you to leave my property. I won't ask how you got here, but I'm sure you'll find a way back."

His voice is heavy with sarcasm. As he speaks he takes a step forwards. Gabriel seems to think he's been given the okay to attack and leaps towards me, growling ferociously. For a second I feel certain I'm about to die and I fall back on the ground in terror. The chain round Gabriel's neck tightens only just in time. I feel his hot, stinking dog breath on my face and his strangled growl is loud in my head. Crawford pulls him back. I'm so scared I want to throw up.

"So sorry. Gabriel doesn't seem to like aberrations." He smiles at me. It's the coldest, most insincere smile I've ever seen. If he hadn't got that dog with him, I'd knee him in the groin.

Mamwyn has managed to maintain her poise throughout this encounter. She didn't even flinch when Gabriel leaped at me, though I did hear a sharp intake of breath. She suddenly draws herself up to her full height and opens her mouth. She starts to chant, using the strange lilting language she spoke in the cave at my first changing. The tone is almost musical, like some ancient song. It's beautiful. Her voice swirls around us, holding us in a reverberating web of sound.

My whole body feels lifted by it. It's like a distillation of all her joy of the sea. I know in my heart that this is part of my legacy, and I'm enthralled by it.

Crawford obviously doesn't hear it the same way I do. His expression changes completely. He looks terrified. He crosses himself and seems to be mumbling prayers under his breath. Gabriel just cocks his head on one side and stares intently at Mamwyn the whole time. As soon as she stops, Crawford stops praying and starts shouting at us. I notice his voice is shaking.

"That's more than enough of your evil witchery, Mrs Pengelly. I want you both out of here, now. Right away." He yanks at Gabriel's chain and turns towards his house.

I scramble to my feet. Crawford looks back at us suddenly. "And if I ever see either of you here again, I'll call the police straight away."

Somehow, I doubt it. He's already spent a lot of time in prison. He's unlikely to want to involve the police.

He strides off purposefully across the lawn. He doesn't look back again. Gabriel trots beside him obediently, without a trace of his former viciousness. The dog doesn't turn to look at us either.

"That was amazing. What was it? How did you do it?"

"Let's get away from here first." She sounds sad.

Out in the narrow lane, we walk quickly back down the hill in the deep twilight gloom. Once we've walked far enough from Crawford's place to be well out of earshot, Mamwyn feels it's safe enough to tell me.

"The chant is something all sea people learn. It's to honour the skin and protect it from harm."

No wonder she sounded so sad. It's going to be even more difficult to get Mum's skin back now Crawford knows we're looking for it. He's bound to keep a more watchful eye on the house – or worse, he might try to destroy the skin. I can't bear to think what would happen if he did. We walk on in silence for a short while. I'm about to say something when I hear the crows suddenly cawing an alarm.

"What's up with them? It's nearly dark – don't crows sleep?"

Mamwyn looks at me, her eyes glittering in the darkness.

"He's following us."

"What are we going to do?" My pulse starts racing. My fear of Gabriel comes back tenfold.

Mamwyn stops dead.

"We should wait here."

"Here? But we're in the middle of the road."

"Better than leading him to that place where we hid the skins."

She's right. That's the last thing we want. I think fast.

"Let's go to the car park. If we're lucky he won't see us. It has to be better than waiting here!"

Our eyes have grown accustomed to the gathering

darkness. We start walking faster, heading for the car park. Behind us is only silence, but I sense that Crawford and Gabriel are coming. So does Mamwyn. I reach in the cagoule pocket for the wind charm. Feeling the lumpy outlines of the remaining knots is strangely reassuring.

We get to the deserted car park. I can see much better than I expected. The moon is nearly full, and has risen above the trees, casting a faint silver glow over everything. My heart sinks. Crawford will find us all too easily.

"Quick. Let's get in that covered picnic area." Without waiting for Mamwyn, I head for the thatched shelter in the car park. I know Gabriel will have no problem finding us, but Crawford won't be able to see us so clearly in there. By the time Mamwyn catches up with me, I've already got the charm out of my pocket and I'm trying to stay calm as I pull at the knotted fabric. The night is so still, we soon hear the sound of Gabriel's excited whining from further up the lane. I have to get this knot undone. Mamwyn watches me without saying a word.

I hear the whine again, closer this time. They've nearly reached the car park. If we're lucky they'll go to the beach first. I pray that Gabriel doesn't catch our scent straight away. The knot is gradually loosening in my fingers. I don't know what to expect when I finally manage to untie it. I straighten out the fabric where the knot was.

As we stare across the dark tarmac, Crawford and the

dog suddenly come into view. They're silhouetted against the entrance in the moonlight, only a few metres away. Gabriel is straining at his chain in our direction.

From out of nowhere comes a rumble of thunder. I see Crawford look up at the sky, surprised. A fast-moving cloud bank covers the moon and now everything is much darker. Lightning flashes across the sky overhead, illuminating the man and his dog again. Another crack of thunder, much closer. Rain starts to spit down onto the gravel, slow at first then pouring from the sky in torrents. I can no longer make out Crawford or the dog at all.

For a moment Mamwyn and I stand at the entrance of the shelter, staring out into the thunderstorm. There's no sign of life.

We keep watching, waiting to see if Crawford finds us. Seconds tick by. Then minutes.

"I think they've gone." The sound of the rain is so loud, I almost have to shout to make Mamwyn hear.

"Shhh!" she hisses.

We stay silent for a few more moments. The heavy rain is unceasing. Finally Mamwyn feels it's safe to talk.

"Powerful charm you've got there. Did Robert give it to you?"

I nod.

"Thank him next time you see him. Let's go and check if the lane is clear."

We step out into the downpour. Within seconds we're both soaked through. The thin nylon cagoule offers no protection against the weather and Mamwyn's jumper dress must feel like she's wearing a wet flannel. It's freezing cold. We cross to the car park entrance and look back up the lane towards Crawford's place. The road is empty. A newly formed river of rainwater washes down the slope.

"We'd better check the beach as well," says Mamwyn.

I know she's right. We need to make sure he's not waiting for us there before collecting the skins. We walk down towards the beach as quickly as we can in our slippery wet flip-flops, and stand next to the holiday cottages. We scour the beach. As far as we can make out, it's empty.

"I think he's gone home," I say, my teeth chattering in the cold.

"Okay. But keep a careful look out. He might come back."

We head for the derelict cottage behind the hedgerow. It's so dark now, it takes me a while to find the entrance to it in the hedge.

"You go in," says Mamwyn. "I'll keep watch."

I hesitate. Going into this creepy ruin at night is not something I want to do by myself. But she's right. Crawford finding us here would be worse. I leave her outside and push through the foliage, scratching my arms on brambles and twigs on my way in. I stumble clumsily onto the uneven cottage floor. There's some degree of shelter from the weather inside, even though there's no roof. The stunted, overhanging ash trees keep some of the rain off, but the leaves constantly drip cold water down my back. It's pitch dark. The dense ivy covering the wall feels like some brooding presence in here with me. I put my hands into the wet leaves, searching for the bag. I come out in a cold sweat as I struggle to find it.

Lightning flashes overhead. I take a few breaths and hear the rumble of thunder. The storm is moving away. I must hurry. I remember how earlier I could see the faint swirling light from the skins through the green plastic. I stop my frantic scrabbling and take a step back on the stone-littered floor of the ruin. I scan the ivy. Almost immediately I spot a faint, pulsing light near the top of the wall. It's as if the skins are alive. As I pull down the bag, showering myself with even more freezing water in the process, I think about Mum's sealskin, shut away in that lead-lined chest. The awful, dead feeling I got from the lead.

"What are you doing in there? Are you okay?" Mamwyn's muffled voice makes me jump.

"Coming! Sorry, it took me a while to find them." I bend down and scramble back out onto the lane, clutching the bag close to my heart.

"We'd better hurry. Not sure how long the rain will keep him away."

She's right. We both keep turning to look back up the lane as we head for the beach. I want to run, but I'm not sure Mamwyn could manage. We're already walking as fast as we can.

We pass the holiday cottages, dark and empty. The beach still looks deserted, but I'm afraid to leave the houses and step into the open.

"Come on. No time to waste. We need to get down to the shoreline."

Now we run. The rain is still bucketing down on the wet sand, which means we can't see very far. I take some small comfort thinking that at least Crawford won't be able to see much in this weather either. I try not to think about Gabriel.

On the shoreline, Mamwyn takes the carefully rolled skins out of the bag and gives me mine. I feel a surge of joy to have it back in my hands. We quickly take off our wet clothes and I hold my skin up against my body, shivering in the cold. I take the wind charm out of the cagoule pocket before handing my wet things to Mamwyn, and she shoves the clothes into the plastic bag as fast as she can.

"Push yourself into your skin." Mamwyn sounds slightly panicky. Her tone gets me worried and I can't concentrate.

"Let go of your thinking." She sounds a little calmer, but

maybe that's just for my benefit. "If you want to keep that charm you're holding, put it in your mouth and hold it with your teeth."

I do as she says, then bury myself in the soft, swirling pattern of the fur. It doesn't feel wet now it's up close. It still has the familiar smell of earth and sea, but with an added hint of dank ivy. The lights come up to my eyes and spiral round. I feel the spasms of pain as the muscles pull and contract and the bones grow and change.

Toc!

I'm on my belly at the edge of the sea. Mamwyn is here too, dragging the plastic bag with her to get it off the beach. As we lumber forwards into the waves, I'm sure I can hear the sound of Gabriel barking somewhere behind us on the beach. Then we are underwater and swimming away from the shore as fast as we can.

We haven't got very far before Mamwyn has to let go of the bag. She didn't have time to knot the top, so it's filled up with water and looks too heavy to manage. As the bag sinks down in the dark towards the seabed, a flip-flop escapes and bobs up on the surface. We keep swimming out to the open water.

The storm has brought a bigger swell to the ocean. I follow Mamwyn closely. Once we're away from Porthenys, we slow down to an easier pace.

I can see surprisingly well, far better than I'd normally be able to in the dark underwater, but I can't help feeling scared of what might be out there. What creatures come out at night? We stay close to the surface, keeping as much distance as we can between us and the currents that suck round the Pig Stacks.

I hear a sudden whisper of movement. A shoal of fish, turning as one away from us in the dark. Mackerel. I can smell them. I wonder if they ever sleep. Maybe they're sleeping now? I hope that means it's safe out here.

A flash of bubbles, followed closely by another. I'm paralysed by fear as a couple of large shapes dart past us. It's terrifying in the darkness. What were they? Sharks? Mamwyn stops and circles round me. Then the shapes are back again, almost touching us as they swim past. I hear the reassuring clicks and whirrs. Porpoises. They seem to be curious. Maybe we look different from other seals? My heart lifts as they swim right up to us, chattering and clicking in the dark as they approach. Mamwyn swims with them and they circle round together. I'm not sure whether to join them or not, but before I can decide, the porpoises swim off into the black ocean as fast as they came, and are gone.

Mamwyn and I journey on, keeping close to the shoreline. I see things in the water from time to time. Cuttlefish with saucer eyes pulsate to each other on the sandy seabed. I try to stop being afraid of everything. This is part of my world now, and in time I'll come to know it better.

As we get close to the beach by the cave, I think I glimpse something moving through a bed of kelp way below me. The dark outline of something big. Stupidly I open my mouth. I'm so busy trying to see what it is, that it's a few seconds before I notice Robert's charm floating down towards it in the depths. I dive down to retrieve it immediately, still feeling unnerved by what I thought I saw.

As I reach the kelp, I'm fully aware how easy it would be for any number of creatures to hide in there, especially in the dark. It's like a forest. The seaweed grows several metres tall from the seabed. My heart's racing.

Suddenly I completely lose sight of Robert's charm. Scanning desperately in the dark, I spot it again floating down through the topmost fronds. I race to grab it, heart pounding against my ribcage. I can't bear to lose it after all we've been through tonight, but at the same time I'm certain there's something else down here.

As I snatch the charm back with my teeth, I get the prickling sensation that I'm being watched. I look down. A face peers up at me, and I freeze in terror. Beams of moonlight filter down from above, and all at once I can make out what it is. A bull seal, the patterns in his pelt swirling silver in the light. So close. He's massive. We stare at each other for a second, then he starts to glide up through the kelp towards me.

He's probably just curious, but I'm so scared I nearly drop the charm again. I turn away, swimming as fast as I can to try to catch up with Mamwyn. I surface for air. The sky has cleared and moonlight silvers the water. I see no trace of the bull seal, but the adrenalin coursing through my body has made me really tense. I can't see Mamwyn either. For a moment I panic.

I dive under and swim fast towards the shore. Suddenly I catch a glimpse of Mamwyn again. She's some way ahead of me, close to the beach. I speed through the water to catch her up, not daring to look back. She sees me and circles round, the familiar patterns on her pelt faintly shimmering, reassuring me I'm safe.

As I pull myself out onto the rocks by our cave, I stare up at the moon shining bright on the water. Then the stars spiral together and the pain starts.

A few minutes later, I spit the sea-soaked wind charm out of my mouth onto the sand and pick it up. My jaws still ache slightly with the tension of holding it in my mouth all that way.

Mamwyn and I pick our way as quickly as we can across the rocky beach, holding our sealskins against our bodies to keep warm, and head back to the total darkness and safety of the cave. I glance back at the water. It looks so calm out there now. As far as I can see, there's no sign of the bull seal. I breathe a sigh of relief.

We climb back up the steep stone steps into the kitchen. The warmth is really comforting after struggling back along the cold tunnel wearing only Mamwyn's old dressing gown. I reckon she can't be any warmer in that stupid housecoat either.

Mamwyn pulls the stone back into place in the floor, and places the mat over it before bustling round and preparing food. I'm amazed at her energy, especially as I know she's done the difficult journey to Porthenys twice today.

I'm so tired I can hardly keep my eyes open, but when I look at the clock, it's only eight. I can't believe it. I feel as though we've been gone much longer.

"I'd better call Dad and tell him I'm staying."

"Okay. I'll have this ready in about twenty minutes."

I go upstairs and change back into my own clothes. Then I find my phone and go outside. There's hardly any signal inside Mamwyn's cottage.

"Dad?"

"Danni, you left the bike lights behind!"

"I know. Sorry. I'll stay here and come back first thing in the morning."

"Do you want me to come and pick you up now? I can fit the bike in the back of the car if you like."

"No, Mamwyn's just started cooking for me. I'll be fine. Don't worry."

"Well if you're sure." Dad sounds quite relieved he doesn't have to come out.

"The weather's a bit unpredictable tonight anyway, Dad. You don't want to get caught in a storm."

"What do you mean? It's a lovely night. Nice moon and hardly a breeze."

"Yes, it's okay now, but earlier – didn't it rain there?"

"No, not a drop. And it rained in Ancrows? How strange. The weather round here is so localized, it amazes me sometimes."

I think about the cracking thunder and lightning in Porthenys. It's not that far away. Was it really only in that one place?

I'm so glad I made the effort to bring the charm back with me. Mamwyn's right. I must thank Robert next time I see him.

chapter 28

Next morning, I open my eyes and gaze at the wooden trunk next to Mum's old bed. I can hear Mamwyn up already, clattering plates in the kitchen. I must have slept heavily.

I blink blearily in the light filtering through the curtains and my eyes focus on the ugly jagged hole in the front of the trunk. Someone must have been desperate to open it if they were that clumsy with their tools.

Suddenly I picture my grandfather's gold chain on the table downstairs in the kitchen. There's a rusty old key on the chain alongside the crucifix. Could it be the missing key?

Mamwyn was so cagey when I asked how much Joseph knew about the changing, I had a feeling there was something she wasn't telling me. I dress quickly and run downstairs.

"Thought I heard you getting up. Fancy a cooked breakfast?" Mamwyn picks up a box of eggs.

"Yes, thanks, that'd be lovely." I'm starving after yesterday and the thought of bacon and eggs is making my mouth water. But I can't wait to ask. "Mamwyn, you know the trunk in Mum's old room?"

"What about it?" She sounds wary.

"The key on the chain. Is that the key to the chest upstairs?"

"Maybe. Too late to fix it now though."

"How come it's on the chain? What happened?"

Mamwyn turns her back to me and pulls a frying pan down onto one of the rings on the old range. She doesn't reply.

I think back to when I asked her how much my grandfather knew about sea people. I can't let it go.

"So what was in the chest?"

She turns to look at me. "My sealskin," she says, her voice dropping to a whisper.

I stare at her. "You mean, my grandfather found the cave?"

"Yes. But it was all Crawford's doing. When Joseph

became one of the Chosen, Crawford told him to find out all he could about sea people. Said he could help to save us." Mamwyn's voice cracks with emotion. "Like we needed saving!"

"So Joseph searched the cave and found the sealskin?" I'm still trying to understand how my grandfather could possibly have sided with someone as horrible as Crawford.

She nods sadly. "I was out in the village at the time. Joseph was asleep when I went out – or at least I thought he was. By the time I came back, he'd brought the skin up and locked it in the trunk. I think he meant to give it to Crawford when he next saw him – and to stop me getting it back, he put the key on the chain with his crucifix."

"Was that the same day he…" I try to think how to ask without upsetting Mamwyn even more. "…went fishing?"

"It was the day he drowned, yes. He went out in a storm. He was trying to prove a point – that he didn't need me to keep him safe out there."

She didn't save him.

Mum's words come back to me and suddenly I realize – Mum can't have known.

"Why didn't you tell Mum? You know she blamed you for not saving him!"

Mamwyn puts a little oil in the pan to heat. Then she turns round to look at me.

"I didn't want her to think ill of her father. She'd just lost him, remember. She had enough to cope with already. I didn't want her to know it was his own pig-headedness that kept me from saving him."

"How come Mum didn't work it out for herself? Didn't she ask why you cut out the lock?"

"I told her I'd lost the key and there was something I needed in there. The chest used to be in our bedroom, so she didn't notice for a while." She pauses. "It wasn't Joseph's fault, you know, not really. It was all down to Crawford, telling him the old ways were evil, the work of the devil. Crawford was a persuasive man, and Joseph believed him."

The mention of Crawford brings the events of last night flooding back to me.

Suddenly I don't feel like eating breakfast any more.

"Do you think Mum realized the truth when she found the chain? Maybe she saw the key and finally understood that you couldn't save him?"

"It's possible, I suppose. Perhaps I should have told her back then, I don't know. It's too late now anyway." Mamwyn's voice is wobbly again.

I don't say anything. All this time Mum had been blaming Mamwyn. No wonder the current pulled her into the rocks. She must have been so shocked and upset.

Crawford has a lot to answer for. In the past he pulled

my family apart at the seams. And he's still intent on our destruction.

I think he's come back to finish what he started.

Cycling back to Dad's on Michelle's bike, I go over everything Mamwyn and I talked about before I left. We're both positive Crawford has Mum's sealskin in his house. We have to find an opportunity to break in to get it back, as soon as possible.

The biggest problem is that Crawford knows about us now. He'll be on constant lookout. And he's got Gabriel.

I start wondering what he would do if he caught me breaking in. I remember the stuffed animals and I shudder. He must have killed them with something. I bet he's got a rifle.

Suddenly a shotgun goes off right next to me and I nearly fall off the bike in fright. I crane my neck round to try to see who's shooting, and realize it's just a builder chucking bricks into a skip. If I'm this jumpy just thinking about breaking into Crawford's house, I hate to think how terrifying it will be when we actually have to do it.

I wish I could tell Elliot what happened last night. I bet he'd help us. I'm already beginning to find keeping the oath of secrecy is more difficult than I thought.

I reach the steep hill rising out of the village and try to concentrate on cycling for a while.

* * *

Back at Dad's, I spend the rest of the day pretending to do schoolwork, but not actually doing any at all. I scour the internet and read as much as I can about Crawford. Compared with trying to get Mum's sealskin back, school seems so unimportant. I can catch up later.

I get a message from Elliot around lunchtime asking if he can pick me up from Dad's later, which cheers me up despite everything. I message back to say yes. It'll be really great to see him and think about something other than Crawford for an hour or two.

By four o'clock I've got a headache, so I go down to help in the shop to try and take my mind off everything. It doesn't really work as I'm still thinking about how Mamwyn and I can get Mum's sealskin back, but at least the headache goes away.

Dad and I eat our supper soon after we close up.

"Are you going out tonight, Danni?" he asks, shoving his last forkful of baked potato into his mouth.

"I'm meeting up with Elliot if that's okay?" I'm worried Dad might want me to stay in after being at Mamwyn's all last night.

Fortunately he seems pleased.

"It'll be good for you to get out and see someone your own age. Can't be much fun being cooped up on your own all day."

"You're here, Dad. And I did serve a few customers this afternoon."

"Well I reckon you deserve a break. What time are you going out? I'd walk round with you to give Jackson a run, only the England versus Germany match starts in a few minutes."

I smile. No wonder Dad's so keen on me seeing Elliot. He wants me out of the way so he can enjoy the game in peace. I just have time to help him clear away the plates, when the bell rings downstairs.

"That'll be Elliot – I'll get it."

"Great. See you later, love. Have a nice evening. Would it be okay for you to take Jackson?"

I bound down the stairs to open the door. Elliot smiles at me and I go to give him a hug. But as I get close, he suddenly doubles up in pain, gripping his chest. Jackson runs up to him and tries to lick his face.

"Elliot? What's wrong? Jackson, come here!" I go to help Elliot up. As soon as I touch him, his breath rasps more sharply and he flinches away.

He tries to speak. "Sorry – dunno what's up – fine till I got here—"

I crouch down to see what's wrong, but he immediately raises his arms in front of his face as though he thinks I'm going to hit him. I can't believe this is happening. I let him stand up shakily by himself. He takes several steps back from me. I can see he's still having trouble breathing. I start to panic. What's going on?

"Look, Danni – something's up – can't breathe. Maybe – some fresh air? Let's walk – to – castle."

He tries to smile, but I can see he's in real pain. I'm scared.

"I'll call Dad. You need to see a doctor."

"Nah – I'll be fine. Let's just walk."

"Are you sure?"

He nods and turns back up the path. I follow him, slightly reluctantly. I still think he should see a doctor. When we get to the pavement we walk together, but a few steps apart from each other. Jackson strains ahead of us, pulling on his lead. I'm upset and don't know what to say. Elliot is careful to keep the distance between us. If I get too close, he flinches and quickly moves away. It's horrible. I've no idea what's happening.

"Is it me, Elliot? Is there something you're trying to tell me?" I try my best not to sound as upset as I feel.

His mouth is set in a grim line. "I don't know what's wrong, Danni. I've been looking forward to seeing you all day, but now it's agony even trying to breathe if I go near you."

I hear a sudden scuffling in someone's driveway as we pass, and look to see what it is. Jackson starts whining excitedly and straining towards the place the sound came from.

"What's wrong?"

"Thought I heard something. Looks like Jackson did too."

Someone coughs in the darkness. A shape looms towards us and unthinkingly I clutch Elliot's arm. He yelps and makes a choking sound in his throat. I let go immediately, and turn instead to face whoever is out there.

"Don't worry, girl. It's only me."

It's Robert. He bends down to pet Jackson, who is delighted to see him and jumps up at him excitedly. But I'm furious.

"You nearly frightened the life out of me. Are you following me or something?"

"Sorry, girl." Robert sounds hurt, and I immediately feel guilty, especially when I think about the wind charm he gave me. If it wasn't for that, I don't know what would have happened last night.

"No, it's me who should apologize, Robert. I didn't mean to shout at you. I'm just upset..." I can't think what else to say.

"It's the boy, isn't it? Where's the pain, boy?"

"In my chest. Can't breathe. Thought the fresh air would clear it."

"Hasn't though, has it? I bin watching youse. Never

thought it, even of Beryl. Putting a curse on one of her own."

Elliot glances at me but doesn't say anything.

"Elliot? What does he mean?"

Robert answers for him. "Reckon she doesn't want him seeing you, girl. So she's made a binding curse to put a stop to it."

I stare at Elliot. "Is that true? Is this something your Aunty Bea has done?"

Elliot avoids my gaze.

"I don't know for sure, but she threatened something a few days ago. I ignored it at the time because I didn't think she was serious. I know about my family's reputation, of course, but never realized a curse could affect you like this." His voice trails off and he rubs his ribcage tentatively. "Now I don't know what to think."

I don't say anything. I've already learned how powerful a weather charm can be, so I'm not surprised a curse can be too. But I'm upset his Aunty Bea could do this to him because of me.

"You needs to nail it, son. That'll hold it for a bit."

I look at Robert in surprise. "Nail it? What do you mean?"

"The boy has to do it, cos she's put the curse on him. Get some nails, boy. Three. Got to be iron. Nail them into the ground around her house. Keeps the curse contained.

Front door, back door, garden gate. 'S only a temporary measure, mind. You need to find the poppet."

"Poppet? You mean she's made one of those figures – of Elliot?" I'm horrified. I wonder what she did to the figure to cause him this much pain.

Robert sighs. "Reckon so, don't youse, boy?"

Elliot just nods. He looks really upset and I'm not surprised.

"You'll need to find it, son – and most likely she'll have hidden it well. Could be under a loose floorboard somewhere, or perhaps up a chimney. Check up all the fireplaces."

I can't get the image of some kind of voodoo doll out of my mind. "What kind of person does something like this to someone?"

"His family." Robert points at Elliot, then he seems to think about what he's just said. "If youse don't mind me saying, boy. It's just what I heard, tha's all."

"That's okay. I already told Danni my family legacy." Elliot sounds close to tears. I desperately want to reach out to him, but I can't even get close.

"Don't mean you have to take that path though, does it, boy?" Robert speaks softly. "You can put your skill to good use instead maybes."

"Thanks, Robert, but I don't think I've got those kind of skills, thank goodness."

"Maybe not." Robert's turquoise blue eyes gaze at Elliot thoughtfully. "'S hard to say."

"From what you've told me, it sounds like I need to get into Aunty Bea's house when she's not there. That shouldn't be too difficult. She's always round at our place. You think the poppet might be either under the floorboards or up a chimney?"

"So I bin told. Some place not too obvious, see. Nail it first though. Keeps the curse in her house. Once you've taken it out of the building, you needs to destroy it as soon as you can, cos it won't be contained any more."

"Maybe I can help you?" I offer.

"No!"

"No way!"

Robert and Elliot are in agreement.

"Not you, girl. Maybe some other friend of his, but not youse. Far too dangerous."

"I'll do it myself." Elliot sounds resolute.

"I'd help, boy, but I don't like to spend too much time in Ancrows if I'm honest. I stays on the outskirts, even though I was born there."

"That's nice of you but don't worry – I'll be fine."

I have a sudden idea. "What about Levi? If he's coming this weekend, I'm sure he'd help you if he can."

"Thanks, Danni, but how could I possibly explain this to him? He'll think my family are all plain crazy. I'm beginning to wonder myself." He attempts a smile.

Poor Elliot. I totally understand where he's coming from. If I told anyone even half of what's going on in my life, I'd be dumped in the psychiatric ward alongside Mum.

The distant rumble of an approaching bus cuts into the silence. Robert shuffles his feet.

"Have to be going, that'll be the last bus. When you finds the figure, chuck it into a fire, okay, boy? Soon as you can. The longer you leaves it, the more the curse will fester. Burning's the best thing for it. Let me know how you gets on, won't youse?"

"Thanks, Robert, I will."

"I'll look out for youse if I can."

We watch Robert as he walks off quickly towards the bus stop. A faint smell of earth and leaf mould hangs in the air after he's left us. No sherry though, as far as I can tell. Maybe he ran out of money to buy it.

Neither Elliot nor I say anything. We listen to the bus engine throbbing as it waits at the bus stop in the village, and a few minutes later we hear it grinding into full throttle as it heads off into the night.

"We may as well go back." Elliot sounds subdued.

"Wish I could help you with Aunty Bea."

"Well you can't."

We wander back down the lane. I walk on the pavement and he walks in the middle of the road, to avoid getting the pain back. The atmosphere between us is strained. We reach the main street again without either of us having said a word. Elliot breaks the silence.

"Danni, it's difficult to talk about this now and I don't feel great. Let's just go home. I'll go over to Ancrows as soon as I get the time."

"Are you going to do the iron nails thing?"

"Does it sound crazy?"

"Not to me."

"Look, I'll call you. I hope I can do it tomorrow. I get some free study time at school on Fridays. If not, it's going to be difficult working in the shop on Saturday if you're around." He starts to walk away.

I stand at the crossroads and watch him. He doesn't even turn around again. I don't want to go back in the house so soon. The match won't even have reached half-time. Jackson sits down on the pavement and yawns.

"Sorry, Jackson. Not much of a walk tonight, eh?" I have an urge to turn out of the village and keep on going. I've never felt so isolated in my life. Now Elliot's gone, I can't hold my tears back any longer. I walk slowly back to the shop and go round to the back door, still feeling really upset. Before I let myself in, I find a tissue buried in my pocket and spend a while in the garden, wiping mascara from under my eyes. I don't want Dad to worry about me.

I can't even begin to explain to him what's wrong. I know he sells all kinds of crystals and magic stuff in the shop, but this is different. I don't think he could cope with it. It's all too real.

Fortunately Dad's glued to the TV when I get upstairs to the flat, so he doesn't notice if I still look blotchy from crying. He takes his eyes off the screen for a moment and glances towards me.

"Hi, love. Levi called while you were out."

"Great. I'll call him." I smile. Talking to Levi is the one thing that might lift my spirits. I fumble in my rucksack for my phone.

Dad realizes what I'm doing and obviously doesn't want my chatting to interrupt the match. "Call him back from the shop phone if you like."

"Thanks, Dad."

I run downstairs.

"Levi?"

"Hey, Danni."

"Dad said you called."

"Yeah, listen, do you think your dad would mind if I come down again tomorrow evening?"

"I'm sure he won't."

"Great. Mum says she'll get the train ticket for me in

return for looking after Cheryl and Syrus in the holiday last week. I'll come after school if that's okay."

"Can't wait. There's been so much weird stuff going on here. I need to see you."

"How's your mum?"

"No change. I'm going to see her on Saturday morning, but you don't have to come with me. Maybe you could see Sarah instead?"

"Not sure. I told Sarah I'd message her and maybe we could meet at that Chill Out club on Saturday night. I figured you'd be going – unless you've fallen out with Elliot or anything?"

"Not really. Hopefully it'll be okay by then."

"Uh-oh. That doesn't sound good. What's happened?"

"You wouldn't believe me if I told you."

"Try me."

"You'll think I'm nuts."

"That's okay. I already know you are."

"Thanks."

"So?"

"So his Aunty Bea's put a curse on him and he can't see me without getting crippling chest pain."

I wait a few minutes for Levi to stop laughing.

"Wow, that's the best excuse I've ever heard."

I don't say anything.

"Sorry, Danni, are you upset?"

"No. I just want you to help him. He needs to find the curse in her house, and burn it. He can't even work in the shop right now. Not if I'm here anyway."

"Bloody hell, you're serious. What's up with that place? Are they all inbred or something?"

I find I'm smiling despite myself.

"Hey, I'm from round here too, you know. Are you calling me inbred?"

"Yeah – I always knew there was something weird about you! High six!"

"Oh very funny."

"Seriously though, I can't wait to hear more about this one!"

"I'll come with Dad to pick you up at the station tomorrow. Think Michelle's back this weekend too. Just let us know what time you're arriving."

I'm surprised how much happier I feel as I switch off the shop lights and go back upstairs. I'm so glad Levi is coming. He might even be able to help Elliot.

Upstairs, the match is still on. I feel exhausted and decide I may as well go to bed. Right now there's nothing I can do to help either Mum or Elliot. Maybe I'll be able to think more clearly in the morning.

chapter 29

The school emails first thing. They want me to send my finished homework by the end of the day, and they've attached shedloads more to do. I feel like telling them to stuff it. I've got more than enough problems without worrying about school as well. I stomp out to the kitchen in a really bad mood.

"What's wrong with you?" Dad is just making a pot of tea.

"Too much to do for school."

"But you've been working hard, so it shouldn't be a problem. Anyway it's Friday and Levi's coming later."

I can't tell Dad I've spent most of the time I was

supposed to be doing schoolwork this week either worrying about Mum, thinking how to break into Crawford's house with Mamwyn, or daydreaming about Elliot.

"They want me to send it today and I haven't done enough."

"Never mind. Just send what you've done. Here, have a cup of tea. You'll be fine."

"*No I won't!*"

Dad ruffles my hair. "Go on, take it. It'll make you feel better."

I attempt a smile and take the cup of tea he offers me. I wander back to my room with it and take a look at my assignments to try to figure out how long it'll take me to do them. I really don't want trouble from the school on top of everything else.

As I drink the tea, I make a chart and divide the subjects I have to complete into time slots. Then I colour in the chart in nice colours to make myself feel like I'm doing something, and try not to think about Elliot and what happened last night.

I finally manage to start working. Once I start, it's not so bad, and it gets easier as the day goes by. At one point I find I'm almost interested in what I'm doing. Almost.

It gets to four o'clock and I decide I've done enough. I email the work to my teachers, then go down to talk to Dad in the shop. He gives me some pricing to do, and insists on playing some mind-numbing New Age meditation music while we're working, despite my protests. Dad says the customers love it, but there isn't a customer in sight. Eventually Dad looks at his watch.

"Danni, will you be all right here for a few minutes while I pop up to the corner shop? We need some more milk. Michelle's mum is dropping her off in a minute and we've got Levi coming later too. Do you want to come with me? We can close now if you'd rather not be here on your own."

"I'll be all right here, Dad. We can lock up when you get back."

He takes some money out of the till and goes out. I turn the music off straight away and search behind the counter to find a price list. Dad's left me with a box full of tiny coloured bottles marked *Faerie Dust*. The shop bell rings while I'm looking. I glance up to smile at the customer. Only it's not a customer. It's Elliot. I gaze at him in amazement.

"Elliot! What are you doing here? Are you sure this is a good idea?" My heart flutters with excitement.

"I had to come to see if it worked." He walks up to the counter and reaches over carefully to brush a wisp of my hair out of my eyes. He doesn't flinch at all. He's breathing normally.

"What's happened?" I ask.

"I just came back from Ancrows. Looks like Robert was right."

"You did the iron nail thing?"

"Yes, but it was much more difficult than I thought because I couldn't tell if she was in or not. And I was worried the neighbours would see me sneaking round the house to hammer them in." He leans over the counter and kisses me quickly on the cheek. "I still feel nervous being near you though. You wouldn't believe how painful it was last night. Sorry if I was a bit weird with you."

The shop bell rings again as Dad walks back in with a couple of cartons of milk.

"Hi, Elliot, nice to see you. Are you staying to eat with us? Michelle will be here soon and we're picking up Levi in a bit."

"No, I can't tonight, Nigel, but thanks for asking – I haven't even been home yet. I just came to ask if I could have tomorrow afternoon off. Got something I need to catch up on. I can be in the shop to cover in the morning though."

"No problem. It's gone pretty quiet in here since half-term. I can manage."

"Thanks. I'd better be off, then. Dad will be expecting me." He turns to me. "Maybe I could meet up with you and Levi later on?" Elliot looks at me and I can tell he feels awkward saying any more with Dad here. I seize the opportunity.

"Hey, wait a minute, Elliot – I'll get Jackson and walk that way with you. Then I'll take him up to the castle ruins for a run before we go to the station."

Elliot smiles.

A minute later we set off, Jackson straining ahead of us on his lead. Outside, it's getting colder as the evening draws in, and the air smells of recently lit coal fires.

"Elliot, I spoke to Levi last night. I told him you might need help getting the poppet from your Aunty Bea's place."

Elliot laughs bitterly. "Bet that took some explaining. I imagine he thought you were joking."

"Only at first. In the end I managed to convince him I wasn't making it up. Anyway, I've got to go and see Mum tomorrow morning, so it would be great if Levi could hang out with you instead. I don't want to drag him to the hospital with me."

"Danni, there's a massive difference between hanging out with me and helping me break into someone's house, even if it's the house of someone I know. I don't want him getting into any trouble."

"But it'll be much easier if you take someone with you. Look, let's all meet up tonight and you can talk to him about it. Maybe he can just keep watch for you or something. Or perhaps we could all help you on Sunday – I'm sure your Aunty Bea will go to church and we could find it then."

Elliot looks worried. "Tomorrow would be better if possible."

"You're only saying that because you want to keep me out of it."

He smiles. "That's partly true. But also I want to get it over with as soon as I can." He looks at me. "Danni, with all this going on, you must wonder what you're doing here. Don't you wish you'd stayed in Graymouth?"

I laugh. "I didn't have any choice. I had to come here."

"Yes, but if you'd had a choice, you'd probably have avoided this place like the plague."

He pushes his dark fringe off his forehead, looking anxious. Just watching him gives me butterflies.

"But if I'd stayed in Graymouth, I'd never have met you," I say.

Elliot stops and turns to face me. His expression softens as he reaches out to pull me into his arms. Suddenly I catch something moving from the corner of my eye. A dark shadow darting into a doorway. It's hard to tell in the gathering dusk, but I'm sure there's someone there.

I mutter under my breath. "Elliot, stay where you are. Grab your chest like you're in pain, like before. Quick, do it now."

For a second Elliot looks mystified, then clasps his hands to his chest and starts wheezing like he's about to die. I step back from him and look round as though I'm seeking help. Fortunately there's no one else about.

I move towards Elliot again and whisper just loud enough for him to hear. "Keep it up. I think it might be your Aunty Bea." I don't need to say more. He sinks down to the pavement, gasping and coughing. I move towards him and he twists away from me as if in terrible pain.

"You could get an Oscar for this," I hiss.

He looks up at me and grins.

"Go away – you're stopping me – breathing!" he gasps. Jackson licks his face enthusiastically. Elliot pushes him away and staggers to his feet.

"Have to get some air. Maybe talk later – if I feel better." He winks at me.

"Okay, be like that – see if I care!" I say it loud and clear, hoping she can hear me. I turn round and walk away quickly, acting as angry and upset as I can, yanking Jackson with me. As soon as I get round the corner, I stop and hide in a side alley between the shops. Jackson sits up and looks at me expectantly, as if he's trying to work out what game we're playing. I wait a couple of minutes, then sneak a look out into the street. There's no one around, so I walk back round towards the place where Elliot and I parted. I'm just in time to see Aunty Bea striding towards the car park.

It's almost as if she senses me watching. She turns and stares straight at me. She must be at least fifty metres away, but I can feel the hatred emanating from her even from where I'm standing. I breathe in sharply. My heart is pounding. I don't even have to pretend I'm afraid. I turn and run, with Jackson scampering along beside me.

chapter 30

Soon after Michelle arrives, we all pile into Dad's car to go to the station. Michelle's looking forward to seeing Levi. She really liked him when they met last week.

Dad waits out in the car for us, and Michelle and I walk through to the empty platform. It's dark now. The ticket office is locked up and the staff have gone home. I look up at the LED information board to see when the train's coming.

"Oh look, there it is!" Michelle's staring up the line. I follow her gaze and we watch the train headlights approaching.

Moments later, Levi is standing on the platform. He grins at Michelle.

"Hi, Michelle. Nice to see you again!"

"You too!" Michelle's eyes sparkle with delight. "Do you need help with your bag?" she asks. It's touching how much she wants to impress Levi.

"Thanks, Michelle, but if you carry it, I'll have to carry you, and then it would be extra heavy."

Michelle giggles, and we all troop out of the station to where Dad's waiting in the car.

We chatter and laugh the whole way back to Cararth. It's great to see Levi. I realize I haven't laughed much recently. Not even with Elliot. I guess there hasn't been much to laugh about.

Levi and I take the opportunity to chat alone for a few minutes while Michelle and Dad make tea.

"Were you serious about me helping Elliot tomorrow?" he asks.

"I'm not sure any more, but ask him when we meet up later. He messaged me when we were on our way to collect you – think he's having second thoughts."

"How come?"

"You've met his Aunty Bea. She's bad news. More than you know. And basically he's going to have to break into her house. He doesn't want to get you into any trouble."

Levi pulls a face. "Tell me more about the poppet thing you were on about. Surely it's not for real?"

"It's too weird, Levi. Apparently Elliot's family have always had a reputation for making them."

Levi raises his eyebrows but doesn't interrupt. I carry on.

"People used to pay his family to make curses. It was like their trade." I catch Levi's alarmed look. "Don't worry, Elliot doesn't have anything to do with it. In fact probably no one has now except his Aunty Bea."

"Did you say his Aunty Bea went to school with your mum?"

"That's right."

He shakes his head in disbelief. "No wonder she didn't want to talk about this place. Anyway, how's Elliot going to get this poppet thing out of her house? What exactly does it look like?"

"Apparently they're usually made of clay or wax – but not always. Elliot told me they sometimes use dolls."

"Ew. That's seriously creepy. How big are they?"

"Not sure. Not that big, I guess. They attach stuff to them."

"What like?"

"People's hair or nail clippings."

"Nasty."

"Then they stick pins and knives in the figures, and hide them away."

"Are you having me on?"

"I wish."

Levi looks serious for a moment.

"I should definitely go along and watch out for him."

"I don't want you getting into trouble, Levi."

"They can't arrest me for just standing around."

"Look, talk to Elliot about it, then decide. I've got to go and see Mum in the morning and Michelle's offered to come with me."

"Michelle's great." Levi smiles.

"Yes and she's brilliant with Mum, just talks to her like nothing's wrong."

"You sure you don't want me to come too?" he asks.

"You can if you like."

"Sounds to me like Elliot needs my help more than you do."

I have to agree with him on that one.

When Levi and I set out to meet Elliot after tea, it's gone eight o'clock. We meet him at the crossroads, and head up the lane towards the castle ruins to give Jackson another run.

Elliot is in a sombre mood. "Levi, I already told Danni it's better you just don't get involved. It's my problem."

But Levi's mind is made up. "Danni's going to the hospital with Michelle, and I can't see Sarah until we all go to the Chill Out in the evening, cos she's busy. You can't leave me to hang out with Nigel and his crystal balls all afternoon."

Elliot manages a smile. "Why not? I have to every Saturday."

"I'm allergic to hippies."

Elliot shakes his head. "I don't want you getting into trouble."

"I'm an expert at avoiding trouble. Ask Danni."

I don't say anything. It's not strictly true. In fact Levi is often in trouble.

I just smile.

We stay chatting for a while and then it starts to rain. The smell of damp earth and wet hedgerow fills the night air around us. Elliot looks back down the lane towards the village.

"I'd better be getting back. It's really good of you to help, Levi."

"I haven't done anything yet."

"Well thanks for the offer. You can change your mind anytime. I'm working in the shop for a bit first thing, so I'll see you both then."

The rain starts to come down harder. "See you tomorrow, Elliot." I reach up and kiss him lightly on the cheek. I'm still nervous about getting close to him right now.

Neither of us can relax until this is over.

Levi and I walk quickly through the rain back to Dad's.

Levi looks worried. "I feel sorry for him, don't you?"

"Yeah, I guess."

"It's like the Dark Ages round here. Surely he doesn't believe the stupid curse thing really works?"

"I'm not so sure. You should have seen him, Levi. He was in agony."

"That's just because he thinks it's going to work, so he makes it happen – what do they call it? Autosuggestion."

"Maybe…but I don't think so."

"I'll be glad when your mum's better and you can come back to Graymouth. Too many strange things go on around here."

"If Mum doesn't get better, I might be stuck here for ever."

"Don't be stupid, of course she will. I'm sure of it."

I wish I could share his optimism. I can't tell Levi, but the problem of getting Mum's sealskin back from Crawford is in the back of my mind the whole time. I still haven't come up with a solution. And I have this really bad feeling time may be running out.

chapter 31

The sealskin screams in the fire. Hurry. Jump through the flames. Choking smoke and dust. Can't – breathe—

"Danni?" Michelle is shaking me. "Danni, wake up!"

I open my eyes. Michelle looks scared.

"What's wrong, Shell?"

"You sounded all weird. Are you all right?"

"I was having a nightmare, that's all. Thanks for waking me!"

Her face relaxes and she smiles. "That's okay. Fancy some breakfast? Race you to the kitchen!"

I smile back. "I think I'll let you win."

My throat feels sore. My mouth is as dry as sandpaper. Funny, I thought Mamwyn said the dreams stopped after the first changing. But that felt so real, just like the ones before. Maybe it takes a while. I'd love to talk to Mamwyn about it, but today I have to go and see Mum. If only Mamwyn had a phone.

Levi and I open up the shop because Dad's gone out briefly with Michelle to buy her some new school shoes. Elliot arrives and gives me a hug before he takes over at the counter for the morning. He looks a bit dishevelled. I don't think he slept very well either.

"So what's the plan later, Elliot?" Levi's already sounding excited.

Elliot looks at him. "Are you sure about this? Please don't feel like you have to come."

"'S fine. Don't worry about it."

Elliot nods. "Okay, so most Saturdays Aunty Bea goes shopping in Bodmin and spends the day in town. But before we do anything, when we get to her place I'll knock on the door to double-check she's not in."

"What if she is?" Levi sounds dubious.

"I'll make some excuse about why I'm there. Showing you round Ancrows' historic harbour or something. I'll tell her I couldn't stay at work because I had sudden chest pain and couldn't breathe." He glances at me when he says that.

I grin. "That's brilliant."

"And if she's out?" asks Levi.

"That's when having you with me would be really useful. You can keep a lookout. You don't have to come in the house – in fact it would be better if you stay out in the lane. I know where she keeps the spare key and hopefully it won't take too long. Robert's given me some idea of the kind of places to look."

"She's got a spare key? Fantastic. It'll be a cinch. No worries."

I know Levi is trying to reassure Elliot, but in reality I don't think he's that confident about it. I'm just glad he's agreeing to go, especially as he thinks the problem is all in Elliot's mind.

Elliot senses my tension. "Don't worry, Danni. Whatever happens, I'll take full responsibility. There's no way I'll let Levi take any blame."

I know he means it, but I still feel anxious. Aunty Bea is a dangerous person to cross. And whatever Levi thinks, the curse is all too real.

Dad and Michelle pull up in the car outside the shop. Dad toots the horn to let me know he's waiting. I say goodbye to Elliot and Levi.

"Make sure you both keep safe this afternoon."

Elliot smiles at me. "We'll try our best. See you later,

Danni. I'll get my dad to give us all a lift over to the Chill Out tonight."

"Thanks. I'm looking forward to it." It's true. I can't wait for this afternoon to be over so I can make sure they're both okay.

"Hope your mum's better today," says Elliot.

"Doubt it, but thanks."

Levi sighs. "You're such a pessimist, Danni. Think positive for a change."

"Okay," I say. "I'll work on it."

I head outside and jump in the car.

Dad pulls up outside Bodmin Hospital and Michelle and I scramble out.

"Are you sure you'll be okay catching the bus back?"

"Of course we will, Dad. We want to look round the shops after we've been to the hospital."

"Well here's some money to cover the bus fare, and maybe a drink in a cafe if you want one." Dad hands me a ten-pound note out of the car window. "Call me if there's a problem."

"Thanks, Dad."

We wave at him as he pulls out of the hospital grounds.

"Okay, let's go. Race you to the lift!" Michelle starts running towards the hospital entrance. I laugh and start running too. Visiting Mum almost seems like fun when Michelle's with me. Almost.

The ward smells of cabbage again. Or maybe it's the drains. It doesn't smell good anyway. There isn't anyone on the reception desk. I'm surprised. There seems to be a lot of banging and crashing going on somewhere, so I guess everyone's busy.

"Do you think we should wait?" Michelle looks anxious.

"It should be okay for us to go along to her room. They know who we are. Maybe they're serving up lunch or something."

I start having doubts as we walk down the corridor. We hear shouting before we even get close.

"LET ME GO! I have to get out of here, PLEASE LET ME GO!"

"Hold her down, can you?"

I glance at Michelle and wonder if she realizes who's doing all the shouting.

"Shell, this doesn't sound too good. Go back and wait for me by the desk, and I'll find out what's wrong." I start to run.

"HELP ME, SOMEBODY!"

It's Mum. Why is she shouting? What's happening?

"Calm down, Mrs Lancaster. Please stop struggling!"

I reach the door of her room. It's open. The male nurse

and a doctor I haven't seen before are holding Mum down on the bed. She's kicking and struggling to get free, and the nurse is holding a syringe in the air, obviously trying to get an opportunity to stick it into Mum.

"What are you doing to her? Stop it! LEAVE HER ALONE!"

Mum hears my voice and stops struggling for a second as she looks towards me. The nurse seizes the opportunity and sticks the syringe in her thigh. There's nothing I can do to stop him.

"Danni! Please tell them. I have to get out of here!" Mum's looking at me. She recognizes me. She knows who I am! So why are they holding her down? I'm paralysed with shock and don't know what to do.

The nurse looks up. "Danni, it would be best if you leave the room for a moment. We've just given your mother a sedative and it'll take a little while to work."

"Why did you do that?" The tears spring to my eyes as I look at them. "She recognized me! She wanted to talk to me!"

"This is her daughter?" the doctor asks the nurse. The nurse nods.

The tears run down my face. "Why did you stop her? Let her go! Please let her go."

The nurse loosens his grip on Mum, but it's too late. I know he thinks he's done the right thing, but he's wrong.

"He's going to burn it – I have to get there – stop him." Mum struggles to sit up, but falls back on the pillow. The drugs are taking effect.

"Danni?" Mum turns to look at me.

"Mum? Tell me about it so I can help."

Mum's eyes are starting to close, but she's struggling to stay awake.

"Fire – today – high tide." Her eyes close. The nurse lets go completely.

High tide? Does she mean the fire is on a beach? Maybe Porthenys beach?

"WHERE? Mum, where's the fire? YOU HAVE TO TELL ME!" I shake her to try to keep her awake.

She rolls her eyes and mumbles. "By…gravestones…"

"It's okay, Mum. I'll go, don't worry." The tears are pouring down my face.

"She's been having terrible nightmares." The doctor, a young sandy-haired man with freckles, looks at me, concerned. "I'm so sorry you had to witness this, but your mother was very agitated and we had to give her a sedative to calm her down. She'll be fine."

"No she won't! You don't understand!"

I notice the nurse is looking intently towards the door and I turn to follow his gaze. Through my tears, I see Michelle standing in the doorway.

"Danni? What's wrong? What's happening?" She runs

over and hugs me round the waist.

"It was Mum – she recognized me! But they put her to sleep before I could talk to her."

Michelle squeezes me tightly. "Don't worry. She'll wake up again. We can wait here."

I look at Mum. The nurse has sorted her bedding and tried to help her into a comfortable sleeping position. But Mum's face is still twitching and she looks like she's straining to open her eyes. Every so often they flicker and the whites show for a second and she moans in her drug-induced sleep. The doctor turns to us.

"It would be much better if you could both come back later. The sedative is quite strong and she may be asleep for a while. But please don't worry, it seems as though she's starting to make a recovery." He smiles at me encouragingly.

I nod in acknowledgement, and leave the room quietly, taking Michelle with me. As we walk along the corridor holding hands, my mind is whirring. How come Mum could suddenly talk to me properly and knew my name? Since her sealskin's been locked away, she hasn't even been able to recognize me.

And what did she mean, *gravestones*? Was she thinking of the church outside Ancrows where her father's memorial is?

I remember my dream from this morning. The sealskin

screaming. The fire. Mum's not the only one who has nightmares. Something Mamwyn said comes back to me.

Foretelling is part of the gift.

Suddenly it clicks. I think I can guess what's happened. Crawford must have taken the skin out of the lead-lined chest in his study, which is why Mum came back to her senses – at least, she did until they sedated her.

There's no way Crawford has had a change of heart and decided to give the skin back to her. Piecing together what Mum was trying to tell me, I reckon he's taken it out because he intends to burn it. At high tide. So when's that?

I'm breaking out in a sweat and I feel like I can't breathe.

I have to stop him.

Something tells me he wants to finish his mission back in the village where he started. Even though it's a long shot, I'm going with my hunch that he'll be in the church outside Ancrows. I need to get there straight away to find out if I'm right.

I just hope I'm not already too late.

chapter 32

As we go down in the lift, I let go of Michelle's hand and try to explain a little of what's going on.

"Listen, Shell, Mum needs me to get something for her and I have to leave Bodmin right away and get over to Ancrows. Can we save going shopping for another day?"

"Of course. Come on, let's run to the bus station."

"The trouble is, I need Dad to pick you up." I catch her expression. "Sorry, but I have to do this alone – I'll phone him and see if he can come and collect you."

"Why do you have to be alone? I don't understand."

"It's too dangerous."

"So what about you? If it's dangerous, you need me with you."

"No – I really can't risk it. I'm not being mean, honestly. It's just Dad would never forgive me if anything happened to you."

Michelle is upset. She's practically in tears. "So how come you're going?"

"It's a long story. Let me call Dad a minute. Then I'll try to explain." I feel terrible upsetting her like this. I smile to reassure her, but she looks pale and worried.

I listen to the phone ringing at the other end of the line. It goes on and on for ages. I look at Michelle and raise my eyebrows and roll my eyes. She manages a weak smile. Finally the answerphone cuts in and I have to leave a message.

"Dad? It's Danni. Guess you're busy in the shop. Look, I have to go to Ancrows to get something for Mum. I was wondering if you could pick Michelle up – it's really important or I wouldn't ask. Sorry about this." I try to think what to say so he doesn't get too worried. "Um, Dad, if I don't hear from you, I'll try and get hold of Levi and he can look after her for a bit while I sort it out. Um, bye, Dad. Hope to hear back from you soon."

Damn. I definitely don't want Michelle getting involved in this mess. I call Levi. He and Elliot should already be in Ancrows at Aunty Bea's by now. The call cuts straight to his answerphone so he must have switched his phone off. Of course he has. He's breaking into someone's house. I leave a message.

"Levi? Listen, something important's come up. It's a serious problem to do with Mum. I have to get something of hers back off someone – oh, you met him in fact. Remember the minister on the beach that day? Er, maybe you could look after Michelle for a bit for me?" I'm just hoping Levi can read between the lines and realize why I don't want to take Michelle anywhere near Crawford. "Call me back when you pick this up. We're about to catch the bus to Ancrows, so hope to meet you there in a bit. Bye."

I turn to Michelle. "Do you mind coming to Ancrows with me? With any luck Levi will get that message before we get there. If not, I think we can find him."

"Danni, I told you – I want to come."

"I'm so sorry about the shopping. I was looking forward to it."

"But you weren't expecting that thing that happened with your mum, were you?"

"No, I wasn't."

"What did she mean about him going to burn it? Did she mean the man you're going to see? What's he going to burn?"

Michelle must have heard more than I realized.

"You know Mum used to live in Ancrows but she never told me?"

She nods.

"The reason she left was because she witnessed a horrible crime. She went to court to testify against the criminal. And now this man has come back and taken something of hers that means a lot to her, and she thinks he's going to burn it."

"Why? What is it?"

This is going to be harder to explain.

"Let's find the right bus first."

What am I going to say? I'll have to think of something. But right now my biggest worry is not getting to Ancrows in time to stop Crawford. Again I wish Mamwyn had a phone, so she could help. And what am I going to do about Michelle? I just hope either Dad or Levi call me while we're on the bus.

The bus rumbles out of the bus station. Michelle and I sit at the front together.

"So what did the man take?"

"Look, I made a promise that I'd never talk about this to anyone, Shell. But you're my sister, so I'll try to explain part of it at least. It's something that Mum's had since she was a girl. This man came to Ancrows when she was young. Believe it or not, he was a minister."

"Not the Chosen minister?" Michelle's eyes widen.

"You've heard of him?"

"Of course. Everyone knows. He murdered a boy. My teacher said."

"Really? Your teacher told you about him?"

"We did a school trip to Ancrows. It was silly because some children in my class live there anyway. The teacher told us about Ancrows in the old days and what happened in the chapel."

"Well it wasn't as long ago as you might think. Apparently my mum was there at the time."

Michelle's eyes are like saucers. "No! Really? When the boy was killed?"

I nod. I hope I haven't said too much.

"Your poor mum."

"I know. It must have been terrible for her. That's why she never told me about her past."

"And now that minister has something of your mum's?"

"That's right."

She's quiet for a minute.

"How did he get it?"

"He's moved back to this area. He found Mum on the beach the day she went missing. She'd hit her head so she probably wasn't even awake."

"But you can't tell me what he took?"

"No. Sorry. That's the only bit I can't tell you, but you'd

think it was silly, even if I could. It's just something that means a lot to her, but isn't really valuable or anything." My mind fumbles for an example. "Like if it was us and the man was going to destroy Jackson or something."

Michelle gasps in horror. "Please let me help you, Danni."

"It's too dangerous."

"Well you shouldn't go either then. Why don't you call the police?"

I think about it for a moment.

"Shell, the truth is I don't even know if he's going to be there. Maybe the doctor was right and Mum's just been having nightmares. But I have to go and find out."

"Okay." She seems to accept what I've told her.

"I'll call Levi again."

I get my phone out. Levi doesn't answer.

Hopefully someone will pick up soon. My sense of foreboding is growing stronger by the minute. When the hell is high tide? I try searching my phone to find out, but I can't get enough signal.

The bus pulls up in Ancrows. Michelle and I get off. I haven't heard back from Dad or Levi yet.

"Maybe we should see if my grandmother is in?" I'm not sure how Dad would feel if I left Michelle with someone she doesn't know, but I can't think of an alternative.

"Don't you want to see if you can find that man first?"

Of course I do. I'm desperate to find out if I'm right about the graveyard by the church, but I can't risk taking Michelle. Before I can reply, my phone rings. It's Levi.

"Danni – got your message. Where are you?"

"We've just got off the bus. Where are you?"

"We're getting away from this cottage as fast as we can. Man, this place is weird. We'll head down to the bus stop and meet you there."

"Great."

I breathe a sigh of relief. At least I don't have to involve Michelle, whatever happens.

Michelle spots them first. She waves at Elliot and Levi walking together down the main street. Thank goodness they're okay. As the gap between us narrows, I start running towards them. I'm so pleased to see them both. But as I reach out to give Elliot a hug, he suddenly stops and grabs at his chest. He crouches down on the pavement, gasping with the effort of trying to breathe.

Of course. They've taken the poppet out of the house, but they haven't had a chance to destroy it yet. Elliot's probably got it with him. I was so busy thinking about Mum, I'd almost forgotten about it. I step back quickly.

Levi looks totally bewildered and bends down to ask Elliot what's wrong.

I look round furtively, hoping we're not attracting too

much attention, and my eye is caught by a plume of smoke rising from behind the houses in the main street. It takes a few seconds for the information to sink in. Then I realize. I think it's coming from somewhere by Ancrows chapel. My blood starts racing. Was I wrong about the church? Would Crawford risk going back to the very same chapel where he killed the boy? I turn to the others.

"This might sound like a stupid question, but does anyone know when it's high tide?"

Elliot is still crouching on the pavement, trying to massage his ribs. He looks up at me warily then checks his watch. "Should be getting to high tide about now. Well, within the next hour anyway. Why? Is it important?"

I'm amazed. "How do you know that?"

"Dad's out fishing, and he was talking about it this morning. High tide's a good time to fish. It's the highest spring tide of the year today because of the full moon and the spring equinox."

Immediately I think back to Crawford and Aunty Bea in the cafe together. I'm sure they said something about a spring tide. And consecrated ground. Ancrows chapel is where Crawford used to preach. Aunty Bea used to go there too. That's where he's gone to burn the skin.

I stare at Elliot. I want to ask him loads more questions, but there's no time. I have to move fast.

"Can you two look after Shell for me? I just need to

check something." I attempt to smile reassuringly. "I'll be right back."

But Michelle has noticed the smoke too. She points up the road.

"Oh look, there's a fire!"

"I know. I saw it. Stay here with Levi. I'll be back as soon as I can."

Levi looks completely bewildered. "Danni, what the hell is going on? Where are you going?"

"Don't worry, it's probably nothing. I just need to take a look. If I'm not back in ten minutes, come up and find me – but leave Michelle with Elliot."

Elliot gazes up the road for a moment, then looks at me. "If you're going to the chapel, you definitely can't go on your own."

I choose to ignore him. "Won't be long!" I say, and start to run up the hill.

chapter 33

By the time I reach the chapel car park, the smoke pluming up into the sky is getting thicker. It's clearly coming from somewhere behind the building. My breath catches in a strangled sob at the sight. Now I wish I wasn't alone. Maybe I should have listened to Elliot. My pulse is racing.

I wonder briefly if Mamwyn sensed the danger, the same as Mum and I did. Since she's not here, I guess she can't have done. I'm not sure what to do, and I'm worried that I might be too late already.

I reach into my pocket for a tissue and pull out a strip of blue canvas. The weather charm from Robert. Thank goodness I managed to keep it after that trip to Porthenys.

There's only one knot left. I stuff it back in my pocket, holding it in my fingers to make myself feel better. It's the only help I've got with me.

I stare at the building. The place looks different in the daylight. I need to find a way to get round the back. Then I notice a narrow cobbled passage at the side of the chapel, and run towards it. I'm already panting with exertion from running up the hill and stumble down the passage in such a hurry that I graze my elbow badly on the lichen-covered stone wall. It stings like crazy, but I can't stop to look at it now. The acrid smell of smoke starts to fill my nostrils, making me want to cough.

I race round the corner and suddenly find myself in a graveyard I didn't even know existed. It's about the size of a small schoolyard, and it looks unkempt, with brambles and weeds growing in clumps everywhere. Several of the old gravestones have fallen over. My eye is drawn to a group of people standing round a blazing bonfire. Their heads are bent and they seem to be praying. I spot Crawford. He's got Gabriel with him. My blood freezes. No one has seen me yet. As I watch, Crawford reaches down to a large canvas shopping bag on the ground and pulls something out. It's the sealskin. I almost cry out in dismay.

Elliot's Aunty Bea is standing next to him. She must sense someone is watching because she looks up. She stares straight at me. Even from here I can feel her fear and hatred.

"Look, Cyril! That girl is here."

Crawford looks up. The men with him stare at me too. One of them looks familiar, and I'm not sure why. Then he does the weird hand in front of his face gesture three times and spits, and I remember. He was standing outside Cararth Crystals looking into the shop that day.

For a brief moment, Crawford looks wary. Then he starts shouting at me.

"Stay away! You can't come here! This is a place of God."

"Me stay away? What about you, after what you did?" My voice is shaky, but I'm so angry I want to go over and punch him. I step closer. "Here in this chapel, wasn't it? I bet Mrs Goodwin doesn't know you're here, does she? She's the minister here now, not you. I'm going to call the police." I reach in my pocket. I wish I could stop my hand trembling.

Gabriel snarls a warning.

"Go to hell, you evil witch!" shrieks Aunty Bea. "What we're doing here is none of your business. It's God's work."

That does it. I'm so angry I start walking towards her. "Call *me* evil? What about you? Have you told your friends here about the curses you make?"

Crawford puts his arm out protectively in front of Aunty Bea.

"Beryl is one of God's Chosen. She only uses her skills for the greater good. Unlike you." His voice is full of menace.

I stop where I am. My legs are shaking with fear, but I can't let it go. "You reckon? So cursing her own nephew is for the greater good?"

Aunty Bea and Crawford just glare at me, eyes filled with hatred. Then Gabriel snarls, baring his teeth. He starts walking towards me, ears pinned back, hackles raised. I try not to move, hoping the hateful dog is on a lead.

I'm not in luck.

"Gabriel, get her!" Crawford points at me. The dog needs no further encouragement and runs straight for me, growling.

There's no escape. I don't stand a chance. I have the sickening realization too late – I should have called the police while I still could.

As Gabriel jumps towards my throat, I lose my balance and fall backwards. My head smashes against a gravestone as I fall.

Everything goes dark.

I hear sounds, but they seem far away. It's as if someone's stuck my head down a toilet bowl and is holding me underwater. My mouth is filled with thick, salty liquid. Blood. I'm trying not to swallow, but there's so much blood in my mouth, it's hard to breathe. I've bitten my tongue badly, and it's incredibly painful.

I'm still holding something in my hand. I open my eyes blearily and see the knotted canvas. I picture Robert's turquoise blue eyes gazing at me by my grandfather's memorial in the cemetery that day. *The last knot, he's for when youse in real trouble.*

From the corner of my eye I can see Crawford, holding up the sealskin. He's chanting some prayer in Latin. What's he waiting for? The others have their heads bent in prayer. I must have been out for a while as they seem to have forgotten about me.

There are four of them altogether. Against one of me. That's not good odds. Worse, there's Gabriel, now curled up at Crawford's feet. Luckily for me, he must have been satisfied with knocking me out. When he leaped at me, I honestly thought he was going to rip my throat open. Amazingly, I don't think I've been bitten anywhere.

I wonder why no one is looking at me. The pain in my head is terrible and I'm finding it hard to think straight. Maybe they think I'm dead or something?

I spit out the blood as quietly as I can, and start working at the knot with my fingers. I try my hardest not to attract attention. The prayer drones on. I glance up. The sealskin swirls and vibrates in Crawford's hands. There's a ringing sound in my ears. I'm not sure if it's because my head's throbbing from the fall, or if the skin is calling to me. I think it's the skin. My heart lurches in despair. He's going to drop it into the fire soon. I know it.

Crawford holds the sealskin up higher. He's almost shouting now, and it sounds like he's getting near the end of his prayer. My fingers work frantically at the knot, and finally it comes free.

Nothing happens. Nothing at all. I don't know what I expected, but the disappointment I feel is intense. I really thought it would work, the same as when I undid the first two. The air is ominously still and silent.

I ache all over. I strain every muscle in my body in a feeble attempt to get up off the ground to try to stop Crawford. I feel a breeze picking up and look hopefully at the sky.

The dog must have seen me moving. He stands up and growls deep in his throat. I hardly dare breathe as he paces towards me again. Within seconds he's so close, I can see cords of drool hanging from his jaws. I curl into a fetal position by the gravestone and scrunch my eyes shut in terror.

"What have you done to her? Touch her again and I'll throw you in the fire, you mad bastard!"

I recognize the voice instantly. Levi. I half open one eye and squint up at him. I close it again quickly to try to stop the sensation that the whole graveyard is spinning. I feel really dizzy.

I hear a blood-curdling snarl from Gabriel right by my ear, followed by a yell from Levi and then a sickening thump. Gabriel yelps and whines. I snap my eyes open and see drops of blood splattering onto my arm.

I look up to see where it's coming from. Levi is clutching his hand, the blood dripping down from between his fingers. No wonder he kicked the dog. The bite wound must be deep. I glance round cautiously, but can't see Gabriel anywhere.

"You're bleeding!"

"You don't look so good yourself." He smiles at me, then winces as he tries to move his fingers.

I wipe my hand over my face. It comes away covered in blood. My mouth is still full of the metallic, salty taste. I try to spit, but my tongue is so swollen, the blood just dribbles down my chin. I'm still really groggy and it takes a minute to remember. Crawford! I have to stop him. As I struggle up off the ground with Levi's help, I sense the wind is picking up.

I look over to see if Crawford's still on the other side of the fire, and immediately spot Aunty Bea, pointing at us and shouting. There's an eerie whistling noise coming from somewhere. It takes a moment to realize it's the sound of the wind blowing down the side of the chapel. The smoke billows round us, making my eyes sting. Levi and I both start to cough, and my tongue throbs painfully with the effort. I look for Crawford again through the stinging smoke, desperate to see if he's still holding the sealskin.

The fire flares suddenly, as though someone just poured petrol on it, and I can't make out anything beyond it. I have to grab the skin before Crawford throws it in the fire. Or has he done it already?

"What the hell's going on?" Levi shouts above the gale. I shake my head. I've no idea what's happening. The choking smoke funnels upwards and swirls round, high above the chapel, and the force of the wind makes it practically impossible to move. It screeches around us with hurricane strength, filling the air with rubbish and debris.

I can hardly stand up in this. The fire roars. Sparks rise like orange stars into the air, swirling higher and higher, catching in the trees and the tiles on the chapel roof.

We're trapped in a whirlwind. Loose tiles are lifted and swept up into the vortex. I watch in disbelief as they spiral above the churchyard, then plummet back down to the ground. Within seconds, sparks catch hold in the exposed rafters and the chapel roof bursts into flame. Someone is shouting.

"It's the girl's devilry. Stand your ground. It's nearly time. The tide is about to turn!"

Crawford is bellowing to make himself heard above the howling wind and crashing tiles but I can only just make out the words. I still can't see him through the smoke, but

I'm desperately hoping *nearly time* means he's still holding the sealskin.

"Danni, we have to get out of here."

I can't leave. If I can make myself move at all, I need my strength to try to stop Crawford.

"You run for it, Levi. I can't go anywhere. I feel too sick."

"I'm not going without you. Come on!" Levi grabs my arm and tries to pull me with him, struggling against the wind.

"Wait a minute!" I shout, shaking him off and looking back at the fire.

The smoke thins for a second and I suddenly spot Crawford. He's still standing on the other side of the flames, his coat pulled over his head to protect himself from the falling debris, clutching the sealskin in his hands. Gabriel is running round at his feet, barking in the chaos. I feel a glimmer of hope. I was right. Whatever they're waiting for, he hasn't thrown it in the fire yet. Aunty Bea ducks and weaves around him, shrieking like a hyena as she tries to avoid the tiles falling like missiles from the sky.

All at once Crawford catches sight of me. He crosses himself quickly, and lifts the skin higher.

"Is it time?" he shouts at Aunty Bea.

"Yes, the tide is turning!" I've no idea how she knows, but I know what's coming.

"Do it now!" she shouts, ducking to avoid another falling tile.

Crawford glares at me in triumph, and thrusts the skin into the raging fire.

I hear a desperate wailing sound and realize it's coming from me. Somehow I'm managing to run. Then without a second thought, I jump into the flames.

The world goes silent. I'm surrounded by dancing flames but hear nothing, feel nothing. In front of me the sealskin rests on the embers, the patterned fur swirling, alive. I have to save it. I reach out, and for a minute everything goes into slow motion. I don't know why I can't feel the heat. From the outside, the fire felt like a furnace. Strangely, I catch a faint scent of brine and seaweed. It's as if I'm somehow in the eye of the storm, protected from the searing flame and smoke.

"Are you crazy? Get out of the bloody fire!" Levi grabs my arm and pulls so hard it nearly comes out of its socket. The shouting and the heat and roar and stink of the furnace comes back. He's pulled me clear.

I'm holding the sealskin.

"You're lucky you weren't burned to a crisp, you moron! Come on. We've got to run for it." Levi grips my arm like a vice as he tries to pull me away. I turn and see Crawford and his cronies coming round the fire and heading towards us. Even as I start to run, I wonder what's happened to the dog. My heart's pounding and my tongue is so swollen, it feels like it's choking me. We have to get out of here.

"Don't turn round, just RUN!" Levi shouts at me.

We stumble across the churchyard as fast as we can. Levi doesn't let go of my wrist and yanks me down the alley towards the car park. Behind us I can hear people shouting above the roar of the wind. I hear something else. A low, menacing growl. A tile shifts and falls from the burning roof and I duck. Behind me, a sudden yelp of pain. Got to keep running.

Levi pulls me round the corner and lets go of my wrist. We're in the car park in front of the chapel. A few metres across the tarmac, I can see Elliot trying to hold back a struggling Michelle, and behind them lots of other people who must have been drawn here by the smoke and noise. I hear sirens approaching. I look round frantically. There's nowhere to hide the skin. Crawford will seize it back again. All the pain and effort will be for nothing.

A figure darts towards me from the shadows of the chapel porch and grabs my sleeve.

"Wha's going on, girl? You called in the weather. Are you all right?" Robert's turquoise eyes gaze at me in concern as the wind swirls plastic bags and sheets of newspaper around our heads.

I could cry with relief. I thrust the sealskin into his hands. "Take this, could you? Hide it for me."

"I will, girl, don't youse worry." He stuffs it down the front of his jacket.

A dog barks and I twist round to see Gabriel racing across the tarmac towards us. He's limping slightly, but that's hardly slowing him down at all. I turn back to Robert in panic. But no one's there. He's gone.

"Danni, look out!" Michelle runs towards me, her arms reaching out to try to stop Gabriel. She's broken free of Elliot, and I see him sink down on the tarmac behind her. Of course. I'm here. He can't breathe. He's still got the poppet and the curse is unbroken. Sirens shriek louder and car tyres squeal.

For a second, Michelle is between me and the dog. Gabriel leaps through the air, and his jaws clamp over her outstretched arm.

"No, Gabriel, stop!"

Crawford calls his dog too late. Gabriel has bitten deep and Michelle screams in shock and pain.

"Shell! Noooo!" I wrap my arms around her. "Duck down!" We crouch on the tarmac as Gabriel leaps and snaps at my back and neck. I frantically try to shelter Michelle.

"Gabriel! Here, boy! Come here, NOW!" Finally the dog obeys his master and the frenzied snarling stops.

A terrified Michelle looks up at me, eyes filled with tears. "I'm sorry, Danni. You told me to stay away."

"No, I'm sorry. I shouldn't have brought you to Ancrows with me. It's all my fault."

"I wanted to come." She's trying to be brave but the tears spill down her cheeks and she's as white as a sheet. It wrenches my heart to see her like this.

"Don't worry, we'll get you to a doctor straight away." I look at her arm. Blood has filled the bite marks where Gabriel's teeth locked on. Poor, sweet Michelle. I have to get her out of here.

I look up. People in the crowd are already running forward to help us. A police car swerves round the corner into the car park, sirens wailing and lights flashing. It pulls up right in front of the chapel and two policemen jump out of the car. They look up at the burning building and move quickly. One of them grabs a megaphone from the back seat and shouts into it.

"Could everyone move back, please? This building is unsafe." He holds his arms out like a barrier to stop the crowd advancing any closer.

"What's happened here?" the other policeman asks Crawford.

"He didn't mean to bite her, officer. He was upset by the fire!" Crawford looks panicked by the appearance of the policeman. He's desperately holding a snarling Gabriel back by the collar. Aunty Bea stands beside him, glaring at us.

"Oh? And he didn't mean to bite me either, I suppose?"

I didn't realize Levi was standing right next to us. When I look up at him, I can clearly see the flesh on his hand is torn and bleeding. It must be agony.

The policeman talks into his radio. "Can we have ambulance backup straight away? Ancrows Chapel. Send a dog handler too, if you can find one." As he speaks, the distinctive clanging of approaching fire engines rises above the hubbub, growing louder and louder. The crowd moves further back as two fire engines pull into the car park, blue lights flashing. Firemen jump out and set to work immediately, unreeling the long fire hoses coiled inside the trucks.

The policeman turns back to Crawford. "I'm sorry, sir, but we'll have to take your dog to the police pound. It's against the law to keep an animal that endangers or harms the public. If anyone presses charges, he may have to be destroyed."

"No! Not Gabriel, he's a good boy!" Crawford is so distraught, I can see tears in his eyes. "Please don't take him away from me."

Just for one, tiny split second, I almost feel sorry for him. It doesn't last.

"It's all that evil girl's fault. She set fire to the chapel." Crawford points at me.

The policeman looks at me with increased interest. "Is this true?"

"Of course it's not. He started the fire. I only went round to see where the smoke was coming from."

"And she stole something valuable from me, officer."

The policeman scrutinizes me for a moment. After what we've just been through, I guess I don't look too good right now. The parts of me I can see are filthy with soot from the smoke and smeared with blood. My clothes are all singed, and my knee's sticking out of a big hole burned in the front of my jeans. Worse, Crawford looks unscathed, the picture of a normal, respectable minister of the church.

"He's a liar. And a killer. Do you know who he is?" Even as I'm saying it, I know the policeman thinks I'm the liar, not Crawford.

"I think we've heard quite enough from you, young lady. Let's move away from the chapel building now. When you've seen the paramedics, we'd like to ask you a few questions."

"That's so unfair!" Levi is furious. I glare at him to stop him saying any more, but he doesn't notice. "That so-called minister started all this. He's totally insane. Danni had nothing to do with it. I can testify for her."

The policeman looks at Levi carefully. I have to admit, I've seen Levi looking better. Wild eyed, bleeding, and dirty from the fire, he looks far more suspect than Crawford.

"I think you'd better come in for questioning too, sir."

The policeman gets out his notebook. "Now before the ambulance comes, I'd like you to tell me your names and where you both live."

The wind has finally died down, and I feel exhausted. The paramedics have been amazing. They managed to get Michelle, Levi and me away from the police and into an ambulance.

"You look like casualties from a war zone." The female paramedic smiles at us. "We must get you to the hospital so we can patch you up."

At that moment, I hear shouting outside.

"You have to let me see them! They're my friends. Please let me past."

"I'm sorry, sir, I can't let you through right now."

I jump out of the ambulance, then wince with pain. I must have twisted my ankle at some point.

"Elliot? Where did you get to?"

"Danni! You look terrible! Are you okay?"

The policeman realizes we know each other and lets Elliot through. He runs straight up to me and gives me a massive hug.

"Ouch!"

"God, I'm sorry – have I hurt you?"

"No, I just seem to hurt everywhere." I smile. He looks so worried, I want to reassure him I'm all right.

Suddenly I realize. He's right next to me and he's okay. He can breathe.

"Hey, how come you can get this close?"

"That's why I only just found you. I had to throw that thing into the fire to destroy it. It was horrible, Danni. She'd made it with wax, and stuck a couple of big spikes through the head and heart. You could tell she'd been working it, pushing the spikes in different places. Ask Levi. Anyway, I just saw Aunty Bea and told her not to come round to the house again. Ever. Not that she'll take any notice of course."

Across the car park, tiles clatter down from the chapel roof. The air is filled with smoke and dust and the stench of burning. A policeman comes over to us.

"Could you all leave now, please. The building is becoming unstable and we want everyone out of here." He walks off to try to disperse the crowd. I grab Elliot's hand and take him to the ambulance.

"Can he come with us, please?"

The paramedic looks at us for a moment. "He doesn't look very injured."

"No, he's not. But he's had problems breathing."

She nods. "Okay, I guess so. Come on then, jump in. Time we got you all to the hospital."

I look at Elliot. "Have you got your phone? Would you mind calling Dad? I really can't face explaining anything just yet."

chapter 34

"Why didn't you just stay in Bodmin?"

Dad's trying not to shout at me because the nurse has told him I have concussion. But I can tell he's angry. I'm not surprised. Michelle is having twelve stitches. She's trying to be brave about it but her lower lip trembles.

"It wasn't Danni's fault. Her mum wanted her to go to Ancrows."

For a moment Dad looks confused. He looks at me. "Did she? I thought she was still in a stupor, or whatever the doctors call it. How do you know?"

"It's a long story, Dad. Wait until we get home and I'll

start at the beginning. I'm just really sorry Michelle got dragged into it."

Dad looks slightly appeased. "And what about the police? When I arrived, they told me they want you and Levi in for questioning."

"Can they wait until tomorrow?" I'm so tired, and my head is throbbing.

The nurse who's patiently stitching Michelle's arm decides for us.

"I don't think you should have to see anyone until you've had a good night's rest. The police can wait. I've told them you've got a minor concussion and you need to stay calm."

I smile at her. "Thanks."

"Anyway, look at your brave little sister here. She certainly needs to get home. She's had a nasty shock, haven't you, darling?"

Michelle nods. "Have we got any ice cream in the freezer?" she asks hopefully.

Dad shakes his head.

I look at them both and make a snap decision. "I'll go and ask Elliot to get some for us. I think we need it. Is that okay, Dad?"

"Yes, good idea. Here's some money. Don't be long, will you?"

"I won't." I grin at Michelle. "I'm guessing chocolate ice cream?"

Her face lights up. "Yes, please."

"There, that's the last one!" says the nurse. "No more stitches. We just need to talk to Dad so he knows how to change the dressing."

I take the opportunity to slip out to the waiting room to find Elliot. I also want to find out if Levi's been treated yet. I hope his hand isn't as bad as it looked.

The waiting room is surprisingly empty. The couple of times I've been to A&E in Graymouth, it was far busier than this.

Elliot and Levi are sitting next to each other. Levi waves a heavily bandaged hand at me. He's grinning all over his face. I can't believe he's so cheerful.

"What are you so pleased about? That looks terrible!"

"It may have escaped your attention, Danni, but this is my right hand. I need it to write. Without it, I can't possibly do a chemistry test on Monday. Or maths homework. I'm very upset."

I laugh. "Yeah, looks like it. Hey, can one of you manage to pop round to the supermarket? Michelle's been amazing and she's asking for ice cream for tonight."

"I'll go! I'm the only one round here who's still in one piece." Elliot jumps to his feet. "What sort does she like?"

"Chocolate. Here, take this." I hand him the money Dad

just gave me. "Do you think it'll be enough to get two large tubs?"

"I've got some money too, don't worry." He smiles and leans towards me so he can plant a careful kiss on my sore mouth. It tingles, but in a good way.

"Is your tongue still hurting?"

"I'll live."

He smiles. "You'd better! I won't be long."

I watch him as he hurries out through the exit. I can't help noticing how good he looks in those jeans.

"Hope he gets the expensive sort with chunks of chocolate in it. Reckon we'll be staying in Cararth tonight. We won't be going back to Ancrows to the Chill Out later, that's for sure – so we may as well eat some quality ice cream."

I'd completely forgotten we were supposed to be going out tonight. Even if any of us were in a fit state to go, it's obviously not going to happen in the burned-out chapel building.

"Have you called Sarah?"

"Yeah. She'd already heard about the chapel burning on the local news."

"The news?" I gasp. It hadn't crossed my mind that the fire would make the news.

"Yeah, on the radio. We could even be on TV tonight!"

My heart sinks. "Were there TV cameras at the chapel?"

"Not when we were there. Not that I noticed anyway." Levi looks disappointed.

"Thank goodness for that." I sigh with relief.

"I suppose we weren't exactly looking our best, now you mention it. Oh, Sarah knew that the crazy minister was involved too."

"Crawford? Seriously? How come?"

"Seems like someone recognized him and told the reporters. It gave them a chance to bring up all the back story about the exorcism and him killing the boy on the news."

"Wow. I hope the police will leave us alone now they know who he is."

"So do I. My mum's not going to be too happy if I'm in trouble again."

"You won't be. I'll tell her what happened myself. You were a real star, Levi. Thanks."

Levi grins. "I was, wasn't I? But you gotta tell me why you jumped in the fire like that to save some old rug. You're bloody lucky to be alive!"

I shrug. "It was Mum's. It meant a lot to her. That reminds me. While I'm here, maybe I should just pop round to check on her?"

Levi looks at me steadily. "Okay, but we still have to talk about what happened. If it was your mum's, how come you gave it to the homeless guy?"

"I didn't want Crawford to take it back." I sigh. "Look, I won't be long. We'll talk about it later."

I know Levi wants to ask me loads more questions, and I don't blame him. I've just no idea how to answer them right now.

I hurry out of A&E and round the outside of the building. It's already getting on for six and the light is fading. I reach the main entrance and head straight for the lift. I hope Mum's okay. It was horrible seeing her like that this morning. Seems like years ago now.

There's a nurse I don't recognize on the ward. I tell her I've come to see Mum. She stares dubiously at my burned jeans for a minute.

"Okay, since you're family. But I think the doctor might be in there with her."

"Thanks!" I practically run down the corridor. I have to catch Mum before anyone sticks any more needles in her. I need to know she's safe. The corridor smells of something sickly sweet like strawberry jelly. I suppose it's better than this morning.

Mum's door is slightly ajar. I push it open. Dr Murphy is standing by Mum's bed, writing something on her clipboard. Mum's fast asleep, but looks far more peaceful than when I last saw her.

"Oh, Danni! Good to see you!" Dr Murphy smiles, then stares at me in amazement. "Whatever have you been doing? You look like you've been beaten up and rolled in a bonfire! And you stink of smoke…"

I shudder inwardly at the mention of fire, but just smile at her. "I'm fine, honestly. How's Mum?"

"Remarkable recovery. Just in time too – I was having problems stopping Mr Albright going ahead with the electroconvulsive therapy treatment. That would be far too dangerous for people like you."

"What do you mean?"

She looks at me for a moment before she answers.

"I've come across a few others like you before, you know. Back home in Ireland. You have exactly the same look. I think you may be different in a way Mr Albright would never understand."

I stare at her in amazement. "So you know about – er, Mum…" I don't know what to say. My mouth opens and shuts like a cod.

"Truth is, Danni, sometimes I see people come into the psychiatric ward that don't really belong here. I couldn't say that to Mr Albright or any of the other medical staff of course." She smiles. "I thought it would probably be up to you to find a way to help her. By the look of you, it was quite a journey."

"You could say that. Thanks for…understanding." I'm so stunned, I can't think of a better way to say it.

"Whatever you've been up to, you look exhausted,

young lady. You should go home and get some rest…"

"Yes, Dad'll be waiting for me – I'd better run. I just wanted to check Mum was okay."

"Come back tomorrow. She'll be fine then, don't worry." She winks at me, and I smile with relief.

I'm still going over my brief conversation with Dr Murphy as Dad drives us all home. What did she say? *I've come across a few others like you before.* I hope I get a chance to talk to Mum about that soon. It might make her feel better about us being sea people, knowing there could be others like us.

"So how was your mum?" Levi interrupts my thoughts.

"She was asleep, but she looked better than she did this morning."

"So what exactly happened earlier?" Dad has calmed down a lot, but he really wants an explanation. "I don't understand."

"I'm not surprised. It's so complicated, Dad. Let's get back and watch the news and I'll tell you all I know about Mum and Crawford."

"Who's Crawford?"

"He was the minister with the Rottweiler that day – do you remember?"

"Oh yes, him. I thought he looked a bit dodgy."

Elliot can't resist butting in. "A bit dodgy? He's the

minister responsible for killing the boy in Ancrows years ago! You must have heard of him."

Now Dad looks totally confused. "Is he? So what's he got to do with Erin?"

I'm beginning to wish I'd talked to Dad a lot more as this whole thing unravelled. It's going to take a while for him to catch up. Suddenly I feel so tired, all I want to do is sleep.

Michelle pokes me. "Don't close your eyes, Danni. They said with a minor concussion you should stay awake for a few hours, remember? Otherwise they were going to keep you in hospital."

"Good thing you're on the case, Shell!" I don't let on how tired I feel. I couldn't bear to go back to A&E.

"It's okay. I'll nudge you every time you close your eyes." Michelle is sitting between Levi and me in the back seat.

"Thanks. I'll try not to blink." I grin at her. Actually I'm touched by her concern. She seems to have managed to shut Dad up as well. He stops asking difficult questions and tells Levi and Elliot they should help Michelle keep an eye on me while he's driving. It's a supreme effort for me not to go to sleep, but it's going to be worth it. I want to spend the evening with my favourite friends and family.

chapter 35

Elliot has his arm round me. It feels warm and comforting. We're sitting on Dad's massive sofa, squashed between Levi and Michelle. Dad's in the armchair. We're all gazing at the TV screen in amazement. The local news is on and the reporter is standing in front of a burned-out doorway. Behind him, Ancrows chapel is a charred and blackened shell. He's interviewing Mrs Goodwin.

"As the minister, Mrs Goodwin, you must be shocked about what's happened here today at your chapel?"

"Of course I'm upset that worshippers won't be able to come for services here for a while – especially since we'd so recently reopened after the twenty-year closure.

But sometimes God works in mysterious ways."

"What do you mean?"

"Well, I always felt the chapel held too many shadows of its terrible past. Now that is gone for ever. The fire has given us the opportunity to create a brand-new building, and have a totally fresh start."

"You're referring, of course, to the notorious child killing that happened in this chapel all those years ago. The reason it was closed for so long in fact."

Mrs Goodwin nods. "Mmm."

"Are you aware that the minister here at that time, indeed the man held responsible for that killing, is currently being questioned by the police? I expect they want to know what he was doing here and why he started this fire!"

"I had heard, of course. But we shouldn't judge Mr Crawford until we know all the facts. The freak storm that blew up may have been partly to blame."

The reporter is quick to agree. "No, you're absolutely right. The weather may have contributed. Thank you for talking to us, Mrs Goodwin."

"No problem." She smiles.

The reporter turns to the camera. "And on that note, let's go back to the studio for the latest updates."

But when it changes back to the studio, the programme moves on to the next news item about a quilt-making contest at the Women's Institute.

Dad turns down the volume and looks at me. "I wish Mum had told me all this stuff about what happened in Ancrows when we were married. It might have explained a lot."

"Dad, she witnessed the exorcism and the killing. She knew the victim. She must have been traumatized by what happened."

"Yes, so you said. I had no idea. I'm still finding it all hard to take on board. I wonder why on earth Crawford came back to this area. And why would he set fire to the church?"

"Dunno. Maybe he didn't mean to. Maybe it was the storm, like they said on TV."

"And what I really don't understand is what you were doing there, Danni. What was that garbled message you left about Mum?"

"I'm sorry, Dad, it must have sounded totally crazy. I was trying to avoid worrying you. But Mum was very upset when Michelle and I visited. She was raving about how Crawford was going to burn something of hers and she wanted me to stop him. I've no idea how she knew, but I had to go and find out if it was true."

Michelle wriggles next to me on the sofa. "Yes, Danni's mum wanted to say more but the nurse stuck a needle in her and she went to sleep."

I'm more than grateful for Michelle's input. When

you're trying to avoid telling the whole truth, it's great when someone backs you up on the detail.

Dad's still trying to catch up. "So when you got to the chapel, Crawford set his dog on you? We should press charges. When I take you to the police station tomorrow, I'm going to ask them about it."

"But then they'll put his dog down. They said so." Michelle looks upset. "And that man will cry. He cried when they said that might happen."

"Darling, the dog bit you, really badly. He attacked Danni, and then bit Levi when he went to help. He's a very dangerous dog."

I think back to the night Mamwyn and I went to Crawford's house. The way Gabriel calmed down after she sang the song to the sealskin.

"It might not be entirely the dog's fault. Really it's down to Crawford," I say.

"Well I'm going to talk to the police about it anyway."

I'm not sure what the police can do about Gabriel, but I'm secretly pleased Dad cares enough to want to stick his oar in. I only hope he wears a better T-shirt.

Despite having a sore tongue and a dull, throbbing headache, it's one of the best evenings I've had in ages. Elliot gets on so well with Dad and Michelle. Levi is on sparkling form too. Maybe it's the ice cream.

My only worry is that we have to go to the police station in the morning to make our statements. Later, when Elliot's gone home and Dad's saying goodnight to Michelle, I grab the chance to talk to Levi.

"Can I ask you a favour?"

"Try me."

"Tell the truth at the police station tomorrow – then our stories will be the same. Except one thing."

"And that is?"

"The rug I got out of the fire. If they ask, I tried to get it out but you dragged me away."

"I was going to ask you more about that rug. What exactly was it? Why did you think it mattered so much to your mum?"

"She'd had it since she was young. She was worrying about it the moment she came round in the hospital earlier today. I know it didn't look like much, but it means a lot to her. Crawford took it off her when she was on the beach that day – he knew how much she treasured it."

Levi looks at me expectantly. "Is that it?"

"Yes, why?"

"It doesn't add up."

"What?"

"I think you're hiding something. You have been for a while, before all this happened today."

"Nothing important, Levi. I can't really talk about it in

detail because it's Mum's family stuff, but trust me, it's nothing bad or criminal."

"That's a shame. It would be so much more interesting if it was. Anyway, I get it – the rug thing must have burned in the fire. You didn't have it in the ambulance anyway…"

I smile at him. "Thanks."

If I'm lucky, the police won't even ask about it.

chapter 36

"I'm afraid Mr Crawford wants to press charges against you." The policeman looks almost apologetic.

"*What?* His dog practically kills me, bites my friend and my sister – and *he* wants to press charges?"

"Don't worry, we know the dog is dangerous. Your father has already expressed his concern about future public safety if the animal isn't kept under control. That's not what this is about."

"So what is it about?"

"Mr Crawford says you stole something from him."

"Rubbish."

"He said it was a valuable sealskin that he had for his

taxidermy hobby. Do you know anything about this?"

I feel a flash of anger. How dare Crawford say it was his?

"He stole it off my mother in the first place. You know she was a witness at his trial years ago? He probably wanted revenge."

"A sealskin? Why would your mother have a sealskin?"

"Her father was a fisherman. He drowned. She doesn't have very much that he left her. So she took it to the beach closest to where his boat sank on the anniversary of his death." So far I haven't told a lie, but I'm having to think on my feet. It's difficult when you've got a head as fuzzy as mine is this morning.

"Are you saying Mr Crawford took it from your mother?"

For some reason, tears start welling up in my eyes. "I think so. I don't know for sure because Mum's been in hospital since that day."

"So where is this sealskin now?"

"Crawford threw it in the fire." The tears spill down my face. I can't help it. For some reason thinking about all this is bringing back the whole horrific episode. The more I think about that fire, the more I can't believe I survived it without burning myself alive.

The policeman speaks gently. "He says you ran off with it."

"That's ridiculous. He's barking mad. He even accused me of causing the fire."

The policeman says nothing. I take that as a good sign. It's true Crawford accused me of starting the fire and they now know he lit the bonfire himself.

"Is that all? Do you think I could go soon? I have to visit Mum in hospital."

The policeman smiles. "You're free to go now, Miss Lancaster. We just needed to clear that up before we proceed with our investigations. Thank you for your cooperation."

I smile at him gratefully. "That's okay."

"And I hope your mother gets better soon," he says kindly, as he switches off the voice recorder.

When we finally get out of Bodmin police station, it's nearly lunchtime and Dad has to take Michelle to her mum's. I'm catching a bus back to his place later when I've visited Mum in hospital.

I give Michelle a big hug. "Hope your arm is better soon, Shell."

"I'm okay, Danni. Will I see you next weekend?"

"Definitely. Even if Mum's better and we go home, I'll be coming back to Cararth to see you and Dad at the weekend."

"Good. I'll look forward to it." She grins at me.

"Me too." I ruffle her hair and give her another squeeze before she gets in the car.

As soon as they drive off, Levi and I start walking down towards the market place. He's arranged to meet Sarah there before he goes back to Graymouth. Now Dad's out the way, I'm anxious to know how he got on at the police station.

"So how did your interview go?"

"It was fine. They were really nice to me. I told them you nearly killed yourself trying to get something out of the fire when Crawford threw it in, and I managed to drag you out and save your life. I'm hoping they're going to give me a medal."

When I look at him, he's grinning from ear to ear.

"In your dreams." I smile. "So when's your train?"

"Four."

"I'll come to the station to see you off. What time are you meeting Sarah?"

He looks at his watch. "Five minutes."

"Okay then – have a good time. And thanks, by the way. See you later."

Levi starts to run, and I turn off towards the hospital.

The ward smells of flowers. That's a first. As I approach Mum's room, I hear voices. One of them is Mum's.

I put my head round the door. Mum is dressed and sitting on the bed. Robert is sitting next to her. They're deep in conversation. They both look up as I open the door wider. Mum gasps in delight when she sees me, and jumps up to give me a massive hug.

"Danni, I'm so, so sorry."

I don't ask why. I just hug her back, for a very long time. "That's okay, Mum. Just try not to do it again, all right?"

She laughs. It's the best sound in the world right now.

"I'd best leave you two to talk. Be seeing you soon, Mary." The way Robert looks at Mum, it's obvious how much he cares about her.

"I'll get in touch as soon as they let me out of here." Mum blushes. I've never seen her like this before.

"And thanks for this." She picks something up from her beside table and holds it out for Robert to see. The heart-shaped stone. So it wasn't Mamwyn who left it. Robert and Mum gaze at each other in a way that makes me feel almost uncomfortable, but I manage to smile at Robert.

"See you, Robert. And thanks for all your help, especially yesterday. You've been amazing."

"Tha's all right, girl." Robert looks at me shyly. "I took that thing you gave me to your grandmother, just so you knows. You take care of your mother now, won't youse?"

"I will."

Robert's already told Mum a lot, but we've still got so much to talk about, I don't know where to start. So I ask about the one thing that's really bothering me.

"Mum, you must have known what was going to happen to me. Why didn't you ever say anything?"

She buries her face in her hands for a moment. "I kept putting it off, Danni. At first it was because I'd never told your dad anything about my past and I wanted to keep you away from Ancrows because of what happened to me. Then as you got older it got more and more difficult to go back on it. To suddenly tell you about your grandmother and everything."

"But what about the changing? When were you thinking of telling me about that?"

She takes her hands away from her face and sighs deeply. "I know it was wrong not to say anything. I was half waiting to see if you got any of the symptoms, secretly hoping that if I just encouraged you to keep swimming, it might not happen. I thought spending so much time in water might be enough. I realise how mad that must sound now. As you got older I worried more and more. And I felt so guilty that I hadn't told you anything, not even about my family."

She looks at me. "I know none of this is any excuse. You must have completely freaked when it started." Her eyes well up and her voice goes all shaky. "I'm really sorry. I don't know if you can ever forgive me. All I can say is I genuinely didn't know I wasn't going to be there for you when it happened."

I give her another hug. "Look, I understand, Mum.

It's not your fault you weren't around. Crawford saw to that. I just wish you'd told me earlier, that's all."

We spend the next hour going through everything that's happened to me while she's been in hospital, and she tells me lots of stuff about her childhood. I get the feeling it's a relief for her to be able to talk about it. She's kept everything bottled up for so long. Finally we get round to talking about the day she went missing.

"It's hard for me to admit it, Danni – but I've always blamed Mam for not saving my father. I knew she was angry with him after he sided with Crawford and became one of the Chosen, but I couldn't believe she was so angry that she didn't go and save him."

I nod. I don't tell her I've already read her diary, so I know about her parents arguing all the time.

"Then I found the key in the wreck. It must have been round his neck when he drowned. I knew instantly what it meant. I was so shocked. And I felt so bad about Mam, the way I've treated her all these years."

"So how come you ended up on the beach?"

"That I don't know, I'm afraid. After I found the chain, I don't remember anything until I woke up in hospital. I guess I must have hit my head on something."

I don't say anything for a moment. I don't want to ask if she remembers Crawford finding her on the beach. I hope not. Just thinking about it makes me shudder.

I'm startled out of my reverie by a quiet tapping on the door. I jump up to open it, expecting a nurse or Dr Murphy.

"Mamwyn!"

"Is it all right for me to come in?" Mamwyn sounds anxious and my heart goes out to her.

"There's no one I'd rather see," I say, and I mean it. We smile at each other.

"I called my grandmother *Mamwyn* too," says Mum, her voice catching with emotion. Tears start spilling down her face. "Oh, Mam, I'm so sorry. I can't believe I kept you two apart."

Mamwyn's eyes well up too. She sniffs and pulls a tissue out of her pocket. She hands one to Mum. "Dry your eyes, Mary love. It was never your fault, I know that."

Looking at them together, I realize they need time to talk to each other. They've a lot of years to make up for.

"Mum, I've got to leave in a minute – I want to see Levi before he goes back to Graymouth. I owe him big time for yesterday."

She nods. "From what you've told me, it sounds like I do, too."

I smile. "I'll come back and see you both later. But before I go – there's one thing that's been really puzzling me. Why was Crawford waiting for the spring tide at the equinox before he tried to burn the sealskin? I couldn't work it out."

Mamwyn doesn't hesitate. "It's the highest tide of the year and the time when the connection between the sea and the land is closest. Though I'm not sure how he'd know that."

"Beryl would have told him, I expect," says Mum. "She's always hated me. She'd know it was a very powerful time and probably their best chance to send the skin back where it came from."

"I'm guessing she just didn't allow for Danni being there," says Mamwyn thoughtfully. "I'm only sorry I didn't make it there in time to help you myself. I knew something was up, but I went to Porthenys to look for Crawford. By the time I realized my mistake, it was too late to get to the fire in time."

I shiver when I think back to the fire. "I couldn't have saved it without Levi, Mamwyn. And Robert's charm was incredible, you should have seen the way the weather changed!"

"Yes, but it was you who pulled the skin out of the flames. You could only do that because you were at your most powerful, like the tide. We are sea people, water is part of who we are. It protects us."

I remember the faint smell of brine and seaweed at the heart of the fire.

"That helps explain why I didn't get burned. Levi couldn't believe it."

"Water is a powerful force. Stronger even than fire," says Mamwyn.

Mum rubs her arms thoughtfully. "If you hadn't saved it, I'd still be stuck in that limbo place. Maybe for ever."

I stare at her a moment. "It's kind of surreal talking like this, Mum. We never used to talk about anything more important than what shift you were working at the supermarket and what we were going to eat for tea later!"

Mum's eyes fill with tears. *Again.*

"What's wrong now?"

"Nothing, Danni. I just can't believe we got through this. I'm so lucky." She insists on squeezing me in another hug, sort of laughing and crying at the same time.

"I hope you'll come and see me again soon as well, Danni." Mamwyn smiles at me.

"Of course I will. Can't wait!"

I check the time quickly. "But right now, I have to go or I'll miss Levi."

As I walk down to the station, I mull over everything Mum and I just talked about. There's such a massive difference between her childhood and mine. Was I really better off not knowing about Ancrows and her past?

However much she wanted to protect me, Mum must have realized she couldn't prevent what was going to happen to me. She knew I'd need to go to Ancrows sooner or later. Surely it would have been better if I'd known from the beginning, like she did when she was growing up?

I think about Mamwyn and the gift of the changing. From now on I want to spend as much time as I can with her, learning the ways of sea people, our language and history. My only worry is how it's going to affect my life in the everyday world, keeping such a huge secret from everyone.

Maybe Mamwyn's right – I think too much.

I realize I'm late to meet Levi and start running. By the time I get to the station, Sarah has already left to meet up with her friends and Levi's sitting on a bench on the platform.

He smiles at me as I plonk myself down next to him. "So how was your mum?"

"She was great. Back to her old self – no, much better in fact. Happy. I never thought of her as happy before."

"Thank goodness for that. You'll finally be coming back to Graymouth."

"Yes, I guess so. Won't be for a few days yet though. Mum needs to be let out of hospital, and she wants us to spend some time with Mamwyn. She feels really bad about the way she kept me away from her."

"Does that mean you'll be staying at your dad's place more often now?"

"Definitely! I want to be here every weekend if I can."

"Pfft! That's just because of Elliot. What about *me*? What am I supposed to do?"

I push him. "Idiot. You can come too, whenever you like. I suppose I can put up with you."

He grins. "Seriously though, how's your mum going to feel about you being here every weekend? She hates it here."

I shrug. "I'm pretty sure Mum's going to feel differently now. Especially since she seems to have a bit of a thing for Robert."

"What, the homeless guy? For real? Wow."

"She went out with him before. Years ago. Before Crawford's trial."

Levi looks thoughtful for a minute. "Danni, when I spent the afternoon with Elliot, he told me a lot of stuff about his family. He had to explain about the way Ancrows used to be, and the curses and everything so I'd understand what we were looking for." He looks at me steadily. "He told me about your family too."

I wonder where this is leading. "What about my family?"

"Why people were afraid of you. Why his Aunty Bea and Crawford hated you. His mum used to tell him stories about the sea people."

"What kind of stories?" Levi has my complete attention. I want to find out exactly how much Elliot knows.

"You have a reputation."

"Thanks!"

"Not *that* kind of reputation."

"So what kind then?"

"That you can change into something else."

I attempt a laugh. "A frog? A princess?"

"A seal."

I'm trying to hide my panic. "Oh that. Yes, I've heard the stories too. Do you think Elliot believes them?"

"Doubt it – he was just telling me what his mother told him." Levi raises an eyebrow. "But that thing you pulled out of the fire…" He pauses a moment and looks up at the departures board. "Oh look, my train's just coming."

Thank goodness he's veered off the subject. I want to keep it that way. "Have you got everything?"

"I think so."

We stand up and move across the platform as the train pulls in with a squealing of brakes. The information announcement crackling over the loudspeaker drowns everything out for a moment. Levi climbs on board, and I breathe a sigh of relief. He leans out of the door before the guard blows his whistle.

"So anyway, Danni—"

"Yes?"

"The rug thing. It was a sealskin, wasn't it? The police said so."

For a moment I can't think of anything to say.

"Yes, but that doesn't mean…" I stammer.

"No, of course not. But I couldn't help wondering." He grins at me. "Will it be okay if I call you Flipper?"

He closes the door quickly and pulls a silly face at me from behind the safety of the glass window. I can't help smiling. Levi was just winding me up. I stick my tongue out at him, and wave as the train moves away into the distance.

My phone beeps. It's a message from Elliot wanting to meet up later. I leave the station and walk out into the sunshine with a big fat grin on my face.

author's note

Deep Water reflects my interest in Celtic myth and folklore, and what I call the old ways – systems of ritual, magic and pagan belief that stretch far back into pre-history. I'm fascinated by the unwritten legacy handed down to us via oral tradition in legends and folk tales, and the clues to our past still visible in the landscape, such as ancient standing stones aligned to reflect the seasonal movements of the sun and the moon. People still use deceptively simple things to create powerful magic – sometimes for good, sometimes for bad, but in a way that is very real to those who believe in it.

Folklore and magic in Deep Water

I have tried to weave some of the Cornish witchcraft and folkloric traditions uncovered in my research into the fabric of *Deep Water*. Poppets (like the one Aunty Bea makes), though similar in many ways to voodoo dolls, are specific to Cornwall, and you can find many real examples in the Witchcraft Museum in Boscastle.

The poppets in the museum were mostly found hidden in chimneys or under floorboards – often by people doing building work in old cottages. The pierced figures (usually wax or clay) were made incorporating nail clippings or hair, presumably of the intended victim.

At one time Boscastle (Ancrows in the story) was known as a place where fishermen could buy weather charms, sold on the quayside by local "wind sellers". Obviously any means of controlling the weather would be invaluable to those whose livelihood depended on going out to sea.

I based the appearance of the weather charm in *Deep Water* on other research into spells involving knotted string or fabric, which were common throughout northern Europe.

Further research

Deep Water was inspired in part by an amazing travel book

called *The People of the Sea,* by David Thomson. Thomson regularly travelled the remote islands of the British Isles nearly a century ago, recording stories of the seal people, told by possibly the last generation who still believed them to be true.

This novel is my contemporary take on the ancient Celtic selkie myth, set in Cornwall. Selkies, and similar mythical beings such as mermaids, occur throughout the Celtic world and beyond.

The idea of shape-shifting is common to almost all cultures worldwide. It's not all about werewolves and vampires and things that are meant to terrify us. Myths are often simply a way of interpreting the complex world around us, a world of infinite possibilities.

Deep Water was inspired by my belief that just because we can't prove something scientifically, it doesn't mean it doesn't exist. And the possibility that such things are real makes the world a far more interesting place.

acknowledgements

Many people have helped me build the story of *Deep Water*, in lots of different ways. Some just by reading it and liking it. Some by coming up with ideas or suggesting ways to improve it – and others (like my family) simply by lifting my spirits when I felt like throwing in the towel. I'm bound to have forgotten someone in the following list, so if it's you – apologies.

Big thanks to Christine O'Brien, Nick Holmes and Alison Powell who were there at the start and encouraged me to grow the story. Also my wonderful Bath Spa University tutors, Julia Green and Nicola Davies, who helped me give it life – along with my amazing (and uber talented) MA group: Clare Furniss, David Hofmeyr, Alex Hart, Blondie Camps and HB Alexander.

I owe a massive debt to Debbie Taylor at Mslexia – and judges Malorie Blackman, Julia Eccleshare and Julia Churchill – for choosing *Deep Water* to win the Mslexia Children's Novel Writing competition in 2013. (You changed my life!)

My favourite readers, who gave me honest feedback and helped me brainstorm plot ideas, include Lottle Sweeney, Eugene Lambert, Olly Perry and Russell Sanderson.

Help with research came from The Museum of Witchcraft in Boscastle (Ancrows by another name) and Marian Green, among many others.

Biggest thanks go to my lovely agent, Ben Illis, for his boundless enthusiasm and support, and basically just being himself. Rebecca Hill at Usborne for commissioning it, my brilliant editor, Sarah Stewart, for helping to make *Deep Water* as good as it can be, and everyone else at Usborne, just for being great.

And last (but by no means least) SF Said – for very timely and much appreciated advice. It saved me resorting to chain-smoking.

For more magical and mysterious
reads, check out

www.usborne.com/fiction